SANGEETA BHARGAVA was born in a remote corner of the Maharashtra region of India and studied in Lucknow. Although she has an MBA in Finance, she soon realised that the business world was not for her and decided to go back to her first love: writing. She is the author of *Letters to my Baby,* a book on pregnancy and baby care. *The World Beyond* is her debut novel. She now lives in London with her husband, two children, 10,000 books and a temperamental laptop.

www.sangeetabhargava.com

By Sangeeta Bhargava

The World Beyond
After the Storm

The World Beyond

SANGEETA BHARGAVA

Allison & Busby Limited
13 Charlotte Mews
London W1T 4EJ
www.allisonandbusby.com

First published in Great Britain by Allison & Busby in 2011.
This paperback edition published by Allison & Busby in 2012.

A CIP catalogue record for this book is available from
the British Library.

10 9 8 7 6 5 4 3 2 1

ISBN 978-0-7490-4058-1

Typeset in 11.5/16 pt Sabon by
Allison & Busby Ltd.

Paper used in this publication is from sustainably managed sources.
All of the wood used is procured from legal sources and is fully traceable.
The producing mill uses schemes such as ISO 14001
to monitor environmental impact.

Printed and bound by
CPI Group (UK) Ltd, Croydon, CR0 4YY

For my father
without whom this book
would not have been possible

Character List

Nawab Wajid Ali Shah/Abba Huzoor/Abbu –
the last king of Avadh

Begum Hazrat Mahal/Ammi –
one of Nawab Wajid Ali Shah's wives

Salim/Chote Nawab –
Nawab Wajid Ali Shah's adopted son

Ahmed – Salim's cousin

Daima – Salim's wet nurse

Nayansukh – Daima's son

Chutki – Daima's daughter

Rachael Bristow – an English girl

Colonel Felix Bristow – Rachael's father

Mrs Margaret Bristow – Rachael's mother

Parvati/Ayah – maidservant

Ram Singh – Parvati's husband

Sudha – Rachael's companion and maid

Christopher Wilson – Rachael's childhood friend

Chapter One

SALIM

It was 1855. The month of Ramzan, the holy month. Prince Salim and Ahmed pushed their way through the bustling narrow by-lanes of Chowk. Chowk – the grand old bazaar of Lucknow, the haunt of the famous courtesans, the hub of the city. There was not a single article in all of Hindustan that could not be found in Chowk. You needed the keen eye of a huntsman, that's all.

A light breeze brought with it the aroma of khus – the cool refreshing smell of summer. Salim paused to look at the rows of decanters in the perfume shop. Ruh gulab ittar – made by distilling the heart of rose petals; musk ittar – procured from the scent that is found in the gland of the male musk deer; jasmine, tuberose, sandalwood . . .

'Which ittar is an aphrodisiac, Salim mia? Musk or rose?' Ahmed asked.

Shrugging his shoulders, Salim moved on. He didn't know, neither did he care to know. If love meant having a dozen wives in your harem like Abba Huzoor, he didn't care. He would sooner man an army than settle squabbles between numerous wives. Just then his ears pricked up, like a deer's at the sound of a tiger's footfall. He could hear the sound of ghungroos and the fall of feet in time with the tabla. A husky voice was reciting the dadra – 'dhaa dhin naa dhaa tin naa'. Looking up at the apartment above the shop, Salim found a eunuch standing in the doorway dressed in a woman's attire.

She winked at him. 'Come upstairs, sweetheart. I'll get you whatever your heart desires.' She bit her lower lip coquettishly and played with her long plait, as she measured him from the top of his nukkedar cap to his short-toed velvet shoes.

Averting his gaze, Salim looked at Ahmed. He was grinning at the eunuch and trying to look past her into the house, hoping to catch a glimpse of the prostitutes who resided there. Shaking his head at his cousin, Salim pulled him roughly as he hurried along. Nay, Ahmed was not just his cousin. He was more than that. He was his brother, his best friend, the keeper of all his secrets.

'Why did you choose today of all days to come here, Salim mia?' Ahmed shouted above the din.

'No, thank you, I don't want any,' Salim said brusquely as he pushed aside the garlands of jasmine a vendor had shoved right in front of his face.

'D'you know what Ahmed-flavoured keema tastes like?' Ahmed asked as he wiped the beads of perspiration from his forehead.

10

Salim's brows knitted together. 'What?'

'Well, you'll come to know today. Because if this crowd doesn't make mincemeat of me, Daima surely will.'

Without bothering to answer, Salim hastened his pace. Daima mustn't come to know he'd been to Chowk. As they passed Talib's Kebabs, Ahmed dawdled and sniffed appreciatively. Salim had to admit – he sure did make the best kebabs in town, the type that melt in your mouth. The pungent smell of fried onions, garlic and grilled meat tickled his taste buds.

'Thank goodness it's the last day of Ramzan,' Ahmed muttered, as he eyed the kebabs one last time.

Salim walked purposefully towards a little shop at the end of the road. It was almost hidden from view by the bangle man's stall.

'Show me those green bangles, bhai jaan,' said one of the women gathered around the stall.

'Bhai jaan, do you have those red ones one size smaller?' said another.

'Bangle man, can you give me two of each colour?' clamoured a third.

Throwing a cursory glance at the women, Salim strode into the music shop. There before him was the choicest collection of musical instruments that had ever been seen in Hindustan. Bade Miyan smiled at him, bowed slightly and pointed to a sarod. Salim's eyes lit up as they rested on the instrument.

As he bent down to pick it up, a slender white hand reached out for it as well. Their hands touched. Salim looked up and found himself gazing into a pair of eyes as blue as the Gomti at the deep end. He could see no more. The woman was clad in a burqa. He looked at her hands again. They were as soft and white as a rabbit. On her little finger she wore a delicate gold ring with a single diamond.

Salim hastily withdrew his hand and with a slight bow said, 'It's all yours, ma'am.'

The woman nodded slightly and their eyes met again. Just then he felt a sharp kick and almost yowled in pain as Ahmed's foot hit the corn on his big toe. But the lady in the burqa was still looking at him, so he suppressed his scream and the urge to slam his fist into Ahmed's face and grinned instead – a broader grin than he had intended. Then, lowering his gaze, he left the shop.

'What if her father was just behind us, Salim mia?' asked Ahmed. 'He'd have surely beaten us up if he had seen you gaping at his daughter like that.'

'Whether her father would've beaten us up or not, you're getting bashed for sure,' Salim said, waving his fist at him. Ahmed ran off laughing with Salim hobbling after him.

Sitting down on the takhat, Salim took off his khurd nau with a curse. He gingerly rubbed the corn on his big toe and cursed Ahmed yet again.

'So finally you're here, Chote Nawab?'

It was Daima. Salim smiled affectionately at her as she gestured to the eunuch Chilmann to bring in the basin. Chilmann, who wore the clothes of a man but swayed like a girl. The butt of all the jokes in the palace.

Salim washed his hands and face.

'Where did you rush off to this morning?' Daima asked, as she stopped pouring water and handed him a towel.

'Bade Miyan wanted me to see the new sarod that was delivered yesterday,' he replied carefully as he wiped his hands. He had never been able to lie to Daima. He looked at her now, noticing for the first time that her hair had begun to match the white of her sari. He waited for the lecture to come – a prince has no business nosing through dilapidated bazaars like a common man.

'Where is it?' she asked.

'Where's what?'

'The sarod . . .'

'Oh. Actually there was a young maiden in the shop . . .'

'So of course, our Chote Nawab let her have it . . .' Daima clicked her tongue. 'This chivalry of yours is going to destroy us one day.'

Salim hugged her from behind. 'There's no need to be so dramatic, Daima. It was just a sarod after all.' Then turning to Chilmann he said, 'Tell Rehman to have Afreen and Toofan saddled by four.'

'You're going out again?' asked Daima.

'I won't be late. And no, I haven't forgotten that it's Chand Raat.'

'Yes, finally, the last day of Ramzan . . . just look at the way all this fasting has made your bones stick out.'

Laughing, Salim took off his cap absent-mindedly and placed it on the stool. Yes, thank goodness the fasting period was almost over. He was missing his hookah.

'And mind you, don't be late for namaz tomorrow . . . you know how it upsets your father.'

'Ya Ali, dare I displease Abba Huzoor on Eid? How is it, Daima? He never misses a namaz, not a single one!'

'Chote Nawab, the day *you* remember to say all the five namaz, Allah mia will be so pleased, he will personally come down from Heaven to bless you.'

Salim grinned. He ran his fingers through his hair as he watched Daima's receding form. She had nursed him as a baby and was the closest he had known of a mother's love, his own mother having died during childbirth. She fawned on him and made sure everyone called him Chote Nawab and paid him the utmost respect, even though he was not the heir apparent. Just an adopted son of the ruler, Nawab Wajid Ali Shah.

He chuckled as he heard Daima chiding someone in the adjoining room. 'Hey you, move those limbs a bit faster . . . otherwise we'll have to serve the feast next Eid.'

Even though she was a devout Hindu, she had comfortably fitted into his Muslim family and commanded as much respect in the palace as any of the begums.

Taking off his angarkha and silk pyjamas, he threw them on the takhat. Chilmann picked them up, folded them carefully and put them away. Salim slipped on a loose cotton kurta and pyjamas. Walking over to his bed, he propped himself on the oblong pillow as two attendants hastened to fan him. He spread his hands over the crisp white sheets. They felt cool and refreshing under his warm moist palms. It was the middle of June and the heat showed no signs of relenting for at least another month. He lay back on the pillow and thought about the girl in the burqa. Her hands were so dainty – just like paneer – soft white cottage cheese. Ya Ali, was he hungry!

It was that time of the year when even the evenings were warm, but twilight sometimes ushered in a cool breeze from the River Gomti. The city of Lucknow yawned and stretched after its afternoon nap and slowly began to deck itself for a night of festivities, on this night of the moon or Chand Raat.

There would be considerable excitement that night, especially among the children, as they competed with one another to be the first to spot the moon. Shops would be open all night to enable people to get on with their last-minute shopping. The women would get busy applying henna to their hands.

As Salim and Ahmed neared the Gomti, they saw some mahouts lead their elephants to bathe in the river. Salim patted Afreen and she trotted to a halt. He watched as the mahouts gave the elephants a thorough wash. They were being primped for the procession to the Jama Masjid tomorrow. Soon oil would be rubbed into their skins. Once that was done, their foreheads, tusks, ears, trunks and feet would be painted with a rainbow of lines and colours and adorned with ornaments. A couple of brass rings would be slipped onto the tusks. Finally their backs would be covered with brightly coloured, embroidered, velvet cloths. On top of that would be placed the gold or silver howdahs.

'Ahmed, isn't that Nayansukh?' Salim asked,

distracted by a figure in red approaching them.

'Nayan who?' said Ahmed.

'Daima's son.'

'Ah, so it is!' replied Ahmed as he trotted up to him. 'Why in Allah's name are you undressing in the middle of the road?' he asked with amusement as he watched Nayansukh tug impatiently at the gold buttons on his coat.

'These angrez are crazy! Make us parade in the heat in bloody coats! I can't even breathe. It's so bloody tight under my arms,' Nayansukh replied, as he finally managed to wriggle out of the coat. He walked over to Salim. 'Salaam, Salim bhai. We ought to wear just vests and lungi in this bloody heat, you know.'

Laughing aloud Salim replied, 'Soldiers marching in just a loincloth! Ya Ali, there's an image!'

Nayansukh slapped Afreen's back and said wistfully, 'Seriously, bhai, I wish I hadn't enlisted in the Company's army.'

'But it was Daima's dream,' Salim said. 'She always wanted to see you as a soldier . . .'

'Aren't you happy?' Ahmed asked.

Nayansukh stroked Afreen's mane and, looking down, replied, 'The salary's fine, but they've taken away our land.'

'No,' Salim said in a lowered voice.

'Yes. Can you imagine Salim bhai? Those bloody firangis took away my ancestral land and I could only stare after them. They took my property from under my nose and all I could do was twiddle my thumb.' He angrily smacked Afreen's rump. Afreen snorted in protest. 'And all thanks to that firangi – what's his name? Dalhousie.' Nayansukh turned his face away and spat on the side of the road. His voice was choked when he spoke again. 'Now where will I find the money for Chutki's marriage?'

Chutki. Daima's little girl, with her small glistening eyes and sharp nose. Who never forgot to tie a rakhi on his arm or put tika on his forehead on bhai dooj. Sometimes Salim felt she was fonder of him than her own brother, Nayansukh.

Touching Nayansukh's shoulder lightly, he said in a quiet voice, 'Don't worry about Chutki. She's my sister too. I'll make sure she has one of the grandest weddings in Lucknow.'

'It's not just me, Salim bhai,' Nayansukh continued. 'Most of the Indian soldiers are unhappy.'

Afreen snorted and swished her tail to drive away the flies that were trying to settle down on her back.

'And know what? Senior Indian sepoys are the most frustrated. They've been in the army for as long as I remember. But they can't get promoted over the most junior English sepoy.' Nayansukh paused and twirled his moustache angrily. 'I swear on Lord Ram, the young dandies are so rude. Makes my blood boil. And if we protest, we are given our marching orders.'

Salim looked at Nayansukh as he continued to twirl his moustache. He knew promotion wasn't the only reason why the Indian soldiers were dissatisfied. There were other issues. Several of them.

Nayansukh broke into his thoughts. 'Where are you two off to?' he asked.

'Going back to the palace to break our fast,' Ahmed replied. His stomach growled as though on cue.

Chuckling, Salim said, 'Ahmed, you'd better not overeat tomorrow. You don't want to spend the next ten days dashing to the hakim like last year.'

'The last day of the fasting period is the most difficult, Salim mia. Ammi has already started cooking for the feast and all those smells coming from the kitchen . . .'

Salim shook his head. Poor Ahmed. He fell silent as they rode towards Kaiserbagh. He thought about Nayansukh and what he had said about Dalhousie's reforms. He smiled scornfully. East India Company. A mere bunch of traders from England. And now, the lord and master of practically all of Hindustan.

He wiped the perspiration from his forehead. How he hated that Dalhousie. It wasn't just because he was a firangi. It was his attitude towards the Indians, his arrogance, his high-handedness that got to him. If only he would leave Hindustan and go back to where he belonged. And take all his whimsical policies with him. He looked at Ahmed. He had grown quiet as well, but his silence had more to do with an empty stomach, Salim suspected. They rode in silence for another five minutes, then Salim abruptly brought Afreen to a halt. He patted her apologetically. She was foaming at the mouth.

'Now what?' Ahmed asked.

Salim didn't answer. His eyes and ears were transfixed to the open window of the bungalow in front of them. An English girl sat at the piano. Salim stood still. He had never heard such feisty music before. He could not see the face of the pianist clearly. But her hands – they were the same slender white hands he had seen that morning – the same ring, the same diamond, glinting in the setting sun. Her fingers were running confidently from one end of the keyboard to the other, dancing merrily as to a lively jig.

'Ya Ali,' he exclaimed incredulously, 'it's the same girl we saw in Chowk this morning!'

Chapter Two

RACHAEL

Everybody clapped as Rachael finished the piece with a flourish. She curtsied slightly and thanked them. Anna took her place on the stool and started playing a ballad.

'That was beautiful, Rachael. Was that Mozart?' asked Mrs Wilson.

'No, Haydn,' Rachael replied as she carelessly flicked a golden lock of hair away from her forehead

'I wish I could practise like you, my love. But I can never find the time. What with the washerwoman always misplacing Christopher's shirts and Kallu forgetting to put up the mosquito nets . . .' Mrs Wilson stopped mid sentence to accept a glass of wine from the waiter. As she thanked him, Rachael excused herself and went outside.

She was relieved to be away from the stultifying heat and the even more stifling conversations within. She did not care how many days the washerwoman took to do the ironing or how slow Kallu was in laying the table. She watched two horsemen disappear into oblivion, whipping up a cloud of dust behind them. What would she not do to saddle up and ride alongside them? She grinned devilishly as she imagined the look of horror on the faces of all the guests at home.

Rachael loved looking at the skyline at this hour. The white palaces and mosques, bedecked with golden minarets, domes and cupolas, looked flushed and pink as the sun set slowly behind them. Like a virgin bride blushing in all her bridal finery. As the incantation of Allah-o-Akbar rose from the mosques, a dozen sparrows flew into the air.

She took a deep breath. The air was laden with the scent of roses and jasmine. She stooped to pick up a rose that had fallen on the lawn and started plucking its petals one by one. 'Yes,' she sighed contentedly. Lucknow certainly was more beautiful than Paris or Constantinople. She wondered what those palaces and mosques looked like from the inside. Did the women wear burqas inside the palace as well? She had heard Nabob Wajid Ali Shah had many begums. She wondered how they lived together. Did they live in harmony like sisters or were they always quarrelling? If only she could spend some time with them. And Urdu – the language they spoke – it sounded so poetic, so rich, so polite. And the way it was written from right to left – it was intriguing. One day, Rachael decided, she would learn to read and write in that language.

Mother, of course, would not approve. She had no interest in India or its people. 'The less I know about these heathens and their ways, the better,' she would say. Rachael pitied her. She had no idea what a treasure trove of excitement she was missing. How narrow and shuttered her life had become.

Rachael propped her elbows on the little wicker gate that led into the garden. The gate creaked in protest against the unaccustomed weight. She thought of the young man she had met in Chowk that morning. He had looked her straight in the eye – unlike the other natives, who never looked a woman in the eye unless she was his mother, wife, sister or a nautch girl. He was no ordinary native – he walked like one who owned the land. Who was he? A prince? But no, he did not wear any jewellery like all the nabobs and princes she had seen. So who *was* he, then? She blushed slightly as she caressed her right hand and remembered how his firm brown hand had touched it.

The following morning, Rachael thought about the previous night's party as Sudha brushed her hair. She would run away from home if Mother made her attend one more party that week. And what made all these social gatherings even more unbearable was whether it was a party or a ball or the theatre, they invariably met the same insipid crowd. Added to that was the matchmaking all the mothers were now indulging in since the day she had turned eighteen.

'Captain O'Reilly has just arrived in Lucknow and he's single. You must invite him next time, dear,' crooned Mrs Palmer.

Another one whispered conspiratorially into Mother's

22

ear, 'Stella's youngest son – what's his name – ah, Thomas – that freckled Rebecca has given him the mitten. He's a free man now.'

For the love of God! Had she told them to look for a suitable boy for her? Did she look desperate? Then why were they so anxious to get her betrothed? Had they nothing better to do? It seemed the only purpose in a woman's life was to go to the altar. And how that thought vexed her.

Sudha stepped aside as she threw back her stool and turned away from the dressing table. She had had enough of this matchmaking. Next time someone said a word about marriage she would scream. Even if it meant being banned from English society for ever.

She went into the dining room and looked around. Breakfast was going to be late. The servants were still busy clearing the mess from yesterday's party. The room smelt of stale food and liquor.

'Oh my God, memsahib, something wrong with puppy,' Ram Singh suddenly exclaimed.

Turning around sharply, she rushed to where Ram Singh was bending over something. Sure enough Brutus was acting in the strangest manner. He was spinning his head rapidly. Then he put his head down on the floor and rubbed it up and down against the carpet. Ayah looked at him and screamed, 'Oh no, he possessed by evil spirit! Someone call the tantric!' She scurried out of the room to call Mother.

Rachael bent down over the puppy. 'What's the matter, baby?' she cooed. She patted his soft black back and tried to scoop him in her arms. But he simply yelped and leapt out. He continued shaking his head, as though trying to rid himself of something.

'What's the matter? What's all this hullabaloo?' said a startled voice from behind. It was Mother – her eyes puffed and still sleepy, hair tousled.

If there was one person who had strongly opposed keeping Brutus in the house, it was Mother. But Brutus had soon won her over. He followed Mother everywhere. He wagged his tail briskly and yelped in delight whenever she got back home. He looked at her with such sorrowful eyes whenever she scolded him that she began to soften. So much so, that now, if there was one person in the entire household who stirred any emotion in Mother, it was Brutus.

If Rachael did not eat her meal, it often went unnoticed. But if Brutus did not eat, one servant was sent right away to summon the vet, another to the market to get some fresh meat and a third was ordered to roll out rotis just as Brutus liked them – thick and soft. And until Mother finally managed to coax Brutus to eat, she would sit with him on her lap, stroking his coat and whispering sweet nothings into his ear.

Smiling sadly, Rachael wondered when was the last time mother had hugged her. It was so long ago it did not matter anymore. Mother's lack of warmth and affection had hurt a lot when she was little. She would break Mother's favourite china or throw tantrums to evoke a reaction from her. But nothing ever worked. Finally she had convinced herself that Mother was her stepmother. Just like Cinderella's.

'What's happened to my Brutus?' There was an edge

of panic in Mother's voice now, as she helplessly watched Brutus running around.

As Rachael moved aside to enable Sudha to lay the table, she spotted something on the floor and picked it up. It looked as if it had been chewed and then spat out. 'Nothing to worry about, Mother,' she announced. Grinning, she held up something green for all to see. 'Brutus has just had his first taste of green chillies.'

Her declaration was greeted with oohs and aahs and mirth. Ayah went to fetch Brutus a bowl of water while Sudha scraped some leftover pudding from the dish for him.

Once Brutus had been fed and watered and lay contentedly on his rug, Mother commenced her tour of the house. 'Sudha, why have these dead flowers not been replaced?' she said, as she lifted the bunch of flowers from the vase in the living room and handed them to her.

'Sorry, memsahib, I do it right away. You see, they alive yesterday.'

'And Ram Singh, I want you to remove all the cobwebs behind the khus mats at once. I felt mortified last night when Mrs Wilson noticed them.'

'Very well, memsahib,' replied Ram Singh.

As Mother lifted a khus mat to point out the cobwebs to Ram Singh, a lizard fell on her. She screamed and shook her garments vigorously to get rid of the hideous creature.

'Mother, pray sit down and have your breakfast. You can instruct them after you've eaten,' said Rachael.

Mother sighed and sat down at the table. 'Oh, these

dim-witted natives. They have again put the wrong cutlery.'

'Pray do not vex yourself, mother. They'll learn eventually. Your breakfast is getting cold.'

But Mother was already marching towards the kitchen. She yanked open the cutlery drawer and, lifting out a spoon, waved it at Ayah. 'This is the spoon—' She could not finish as a cockroach darted out of the drawer. 'What the—?' she gasped, horrified.

Poor Mother. 'You don't like this country much, do you, Mother?' Rachael had asked her once.

'I hate it,' she had barked in reply.

Yes, Mother hated India. She hated the uncouth natives; the heat and the dust; the hot curries and the leathery Indian bread; the smell of perspiration, strong spices and cow dung. Above all she hated the country for swallowing her only son.

Rachael squinted as the glaring sun beat down on her as soon as she stepped out of the house later that day.

'Good afternoon, missy baba,' Ram Singh greeted her.

She smiled and crinkled up her nose. 'Afternoon, Ram Singh.'

She had known Ram Singh since she had learnt to walk. When she was two, Mother had often asked him to keep an eye on her. She would throw her toys out of the window, then clap her hands with glee as he ran outside for the umpteenth time to pick them up.

When she was older, he and his wife Parvati often told her tales from the *Ramayana* and *Mahabharata*.

They would tell her about the cousins, the Pandavas and the Kauravas, and how they waged an eighteen-day war against each other. Or how Lord Ram was the only mortal who could lift the celestial bow to win Sita's hand in marriage. She would listen in awe as the monkey god Hanuman set fire to Lanka with his tail, or Lord Krishna lifted an entire mountain on his little finger to save his fellow villagers from a thunderstorm.

The couple would often quarrel over details. Angrily, Ayah would pull the edge of her sari over her eyes so she could not see her ignoramus husband's face anymore, and stomp off. Ram Singh would shake his head at her receding form, and then continue the tale.

Today, as Rachael passed the servants' quarters, she halted. 'What's that lovely aroma coming from your house, Ram Singh?'

'Missy baba, my son ask wife to make kheer. You like taste some?' he added hesitantly.

'Yes, why not?'

She followed Ram Singh but hesitated at the doorstep. In all the years that she had known him, she'd never been inside his house. Even as a child she had understood it was not the done thing. Sahibs and memsahibs did not mix with the natives. But then Ram Singh and Ayah weren't just any natives. They were almost like family. Rachael lifted her right foot determinedly and entered the house. The door was small and she had to bend down to enter. A peculiar smell greeted her – a mixture of sweat, food, incense and camphor.

'Oh, missy baba, I no knew you come. Welcome,

welcome. You sit, baba, over here. No, here,' Ayah chattered, wringing her hands as she spoke.

'You sure, missy baba, you like to eat in our house?' Ram Singh asked her for the third time.

She now suspected he had invited her out of politeness, but had not expected her to accept the invitation. But she couldn't possibly refuse now. She sat down quietly on the chair that he had dusted and put out for her. He then excused himself and followed his wife to the kitchen.

'Parvati, hurry up and serve food. If barre memsahib and sahib come and find missy baba here, they skin me alive,' Rachael heard him say, and she felt guilty for putting him to such trouble.

She looked around. The room was too small for even one person to live in. The roof was low and there was just one small square window in the entire house. Rachael wondered how Ram Singh and his wife survived in this heat. The only furniture in the room was a charpoy, a wooden table, a chair and a cupboard.

'No, no, no, I'm happy eating on the floor,' Rachael insisted when she saw Ram Singh clearing the clutter from the table. And before he could protest, she had settled down on the threadbare rug on the floor. The floor felt hard, but she said nothing. She did not wish to add more to the couple's discomfiture.

Ayah placed a plate of food before her and started fanning her with a punkah.

'I'm not eating alone. Where's your plate?' Rachael asked.

'Oh no, baba, how can I eat before husband?' Ayah answered shyly as she continued to fan her.

'Ram Singh, come and join me,' Rachael called out to

Ram Singh, who had stationed himself at the door and looked out nervously every two minutes.

'No baba, you eat. I eat later.'

'Look, I'm not going to eat alone. Either you or Ayah eats with me or I'm going.' Rachael started to get up.

'Oh no, missy baba, you know not how bad it is for a guest to leave table without eating,' said Ram Singh. Reluctantly he sat down on a small chatai and gestured to Ayah to bring his food.

Rachael licked her lips. She had never eaten without any cutlery before. She was relieved when Ayah handed her a small teaspoon she had managed to dig out. She spluttered as she took the first mouthful of the vegetable pulao. It was spicy and hot, but oh so delicious. 'Where's Kalyaan?' she asked as she took another mouthful. What was that special aroma – was it the bay leaves, the green cardamoms or the black ones? How come English food always smelt healthy but never exotic like this?

'He eaten and gone to tend the horses,' said Ayah.

Rachael smiled as she thought of Kalyaan. Many an afternoon she had spent with him as a child; until the fateful day when she had that fall. That was the last time she played with him. For thereafter, much to her consternation, she was whisked off every afternoon to Granny Ruth's – that's what everyone called her.

Mother took a siesta every afternoon with clockwork regularity. She locked her bedroom door and nobody, not even Papa, was allowed to disturb her then. And certainly not her. But Rachael could never bring herself to sleep during the day. The world outside beckoned her. She'd creep out of the house and join Ram Singh's son in his games. He'd defeat her at a game of marbles or teach her how to climb a tree. That afternoon, as she was climbing the guava tree, the branch snapped and she had a nasty fall. Mother had to be woken up and, of course, she was not pleased. She was scandalised to learn her daughter had been climbing trees. Rachael had to endure an hour-long lecture on the impropriety of playing with the natives while the nurse tended to her wounds.

Granny Ruth was a frail old woman with a high-pitched nasal accent. At first Rachael abhorred her, until she introduced her to the enchanting world of music. From then on, Rachael began leading a secret life every afternoon, when only she and her piano existed. Her notes would rise to the skies and inhabit a world full of laughter and ecstasy. By the time the afternoon ended, her face would be flushed, fingers aching and eyes starry.

'You not liking food, baba?' Parvati asked.

Looking down at her food, Rachael realised she had been daydreaming. 'Umm . . . What's this?' she asked, pointing to the bowl Ayah had just placed before her.

'Kheer . . . sweet?'

Rachael took a spoonful. A kind of dessert. Tasted a little like rice pudding. Just then she heard the creak of a rusted gate being opened and the sound of horses trotting to a halt and neighing.

'Oh my God, sahib here. I going to be skinned alive,' Ram Singh groaned.

'Shh, listen to me, Ram Singh. Tell me when they are inside the house and I will sneak into my room through the window.'

* * *

Stepping out of Ram Singh's house gingerly, Rachael looked around. No one was about except for the gatekeeper who sat yawning at the post. She glanced across the garden. Everything was still, as though drugged on opium. She lifted her skirts and scurried to the back of the house where her window was, as a hot gust of wind hit her.

Suddenly she heard someone coming. She held her breath and closed her eyes. Then she heard a small bark. She opened her eyes slowly and found Brutus wagging his tail, his tongue hanging out and his little head cocked to one side as he looked at her.

'Oh Brutus, it's you,' she exclaimed as she slowly let out a sigh of relief. Her heart was still thumping rapidly as she reached for the window latch.

'Rachael?'

She froze. It was Papa.

Chapter Three

SALIM

Salim had just returned to his rooms after offering the Eid prayers. He was relieved Daima wasn't around. Despite her warning yesterday, he had managed to oversleep and reach the Jama Masjid late. Although he had slipped into the prayer hall quietly after washing his hands and feet, he had espied Abba Huzoor noticing him from the corner of his eye.

He walked over to the latticed window and looked out into the courtyard below, while the barber prepared his shaving foam. There was a hum of activity – servants ran helter-skelter, completing last-minute preparations for the Eid celebrations. New expensive carpets from Persia were being rolled out in the hall. As usual, food was being prepared in all the six royal kitchens.

Salim sat down on the takhat and the barber began to apply shaving foam to his cheeks. He thought of the girl in the burqa whom he had met the previous day. She had the most beautiful pair of eyes he had ever seen – cool, calm and as blue as the sky at midday. It irked him, however, that the girl for whom he had felt a tug for the first time in his life was not Muslim. She was English. Damn, but she played the piano so well!

Just then Ahmed entered the room. 'Eid Mubarak, Salim mia,' he said.

The barber stepped aside as Salim got up to embrace his friend. 'Eid Mubarak, my friend. Eid Mubarak.'

Salim sat down on the takhat again and the barber recommenced his shaving.

Ahmed walked over to the painting of a European lady in her boudoir that hung on the wall. He ran his finger alongside the frame, then turned to face Salim. 'Can I ask you something, Salim mia?'

'What is it, Ahmed?'

Clearing his throat, Ahmed looked around. 'Salim mia, the girl we saw yesterday. You sure it was the same girl? An English mem in a burqa?' He put a paan in his mouth. 'I think you've lost it, Salim mia. You've started hallucinating. Better start visiting the tawaifs.'

'I'm absolutely sure,' Salim replied, an edge of irritation in his voice.

'But if she was Eng—'

'Look, I don't wish to have anything to do with an Englishwoman. So can we please drop the subject?'

Ahmed's smile vanished. 'Oh well, I must get going. Ammi is waiting for me. I'd just come to wish you "Eid Mubarak",' he mumbled and left the room before Salim could stop him.

The barber wiped Salim's face with a towel, packed

his shaving kit, bowed and backed out of the room. Salim looked out of the window. He sighed as he watched Ahmed dodging the servants at work in the courtyard. He shouldn't have spoken to him in that tone. He could still remember the first time he had met him. It was Eid on that day as well. He was about five years old then. Upset the wind had torn his new kite, he had stomped into the palace.

'The biggest kite in the whole of Avadh,' the shopkeeper had assured him. 'The king of the skies,' he had added with a wink as Salim reluctantly handed him all his eidi.

Some king, Salim thought ruefully. Well, the king was in shreds now. He was about to throw a tantrum for Daima's benefit when he saw him – a boy with a round face and a cheery dimpled smile. His maternal uncle's son, he was told.

'Eid Mubarak,' the boy said.

'Eid Mubarak,' Salim replied. 'How old are you?'

'Four.'

'What?' How could it be? He was plumper and taller than him.

'Here, you can have mine,' the boy said, as he handed a surprised Salim his kite.

Since that day in 1838, the two of them had stuck together like the two drums of the tabla. Each incomplete without the other.

They had got into many scrapes together. They had fallen from the guava tree, been chased by a mad bull, been punished by the moulvi at school. They had tried to learn to whistle through the gap between the teeth when they lost their first baby tooth; they had kept their first fast during Ramzan together; they had even visited Lol Bibi's kotha together at the age of twelve, only to be chased by the gatekeeper. They had been together when Salim had almost killed the woodcutter. Yes, killed him, almost.

An involuntary shiver ran down Salim's back. Even after six long years . . . he pursed his lips, shook his head and tried to think of something else.

Somehow news of their antics had always reached Daima. And always, much of her scolding was directed at Ahmed. She never was fond of him. She felt relatives like him were parasites, a drain on the royal treasury. If only she knew who the real scroungers of the treasury were. Moreover, she firmly believed Chote Nawab could do no wrong.

Ahmed soon got used to her tongue-lashings. The good-natured soul that he was, he would cheerfully listen to her. Like the time when she scolded them for playing in the rain and her vitriolic tongue got the better of her.

'Nothing will happen to you, you son of a rhino,' she scolded, waving her arms accusingly at him. 'But our Chote Nawab here, he's of blue blood. He'll be struck down with pneumonia.'

Ahmed had simply strolled over to the basket of fruit and dug into the juiciest apple. Daima stared at him while he busied himself crunching and slurping the apple and licking the juice that ran down his fingers.

Yes, that was Ahmed. He never answered back, which strangely fuelled Daima's anger even more. For him, there was a simple solution to every problem – food.

Little wonder Eid had always been his favourite festival. As boys, the two of them had loved waiting at night on the terrace to catch sight of the moon; the new clothes, the lip-smacking food. Above all, they had loved hoarding all the money they received as eidi, to buy kites.

They had always been welcome in the kitchen, especially the day before Eid, when the chef could not taste the food because of his fast. In Salim and Ahmed he found willing guinea pigs.

'What else would Chote Nawab like to have?' the chef would ask.

'Anardana pulao,' he would answer, dipping his paratha in the thick sweet and sour mango murabba and licking his fingers. He loved anardana pulao more for its appearance than the taste. Half of each grain of rice was fiery red and the other half white, thus giving them the appearance of pomegranate seeds.

But what Ahmed enjoyed eating most of all as a child was siwaiyaan – vermicelli cooked with milk, sugar and lots of dry fruits and topped with balai, or clotted cream.

Salim ran his finger over the rim of the cut-glass lamp that stood on the stool, then looked out of the outer window facing the palace gates. Ahmed was crawling towards the gates, his shoulders slouched. Salim pursed his lips. He had better make it up to him tomorrow.

Salim took his seat at the dastarkhwan and hastily glanced around. The floor of the banquet hall had been covered with Persian carpets, over which starched white sheets had been spread. Abba Huzoor had taken his seat of honour, flanked by his mother Begum Janab-e-Alia and his wife Begum Khas Mahal. It was difficult to imagine such a big man with so much grace, and yet he was one of the most graceful and dignified men Salim had ever met.

He was, however, glad to be seated far from him. Who'd want to be admonished for being late for prayers on Eid? He stifled a smile as he saw Choti Begum, who sat next to him, looking at Begum Khas Mahal's new gharara with envy. She saw him watching her and showed him the henna on her hands.

'It's beautiful,' he said politely.

'Thank you, Chote Nawab,' she replied, blushing, and looked away. She was not much older than him.

He wrinkled up his nose. He would never let his wife apply henna. It smelt of rotting mint leaves.

The servants started bringing in the trays of food. One of them almost tripped over the edge of the sheet spread out over the carpets.

There were hundreds of delicacies. Several varieties of pulao – anardana pulao, moti pulao where the grains of rice were made to look like pearls; several types of bread: chapattis, parathas, and sheermal – unleavened bread made with milk and butter with saffron on top. There was quarma and zarda and a variety of kebabs; biryani, lentils and fried brinjal. Then there were the murabbas, pickles and chutneys – accompaniments to the main meal. For dessert there was rice pudding, sohan halwa, jalebi, imarti and other sweets. And of course, siwaiyaan, without which Eid would be incomplete.

There were pieces of meat carved in the shape of birds and placed on platefuls of pulao – it seemed they were pecking at the grains of rice.

Stealing another glance at Abba Huzoor, Salim was filled with a mixture of awe and pity. He was wearing a new brocade angharka, a heavy gold necklace, a pearl necklace and earrings. Salim could never bring himself to wear jewellery. Too much of a bother. Abba Huzoor, however, always made the most of such occasions. Perhaps it was to convince himself more than anybody else that he was the ruler of Avadh and not a mere puppet in the hands of the Company.

Salim turned his attention to his little brothers, who were making big plans about their eidi.

'I'm going to buy a hundred marbles,' boasted little Jamaal.

'I'm going to spend all my eidi on jalebi,' Birjis Qadir announced as he stuffed his mouth with gulab jamun.

'That's my marble,' little Salman wailed.

'I was just looking at it,' Jamaal retorted.

Birjis Qadir clapped his hands loudly. A hush fell in the hall and all eyes turned to the little prince, including Abba Huzoor's.

'Jamaal, we order you to give back the marble to Salman,' said Birjis Qadir, looking sternly at his cousin.

Jamaal scowled as Salman yanked the marble out of his hand.

Salim smiled. He patted Birjis Qadir's head lovingly as he helped himself to another shami kebab. 'I think you're fit to be a king,' he said to the little boy. Little did he know his prophesy would soon be fulfilled.

Birjis grinned. He was eleven, the son of Begum Hazrat Mahal, Salim's stepmother and a woman he openly admired.

Salim turned towards the entrance as he heard everyone clapping and cheering. It was the head chef. He entered the hall with a flourish. He held a silver tray with the biggest pie Salim had ever seen. As soon as the pie was cut open, a host of little birds were revealed. There was a sudden cacophony of sounds in the hall – the astonished excited chatter of the children, the amused prattle of the grown-ups and the twitter and flutter of feathers, as the birds tried to fly away.

Looking at all the happy faces, at the sumptuous banquet spread out before him, Salim sighed. Why did lavish preparations like this make him feel as though he was living on borrowed time?

Salim slouched over Afreen as he and Ahmed trotted along. It was the morning after Eid. The festivities were over and had left him feeling bloated and lethargic. Even the air was still and languid. He looked up at the cloudless sky and groaned inwardly. It was going to be even warmer than yesterday. He felt sorry for the servants who were following them on foot.

As they neared the parade ground, Salim looked askance at the marching soldiers. Although they looked smart in the Company's scarlet coats and black trousers, they were sweating copiously. The commanding officer bellowed attention and the sepoys halted in neat rows before the dais, with a click of their heels.

Salim grinned and shook his head as he watched

Nayansukh, who stood right in front of the platoon. He was twitching his nose at the Sikh sepoy who stood right next to him. Must be the smell of the curd they used for their long hair.

The commanding officer now ordered his men to stand at ease. He then shouted, 'First company, first platoon, step forward and pick up your rifles and cart—' He was distracted by a figure approaching him from the west. It was an elderly soldier who was jogging towards the podium, panting.

Salim sat upright and cupped his right hand over his eyes to get a better view. Why, it was Ramu kaka, Nayansukh's uncle. Salim tugged Afreen's rein and brought her to a halt.

While the rest of the soldiers stood still, Ramu kaka walked up to the dais, his hands joined in supplication.

'You're late,' barked the commanding officer who now stood over him.

'It not my fault—' Ramu kaka muttered.

THWACK!

The officer had slapped Ramu kaka right across his cheek. Salim was aghast and looked at Ahmed in disbelief. Ahmed was equally bewildered. With an exclamation of 'Ya Ali', Salim pulled Afreen's rein. He was about to charge into the parade ground when Ahmed put a restraining hand on his arm.

'Don't lose your cool, Salim mia,' he said quietly. 'Remember, this is the Company's army, not your Abba Huzoor's.'

'But how can that firangi slap a man double his age?' Salim asked. 'Does he have no respect?'

The commanding officer raised his hand again. Ramu kaka cowered. Just then another hand stopped the officer's hand in mid flight. It was Nayansukh's.

'This man is old enough to be your father,' Nayansukh hissed slowly through clenched teeth. 'I will break your hand if it goes anywhere near Ramu kaka again.'

The commanding officer turned on Nayansukh. 'How dare you, you uncouth barbari—'

The other firangi soldier, who had been quietly standing on the podium until now, hastily came between the two hostile men. 'Let it go, sir. Don't lower yourself fighting with a native. It's not worth it, sir.'

The commanding officer looked disdainfully at Nayansukh as he straightened his collars. Nayansukh stared back at him defiantly, twirling his moustache. 'Son of a pig,' the commanding officer spat as he walked back to the podium. 'Parade, dismiss,' he bellowed.

Ramu kaka was visibly shaking. Nayansukh took his hand and led him out of the parade ground.

Salim shook his head angrily as he and Ahmed started trotting down the road again. 'These firangis need to be taught a lesson,' he eventually said.

Later that afternoon, Salim sat at the edge of the water, a fishing rod in hand. This was not a good time for fish, the Gomti having shrunk to half its size, but an excellent time for fishing. You could almost catch them with your bare hands while wading through the shallow end.

He turned up his nose as he watched his servant attaching the smelly bait to the hook of his fishing rod.

He looked at Ahmed. He was sitting patiently, waiting for a fish to bite, humming a tune. Salim smiled at him as he threw the line into the water. Ahmed had already forgotten how he had spoken to him yesterday. It was typical of him never to hold a grudge. He was now trying to balance his fishing rod between his knees, as he reached out for another paan.

'Ahmed, stop chewing so much paan else all your teeth will fall out. No one will want to marry you then,' said Salim.

'Start lighting the fire, Salim mia. I think I've caught our dinner,' said Ahmed as he started hauling in his line.

'So we are having grilled sandals for dinner, are we?' Salim hooted, when he saw Ahmed's catch. A wooden sandal. It must belong to one of the priests who bathed in the river every morning.

'These priests should be banned,' Ahmed replied, as he disentangled the slimy sandal from his fishing rod and threw it back in the river, while Salim continued to laugh at him.

Suddenly he grew serious. 'Ahmed, what do you make of the rumours? About the Company taking over Avadh?'

'Don't worry, Salim mia. They're just that – rumours. Annexing Avadh? Not a chance. There's no need for that.' He clicked his betel box shut and placed it next to his cap, on the grass. 'After all, it's a golden goose which lays an egg for the Company whenever it needs funds. And right now it needs loads of money for all the wars it's engaged in.'

'But what if they decide they want all the golden eggs at once?' Salim asked.

'That'd be foolish. The people love the nawab. They would never accept the Company.'

'I wonder . . . Ahmed, remember the royal banquet in honour of the governor general?' he asked. 'When we put a cockroach on one of the English mem's hat?'

'Of course I remember Salim mia. The cockroach kept marching up and down the hat while the mem was unaware of its existence. How all the begums seated behind the purdah hooted with laughter,' Ahmed chuckled.

'And do you recall how we tied fireworks to General Sahib's horse's tail? Ya Ali, how the poor horse baulked and pranced and neighed and tried to throw him off. That got us into real trouble.'

'But nothing like the time we sprinkled coloured powder in the zenana bath on Holi.'

'The way the begums shrieked when their bodies started turning blue,' Salim guffawed.

'And if you hadn't started giggling, we would have never got caught,' said Ahmed.

'Ahmed,' Salim paused and cleared his throat. 'I'm sorry I spoke to you like that yesterday. It's just that – there's no way I'm getting involved with an English girl. No way.'

Ahmed merely nodded his head.

'You saw how they treated Ramu kaka this morning. Besides, they can't be trusted.'

'What?'

'Haven't you seen the number of times the English

have signed treaties with the nawabs of Avadh and then breached them?' Salim stood up and leant against the shisham tree. Turning back to look at Ahmed, he added, 'You know, the first treaty was signed in 1765 between the Company and the nawab. It gave the firangis permission to trade in Avadh without tax.'

He paused and nodded briefly at his servant to begin packing his fishing equipment. 'Then in 1768 another treaty was drawn up which stated that the nawab could not maintain an army of more than thirty-five thousand men. In return, the Company would protect Avadh from outside attack.' He looked across at Ahmed who was pulling in his line. 'And Ahmed, this trend has been going on ever since. These firangis keep drawing treaties and breaking them. They never keep their word.'

'Yes, tha—' Ahmed started to speak.

'Abba Huzoor is too soft,' Salim interrupted. 'If I were the ruler . . . Ah well, let it be. That can never happen.' Salim threw a pebble with full force into the river. 'But seriously, if I were the ruler, contract or no contract, I would send these bloody foreigners packing.'

Chapter Four

RACHAEL

There was a hesitant knock on the door.

'Yes, who is it?' Rachael asked as she lay on her stomach, propped on her elbows, reading her book.

'Missy baba, sahib wanting to see you in study.' It was Ram Singh. He coughed a little before continuing, 'Memsahib there as well.'

Oh dear, what had she done now, she wondered, as she rolled off the bed. Papa summoned her to the study only when it was something crucial. And mother was there as well. It meant she was in deep trouble. What could it be? They must have come to know she'd eaten at Ram Singh's house. When Papa had espied her outside the window yesterday she had told him she was trying to stop the window from rattling. He had seemed convinced. Then why did he want to see her now? Had someone tattled to him? Who could it be? She knew Ram Singh or Ayah would never do that. Then who?

There was another knock.

'Do hurry, missy baba. Sahib getting angrier by the minute.'

Rachael opened the door and walked out, chin up in the air. The soft, wooden, musty smell of books greeted her as she entered the study. Mother sat by the window, arms crossed. Her hair tied back tightly as usual, her thin lips in a straight line. Rachael wondered – when was the last time she had smiled? Papa was pacing the room. How handsome he looked in his Italian suit, she thought with a sigh. If only he'd loosen up a bit.

'You know why you've been summoned here, don't you?' he enquired without any preamble.

'Well, Ram Singh's son had asked Ayah to make some rice pudding yesterday . . .' Rachael offered feebly.

'What has that got to do with it?'

'Well, because the rice pudding smelt so good and it was Eid . . .' She was stalling. She wanted to frame her replies in a way so as not to get Ram Singh into trouble.

Papa went and sat down behind his desk. 'Ram Singh,' he called out in the cold authoritative tone that he reserved for servants.

Rachael pulled at the collar of her dress. It felt rough and uncomfortable against her skin in this heat.

Ram Singh came hurrying. He glanced at her and then at Papa. He looked as though life had been snuffed out of him. 'I'm sorry, sahib,' he began to plead.

'Ram Singh, two cups of tea please and don't take all day to bring it,' Father barked.

'Yes, sahib. Definitely, sahib,' Ram Singh muttered as he left the room.

Papa turned back to Rachael. 'I know jolly well that it was Eid yesterday. It was because of that bloody festival that I got late for the first time in my life!'

'Mr Bristow, your language,' mother chided.

Rachael unfolded her handkerchief and wiped the sweat from her brow and upper lip. 'As I was saying, because it was Eid, it was difficult for me to turn down the invitation.'

Ram Singh re-entered the room with two cups of tea. His hands were shaking as he placed them on the table. He then backed into a corner, hands folded, head lowered, almost invisible.

'Who the hell in his right mind invites an unmarried English girl to Chowk?' thundered Papa.

'Chowk?' Rachael squawked.

'Yes, Chowk! Were you or were you not in Chowk two days back?'

She let out a sigh of relief. At least Ram Singh was safe. She saw his face light up. But . . . but how did Papa know? She had taken all the precautions. Even worn a burqa. Then who could have recognised her?

'Rachael, I want a simple answer. Yes or no?' Papa tapped his fingers on the desk.

'Yes, I was there,' she whispered.

'Speak up, young lady. I did not hear that.'

'Yes, I was in Chowk the day before yesterday,' she replied haughtily, lifting her chin and looking Papa in the eye as she spoke.

Papa picked up his pipe from the desk and lit it,

before turning back to her. Mother grimaced slightly at the smell of tobacco.

'And I'm sure you have a good reason for being there?'

'I'd gone to ask Bade Miyan if he knew someone who might be able to teach me Hindustani music.'

'Do you not know that Chowk is the home of courtesans, and girls from good families never go there?'

Rachael did not say anything. She wiped her moist hands on the side of her dress and looked out of the window.

'What if someone had kidnapped you and sold you to one of those kothas as a nautch girl?' asked Mother, who had hitherto been silent.

Laughing hysterically, Rachael replied, 'Mother, don't be ridiculous.'

'You can't trust these natives, you know. Not after what happened to Richard.'

'Richard died of malaria, Mother. And imagine someone trying to kidnap me – why, I'm taller than most of the men in this city.' She let out another laugh.

'That's enough, young lady.' Papa turned his attention back to Rachael. 'No supper for you tonight and you're not to step out of your room for a week. Your meals will be sent to your room from tomorrow. You can go now.'

Rachael flounced out of the room angrily. She had simply been looking for a music teacher. What was wrong with that? And how dare he treat her as a child!

* * *

Rachael thought she must have dreamt it. No, she was not dreaming – there it was again – a small tap on the window. She looked at the clock. It was past midnight. Who could it be at this hour? After a tussle with the mosquito net, she hastily put on her gown and opened the door.

'Ayah?'

'Shhhhh!' Ayah hissed as she placed the tray she was carrying on the little cane stool. Rachael bolted the door.

'What is—?'

'I bring dinner, missy baba,' she said as she removed the embroidered cloth covering the tray, to reveal chicken stew and bread. 'This is all I can get. Now you eat nicely. I better be going. Big fat rats doing Kathak in my tummy.'

'What? You haven't eaten yet?'

Ayah touched Rachael's chin lightly. 'How can I eat when my missy baba not eaten?' Then she shoved a little decanter into her hands. 'Hide tray under bed when finish. Then spray this ittar all over room. Spice smell go away.'

'Good Lord, you've thought of everything. What would I do without you?' She took Ayah's hands in hers lovingly. 'You're wonderful, Ayah. Kalyaan is so lucky.'

'Unlucky, missy baba. Better not born than born to poor mother.'

Rachael smiled a small smile. Ayah would never understand. As soon as she left, Rachael attacked the food. She was ravenous and it tasted divine. She gulped down a few morsels then coughed and spluttered. Eat slowly Rachael, she told herself. Don't be a glutton. She took a deep breath and drank some water.

Just as she put the last morsel in her mouth, there was a knock on the door. Now what? Wiping the crumbs off her mouth, she hastily pushed the tray under the bed and straightened the sheets. She was about to open the door, when she remembered Ayah's advice about the perfume and quickly sprinkled some all over the room. It was one of those local perfumes. It smelt exotic, albeit a bit too strong. In her haste she tipped the decanter and a small puddle formed on the bed. She covered it with a pillow just as there was another knock.

It was Papa, followed by Ram Singh carrying a tray of food. Rachael looked questioningly from one to the other, then at the tray.

'I know, I know, but I couldn't sleep,' Papa said. 'I kept wondering how my little princess could fall asleep on a hungry stomach.'

'I'm all right. I'm not hungry.'

Papa patted her head, then whispered, 'I know I shouldn't have been so cross. But I was worried about you – you know, gallivanting all over Chowk. That's why I punished you.'

'Pray don't give me any explanations, Papa.'

He pointed to the food that Ram Singh had placed on the stool.

'I don't feel like eating. I just want to sleep.' She stretched and pretended to yawn but brought her hands down abruptly and bit her lips as Father walked to the bed, pushed the pillow aside and sat down. He sniffed the air but did not notice the perfume stain.

'I'm not leaving until you have eaten at least a little,' he said.

Holding her breath, Rachael watched her father cross his legs. His right foot was just a couple of inches away from the tray under the bed.

She looked at the food. It was chicken stew and bread. With pursed lips and a satisfied tummy, she slowly took a bite. 'Well, it's nothing like the nabob's Eid banquet that everyone has been talking about since yesterday, but . . .'

'I heard there were over a hundred different dishes . . .' Rachael said.

'Well, the only thing that buffoon of a nabob does is eat and sing and dance with his innumerable wives. He's becoming as fat as a hippo,' replied Papa.

'Well, for that matter, I've never seen you put in more than four hours of work a day. And that disciple of yours, that Christopher Wilson, he works even less.'

Papa looked grim. He was about to retort but decided to let it go. 'He's also your friend, you know,' he said quietly.

Rachael sighed. Yes, Christopher was her friend. Had been since they were babies. Most English parents sent their children to England when they turned five, but the Wilsons couldn't. They had no family back home. So Christopher stayed. And Mrs Wilson persuaded Papa to let her stay as well. 'Mrs Bristow is too frail to see another child go. Spare her the heartache a second time. Let Rachael grow before her eyes,' she had said. And Papa had agreed.

Christopher and Rachael had got on well, Rachael

had to admit, until of late when he had started getting possessive, as though he owned her. Thanks to Papa who had given him the nod. And the two families were now waiting for him to pop the question. Rachael felt irritated with herself. Even though she was not interested in him, why had she not discouraged him?

'C'mon, have a bit more,' Papa coaxed, as he saw her push the tray aside.

She reluctantly ate another spoonful and felt her stomach protest. If she ate one more morsel, she would either burst or throw up, she was sure of that. She looked at Papa. The lines around his eyes and mouth looked deeper. He was tired. He was not used to staying up so late. But the thought of his hungry daughter had kept him up. She smiled affectionately at him. He was rash and hot-tempered all right, but he loved her immensely.

How well he writes, Rachael thought, as she read 'Ode to the West Wind' for the third time. Sudha came into the room to put away the washing.

'Sudha, tell the punkahwalla I want the fan.'

'But memsahib, why you never pull cord tied to the punkahwalla's big toe?'

'I don't feel right doing that.'

Sudha lifted the khus mat hanging over the open window and called out, 'Hey, Madan, get to work. Memsahib wanting fan.'

Then she started sprinkling water on the khus mats hanging over the doors and windows. The velvet rectangular fan with golden tassels began to swish back and forth as Madan pulled the cords outside the room.

'You know, memsahib, barre sahib not bad. He worry, that's all. You see, Chowk not safe place for English girl.'

Rachael sighed. The fresh cool smell of khus-khus was rejuvenating.

'Barre sahib save me from becoming sati.'

'What's that?' Rachael asked with disinterest. If only she would stop her prattle and let her get back to her book.

'Memsahib, you see, when husband die, the widow burn herself on the funeral pyre an—'

'What?' Rachael closed her book and sat up.

'Yes, memsahib. You see, I no love my husband. I married when I am child. He older than me. I do not like living with him, why I must die with him? I scared and try to run away.' She continued sprinkling water on the khus mats. 'But my family catch me. They drug me and pull me to the fire. I scared, memsahib, and the fire so hot . . .' Sudha stopped speaking. She had finished sprinkling water on the mats and stared straight ahead. She looked pallid, as though reliving the nightmare.

'Then?' Rachael asked softly.

'Then barre sahib come. He order them to stop and bring me here. I beg sahib give me job here otherwise my family surely kill me.'

'I had no idea,' Rachael murmured.

'But now my whole village hating sahib. You see, they feeling English destroying our religion stopping sati.'

Rachael walked over to the basin of water that stood in a corner and splashed cold water over her face again and again. How ghastly! Imagine having to immolate yourself on your husband's pyre for the sake of religion. She shuddered involuntarily. Her eyes fell on the clothes Sudha was folding. 'What's that, Sudha?' she asked, pointing to her father's breeches.

'Oh, those are barre sahibs. You see, I bring them here with the wash by mistake. I take them back now.'

An idea began to formulate in Rachael's mind. 'No, just leave them here,' she said. 'And tell Kalyaan to keep my horse saddled tomorrow morning. I will ride as usual.'

Sudha stopped folding the clothes and looked at Rachael dubiously. 'But memsahib, barre sahib say you cannot—'

'There is no way I'm going to spend another five days languishing in this room.'

'But barre sah—'

'He won't come to know.' Rachael smiled sweetly at her and winked. 'Now go and bring me Papa's riding jacket, braces, as well as his top hat.'

'You getting me into trouble, memsahib,' Sudha muttered as she left the room.

Rachael held Papa's breeches in front of her legs and grinned impishly at her reflection in the mirror. She wondered what it felt like to wear a pair of trousers.

She was up early the next morning. Sudha helped her slip into Papa's breeches. 'Oh no, they're so loose,' she exclaimed.

'You need this, memsahib,' Sudha said as she handed her the braces.

'Ah yes, I forgot.' Rachael heaved a sigh of relief as

Sudha adjusted the braces over her shoulders and back. Carefully she pushed back every single strand of hair that was trying to peek out from beneath the hat. Finally, she put on Papa's riding jacket and looked at herself in the mirror as Sudha left the room.

She crinkled up her nose as she smiled. The breeches were supposed to stop halfway down the calf, but they were almost reaching her ankles. Ah well, it would have to do. She gently tugged the breeches at the thighs and giggled as they ballooned out. Then she put on her boots and took a final look at herself in the mirror.

'Memsahib, barre sahib leave in an hour. You better go now,' Sudha said as she entered the room.

'Yes, I better,' Rachael replied as she tucked in a stray lock of hair underneath the hat. Papa would soon leave for his customary morning ride. Mother was still sleeping. It would be another two hours before she left the room. Rachael would be back home by then and no one would know she was gone. Quietly, she walked over to the main hall and looked out of the window. No one could be seen except the gatekeeper.

She lowered her head and traversed the distance between the house and the stables swiftly. She neither looked to the left nor right and kept her eyes down. Ram Singh and Kalyaan were waiting for her with Chestnut. Rachael patted the horse's back affectionately. Ram Singh helped her onto his back.

'Baba, better coming home soon or we getting skinned alive.'

'I will, I will,' replied Rachael gaily as she trotted towards the gate.

'Salaam, barre sahib,' the gatekeeper saluted.

Rachael nodded her head slightly as she rode off towards Macchi Bhawan. She chuckled to herself as she imagined the look on the gatekeeper's face when the real barre sahib left the house. He would say nothing, of course, out of fear of losing his job.

She took a deep breath as she looked at the lemony sun slowly rising higher in the east. The dew-laden air was fresh at this time of the day. She could hear the sounds of the city waking up: the call of a peacock in the distance, the chime of the temple bells, the call for azan coming from the mosques, the sound of bullock carts and the tinkling of the cows' bells as they were led across the field by the milkman. She felt a freedom she had never felt before. She looked heavenward and closed her eyes. 'Thank you, God, for a perfect day,' she whispered.

Chapter Five

SALIM

Salim shifted his weight from one foot to the other and looked impatiently at the entrance. Now that the festivities of Eid were over, the court was in session again. He wondered why he had been summoned there.

He looked around at the darbar hall of the Safed Baradari. The heavily pillared hall was filled with courtiers smelling strongly of ittar. They all stood with folded arms and were softly murmuring to each other. He felt intimidated and began rubbing his forearm in agitation.

Just then he heard the sound of firing. It was a gun salute in honour of Abba Huzoor. The band began to play and a hush fell in the hall. Musa-ud-Daula stepped forward and announced in a loud sing-song voice, 'His Imperial Majesty, Nawab Wajid Ali Shah, son of Nawab Amjad Ali Shah, has arrived in court.' Everybody stood still with heads lowered and arms folded respectfully.

Entering the hall, Abba Huzoor took his seat on the throne. Two men followed him, each carrying a silver box, which they placed at the side of the throne.

Some individuals stepped forward with gifts they had brought for their king – baskets of mangoes, decanters of perfume, gold and silver cages with rare birds. Abba Huzoor nodded at them. A courtier stepped forward and accepted them on his behalf. Abba Huzoor instructed him to distribute some shawls in return.

Wazir Ali Naqi Khan then stepped forward with another man. Both men raised their right hands to their foreheads and bent down to their waist. 'Your Majesty, please permit me to present before you the famous poet Amirudin,' said the Wazir.

Abba Huzoor smoked his hookah and looked at Amirudin thoughtfully. 'I thought you were the embellishment of the Mughal court? What brings you to our kingdom?'

The poet flushed slightly. Keeping his head lowered he replied, 'Huzoor, as you know, the powers of the Mughal Emperor are now diminished. The Court of Delhi is languishing.' He paused and lowered his head still further while his voice rose. 'Avadh, on the other hand, is at the pinnacle of its glory. Everywhere I go I hear about its achievements . . . I will be grateful if you could permit me to be a part of your esteemed court.'

Looking at him, Abba Huzoor said, 'We always have a special place for talent such as yourself. You're most welcome to be a part of this court.'

'Thank you, Your Majesty,' the poet whispered. He

again raised his right hand to his forehead, bent low and backed out of the hall.

A courtier then stepped forward and opened the silver box that had been placed next to the throne. It was one of the boxes that preceded Abba Huzoor's processions. They enabled the common man to address his grievances to the ruler. The courtier began to read the petition aloud while Abba Huzoor listened to him carefully.

Salim's mind began to wander. He again wondered why Abba Huzoor had summoned him. Was he in trouble? He recalled the events of the last few days. Had he done anything he shouldn't have? He had been late for the morning prayers on Eid. That was all he could think of. Salim drew his breath sharply. Surely not. Why, he was twenty-two. Not a mere lad. He couldn't possibly be reprimanded in front of the others for something as petty as that. Keeping his head lowered, Salim stole a look at the throne sideways. He looked at the sheets of gold covering the throne, the oblong pillow covered in red velvet, the royal insignia of the fish carved boldly on the headrest. Then he looked at Abba Huzoor with a combination of awe and affection.

Once the last petition had been read and instructions given by Abba Huzoor on how to deal with the matter, Ali Naqi Khan stepped forward again.

'His Majesty would now like to present the sword of honour to Kishore for saving his brother from the clutches of the man-eating tigress.'

A scrawny village bumpkin with his left arm in a sling and a bruise on his left cheek stepped forward and grinned shyly. 'Bow down, you fool,' a courtier whispered as he nudged him with his elbow. The boy quickly performed the taslim.

'His left hand has been mauled by that tigress,' whispered the courtier standing next to Salim. 'I don't think he will ever be able to use that hand again.' Salim looked at the boy's arm and shuddered.

The boy grinned again as he was presented with a bejewelled sword. It was hard to decide whether his teeth or the jewels on the sword sparkled more.

'Moolchand Chowdhary, the chief of the village Faizabagh, please step forward,' Musa-ud-Daula announced. An elderly villager stepped forward and bowed low before the king.

'Prince Salim, I would like you to step forward as well,' said Abba Huzoor.

Salim was puzzled. He had never seen this old man before. Nevertheless, he stepped forward.

'Tell the prince your problem,' said Abba Huzoor.

'My Lord,' Moolchand began. Then he looked at Salim and joined his hands. 'My son, we have been ruined. My village has been destroyed . . .' he faltered and wiped his brow with his sleeve. 'Save us, my son, save us.'

Perplexed, and with a slight irritation in his voice, Salim replied, 'Yes, I'll do my best to help you. But tell me clearly what your problem is.'

'It's that tigress. Earlier she used to steal our cattle, but now she has started attacking the villagers. She has killed a dozen men already. Kishore here barely managed to escape with his life.'

'I see,' Salim said quietly.

'The villagers are panicking and fleeing the village. I don't know how to protect them.'

'Salim,' called out Abba Huzoor.

Bowing slightly, Salim answered, 'Yes, Huzoor.'

'We want you to lead the hunt to catch this maneater. You must leave by tomorrow. We cannot waste anymore time.'

'*Me*, Huzoor?' Salim squeaked, brows raised. He cleared his throat. Why did his voice sound like a sheep that has been cornered by a wolf?

'Yes, you, my son. I hope you will not let us down,' said Abba Huzoor.

'Have no doubts, Abbu, it will never come to that,' Salim mumbled.

'We're glad to hear that.' So saying, Abba Huzoor got up, signalled to Ali Naqi Khan to dismiss the court and left the hall.

Salim watched dully as Abba Huzoor walked up to Sambhu, his favourite elephant. The elephant was kneeling just outside the Safed Baradari. As soon as he saw Abba Huzoor, he raised his trunk to his forehead and saluted him. Abbu patted his forehead and settled down on the golden howdah. The party began to move towards Kaiserbagh Palace.

Salim looked dubiously at his reflection in the mirror as Chilmann tied his cummerbund. Lines creased his brow. He was scared. True, he had gone hunting several times before, but it had been confined to Musa Bagh, the royal hunting grounds where the kill had been the spotted deer, sambar, porcupine, black buck, barking deer, hare, even the odd jackal, hyenas and fox. But a tiger? And that too a maneater? Salim swallowed. The words of the woodcutter came to haunt him again. 'You're a coward,' he had said. Salim shivered involuntarily as he remembered the boy who had been honoured at court yesterday. How cruelly he had been assaulted by the tigress. No, he must go and tell Abba Huzoor he couldn't do it. And then? He would never be able to show his face to Abba Huzoor again. More than anything, he had always wanted to prove to Abbu that he was a worthy son. Yes, this was his chance. He *must* kill that tigress no matter what. He had no choice.

'Preparing for war, are we?' Daima demanded as she entered his room.

'Oh, Daima,' Salim chortled, momentarily forgetting his fears. 'I'm going after that maneater. She has already caused much havoc.'

'Why do you have to go? Are all the brave men in Avadh dead? And isn't your Abba Huzoor's hunting party soon to go into the jungles?' Daima asked as she straightened the sheets on the takhat.

'No, I very much doubt it,' said Salim as Chilmann put on his boots. 'Even if he decides to go hunting, it won't be before December. And you know that Abbu can't go off just like that. It will take at least two weeks to get his hunting party together. By then the tigress will destroy I don't know how many more villages.'

Daima said nothing but proceeded to tidy the clutter on his desk.

Salim rose and adjusted his jodhpurs. He picked up his gun, polished the cool metal with his fingers, then brought its tip to his nose. He liked the smell of sulphur. He swirled it proudly before tucking it into his cummerbund. 'And what's more – not only Abba Huzoor, but Hazrat Ammi has also asked me to go. She feels I'm ready to prove my valour.'

'That upstart!' Daima exclaimed. 'That low birth! Had the nawab wrapped around her little finger for years and now she talks about valour and manhood . . . Indeed!'

'That's not true, Daima. She's an amazing woman. She's so intelligent, and her guts – sometimes I wonder whether she's a man. She knows no fear.'

Daima pursed her lips. 'You're getting late . . . Go now.'

Salim chuckled softly.

The heels of his boots clicked loudly as he walked down the stone floor of the corridor. He could not comprehend why Daima didn't like Hazrat Ammi. Maybe it was because she belonged to a poor family. Or perhaps it was because she was one of the few begums who were not scared of her. But if there was one person who could prevent Avadh from falling into the hands of the British, it was Hazrat Ammi.

It was early evening when the hunting party passed the fields of sugar cane on the outskirts of Faizabagh. Salim brought Afreen to a halt. The twenty-odd horsemen accompanying him halted as well. He looked impatiently at the bullock and baggage carts that formed the tail of the hunting party. He had insisted on not bringing any elephants along as they would have slowed them down. But he could not say no to the carts. They were needed to carry all the tents and utensils as well as the servants. And those slowcoaches were even more sluggish than the elephants would have been. Just then, the sound of a bullock cart coming from the direction of the village drew his attention. 'HALT! Who goes there?' he called out.

The driver, clad in a dhoti and vest, approached Salim with joined hands. 'Salaam, Chote Nawab. I've been destroyed, My Lord,' he wailed. 'My wife, my beautiful wife . . .' He stopped speaking to wipe his tears with the edge of the cloth draped across his shoulders.

'Ya Ali, why? What happened to her?' asked Salim.

'She gone to draw water from the well this morning. The tigress appeared out of nowhere. She struck a fatal blow to her face. Her beautiful face . . .'

Salim put a consoling arm on his shoulder. 'I'm sorry, kaka. Don't worry, we'll avenge her death.'

'Good luck to you, Chote Nawab,' the villager replied. 'I take no chances. I take my children far away to safety.'

Looking thoughtfully towards the village, Salim asked, 'Tell me, kaka, do you think the tigress is still in the village?'

'I don't think so, My Lord. She was last seen ambling towards the forest.'

Salim nodded. The villager raised his hand to his forehead, bowed and backed away to his cart.

The baggage carts had caught up with the rest of the hunting party by now. Salim looked at Khurram baba, who had accompanied his father as well as his grandfather on several hunting expeditions. All Salim knew about hunting and the birds and the bees, he had learnt from him. Khurram baba signalled to him and they started moving again.

Soon they were in Faizabagh. The entire village was deserted. Salim stopped under a mango tree. A parrot took flight as he approached, letting a half-eaten mango splat on the ground. He looked around. He could see a diseased stray dog sniffing a rubbish heap intently. A crow cawed atop the roof of a hut. Other than that, there was not a soul to be seen. The silence was eerie.

'Looks like the tigress has scared the hell out of them,' Ahmed said. 'I cannot conceive what might have turned her into a maneater.'

'Some of the villagers who saw her say she was limping,' said Salim. As he and Ahmed trotted up to a nearby well, they noticed some pug marks. Salim drew in a sharp breath. Ahmed dropped his betel box, his mouth falling open as he saw the torn pieces of bloodstained clothes scattered near the well.

Salim turned to his men. The servants were busy feeding the horses. 'Let's not dally,' he ordered brusquely. 'The tigress might still be on the prowl. Start moving.'

There was a sudden drop in light and temperature as they reached the greenish-black woods – the colour of henna that has just been made into a paste. Salim's hunting party trotted around looking for a good spot. Soon they came to a small clearing surrounded by a canopy of dense trees.

'This is perfect. We'll camp here,' said Salim, as he got off his horse.

As the servants got busy setting up the tents as well as the machan for the hunt, Salim and Ahmed ambled through the forest. They came upon a cave partially hidden from view by the branch of a neem tree.

Ahmed peered into the cave. It was dark. He could see nothing. He looked at Salim. 'Shall we?'

Salim nodded.

The two of them pushed the branch aside and walked into the cave. They could still see nothing. Ahmed stepped onto a dry twig. It snapped into two, making him jump. There was a strong, all-pervasive smell in the cave. Wet grass and something else.

'It's the m-m-maneater,' Ahmed stammered.

'Shh.' Salim put a finger to his lips. He could sense some movement. Then a sound. A rumble, that soon grew into a growl. Salim and Ahmed stared straight into the eyes of the tigress. She was gigantic. They stood rooted to the spot. Salim broke out in a cold sweat.

The tigress was not happy to see intruders in her home and let out a terrifying roar. Salim shuddered. The sound must have reverberated for miles around. Her green eyes flashed angrily in the darkness.

Ahmed gulped. 'Salim mia, run!'

The two men ran faster than they had ever run in their entire life. They bolted blindly, slipping, sliding and scrambling through brambles and bushes and thorns. They did not stop until they reached the camp.

There they sat, under a mulberry tree, catching their breath. Salim looked over his shoulder to see if the tigress was following them. Thank goodness, she wasn't. He looked at his torn breeches, at his bleeding knees, at

Ahmed's torn and stained angarkha, at the bruise on the side of his neck.

It was getting dark. The forest was now full of mysterious shadows and whisperings. He felt sorry for the goat, tethered as it was, at the edge of the clearing. The servants were still setting up the machan. Some crickets started clapping their wings just as a firefly flashed its light in the darkness.

There was a sudden movement in the grass. Salim became alert. 'Looks like she's found us,' he whispered. It was just a rabbit. It darted off as soon as it saw him. 'Ahmed, the tigress will be upon us any minute now. Let's not tarry.'

He hobbled towards the machan. How long were those incompetent nincompoops going to take to set it up? He had walked a mere ten paces when he felt something behind him. He turned around sharply.

Sure enough, the rusty-brown tigress was stealthily padding towards the goat, its tail shot up in the air. The goat began to bleat hysterically.

Salim jumped onto Afreen's back post-haste while Ahmed ran to fetch his rifle. Snatching his gun, Salim took aim just as the tigress sprang on the goat. The bullet hit her on the thigh. She let out a pained menacing roar.

The servants rushed to the spot upon hearing the roar. One look at the tigress and they froze on the spot, stupefied.

In spite of her limp, the tigress turned towards Salim. Her tail twitched from side to side, accelerating to a furious lashing as she charged towards him. His hands shook violently as he pointed his gun at her and fired.

It missed. Beads of perspiration gathered on his brow. 'Ya Ali,' he muttered as he took aim again. But before he could fire, she had sprung on him with one fluid movement and knocked him off the horse.

Ahmed fired. Although it missed the tigress, the sound distracted her. Her whiskers shot upwards, bristling with fury as she turned to Ahmed and roared again.

Scrambling to his feet, Salim put some distance between himself and his tormentor. 'Khurram baba, my rifle!' he shouted as he threw his empty gun away. He was breathing hard through his open mouth.

Just then Ahmed tripped over a stump and fell. His rifle flew out of his hands. He turned white as he stared at the tigress. She was just a yard away from him. He sat there, petrified, unable to move.

'Quick,' Salim yelled as the tigress inched closer to Ahmed. Two servants rushed to Ahmed and dragged him back into the bushes. Khurram baba came running, a double-barrelled pistol in his hands. Salim snatched the loaded pistol and fired one shot after another till no more bullets were left.

The tigress roared one last time, then lay still. Thick, sticky blood oozed out of her.

Salim sank to the ground and wiped away the perspiration. He looked at the tigress. The black stripes on her coat shimmered. She was almost ten feet long and was at the prime of her life. It was a pity he had to kill something so majestic. He got up and patted Afreen. She was shaken, but otherwise unhurt. The servants gathered around him, praising him for his bravery.

He looked at Ahmed. Ahmed raised his right hand to

his forehead and saluted him. 'I owe you this one, Salim mia,' he said, his voice still quivering. Salim gave him a small smile. Then he lifted the flap of his tent and went in.

No sooner had Salim stepped out of his tent the next morning, than he was greeted by the cook.

'Good morning, Chote Nawab.' The cook raised his right hand to his forehead and bowed. 'When should I serve food?' he asked.

Salim took a deep breath of the crisp morning air before replying. 'I'll be back in an hour. We'll have breakfast and leave shortly after that.'

'Whatever you wish, Chote Nawab.' The cook bowed and left.

As Salim and Ahmed cantered through the woods, Salim looked around. The forest looked different as the morning light filtered feebly through the dense foliage. There was a fresh nip in the light breeze that blew in from the north. It made the leaves on the trees rustle like the ghungroos on a tawaif's feet. The dewdrops on a giant spider's web swayed and sparkled like jewels as they caught the faint sunlight.

'You go ahead, Salim mia,' said Ahmed. 'I'll join you in a few minutes. And take Toofan with you.'

Salim hadn't realised that, while his eyes had been feasting on the grandeurs of Mother Nature, Ahmed's eyes had caught something else. He followed Ahmed's gaze and noticed some village girls in the distance. They were giggling and squealing with laughter as they collected wood and twigs to light the fires at home. He gave a lopsided smile and shook his head as he patted Afreen and took the reins of Toofan in his hands. Ahmed would be back soon. For all his interest in girls, he was as scared of them as a rabbit is of a fox.

As Salim trotted along under the low-lying branch of a peepal tree, someone jumped down from the branch onto Toofan's back and made off with the horse. For a moment Salim stood dumbfounded. Was it the ghost that lived on the peepal tree? The one that the villagers had been talking about? Of course not. It was a thief. Salim kicked Afreen furiously and galloped after the thief. Soon Afreen was abreast of Toofan and Salim managed to get hold of his reins. He tugged hard at them and brought Toofan to a halt. The thief jumped off the horse and was about to make his escape when Salim grabbed hold of him.

'You impertinent thief!' he cried. 'You think you can escape after trying to steal the nawab's horse?'

'I'm not a thief,' the thief mumbled indignantly through clenched teeth. 'I was just borrowing the horse as mine has run away.'

Before Salim had time to reply, he had been punched hard in the stomach with an elbow. He groaned but did not loosen his grip on the thief. In the scuffle that followed, the thief's hat came loose and a waterfall of golden hair came cascading down. Salim stared at the hair and then at the thief in disbelief. His lips parted slightly as he narrowed his eyes to gaze into a pair of deep-blue ones.

Chapter Six

RACHAEL

Rachael couldn't help giggling at the look of shock on her captor's face. He looked so familiar – those eyes, that long black hair, that firm chin. Where had she seen him before? Who was he? He was the only native she had come across who was taller than her. He must be a prince, she decided.

He abruptly let go of her.

'I'd stopped for just two minutes to pick up some wild flowers – you know, those yellow flowers? And the moment I got off the horse, he just galloped away . . .' Rachael trailed off as she found him staring at her hands.

She looked at him perplexed, and nervously played with the ring on her finger. He stared at them even harder, before clutching them.

'Ya Ali, were you playing the piano a few days back at Colonel Bristow's house?' he asked urgently, as he turned her hands over and over, as though looking for a clue to some hidden treasure.

'Yes, I'm his daughter.'

'And were you in Chowk a few days back in a burqa?' he asked as he gently rubbed the diamond on her ring.

Rachael shifted uncomfortably and took her time before answering. She remembered now why he seemed familiar. She had seen him at Bade Miyan's shop.

'Maybe,' she answered softly.

'I knew I'd recognise these hands anywhere.'

'My hands,' said Rachael.

'Yes?'

'You're still holding them.'

'Oh, I'm s-sorry . . .' the prince stuttered as he let go of them.

'Sir, I had no intention of stealing your horse.'

The prince raised a brow.

Fiddling with her ring, Rachael answered, 'I was simply borrowing it as my own horse has run away. So if you would be so kind, lend me a horse and I'll quietly take my leave.'

'I'm afraid not, ma'am,' the prince answered in clipped tones. 'You're my responsibility now. As long as you're with me, you're not going anywhere alone. You shall join us for breakfast and then we shall safely escort you home.' His voice was deep, confident, authoritative.

Rachael groaned inwardly. Now she was in even more trouble. Not only had she left home when she shouldn't have and been stranded in the forest by her runaway horse, but now she was going to be escorted home by the nabob's entourage. She could just imagine the look on Papa's face when he saw her regal homecoming. Not to mention how horrified he was going to be when he saw what she was wearing. It felt so liberating, though, wearing breeches, not having to sit side-saddle in an irritating long skirt over which she often tripped. How she wished she was a man.

She had not intended to stray so far. Since she was taking her meals in her room, she would not be missed as long as she managed to sneak back before late afternoon. After all, everything had worked out smoothly on the last two occasions she had sneaked out of the house. But now she was in big trouble, and all because of that prince! Rachael's forehead creased slightly. What was his name? Not that she cared. If he had not caught her and insisted there was no way she was going out of the jungle alone, she would be home by now. That arrogant man! He had annihilated all chances of getting back home unnoticed.

Walking about restlessly, she hit the trees with the long twig that she had found. She swung it in the air, brandishing it like a sword, then poked the stones lying buried in the earth with it. Then with a sigh she sat down on the stump of a tree and watched the servants bustling about preparing breakfast and laying out the food. There were others who were busy dismantling the machan and folding the tents where the party had slept last night.

The diamond on her ring sparkled as it caught a beam of sunlight filtering in through the leaves of the tree under which she sat. Just then she noticed something glittering at her feet as well. She picked it up and dusted it. It was a black, velvet, bejewelled cap. It must belong to the prince. She put it on and walked over to the watering hole.

Peering down at her reflection, she said in a gruff voice, 'As long as you're with me—'

'Interesting, very interesting,' a voice chuckled behind her.

Rachael hastily turned around. It was the prince. With him was a rotund young man in an angarkha and wide-bottomed pyjamas. He wore a pearl necklace, earrings and a huge stone on his forefinger.

'I've never met anyone like you before. An English girl in men's trousers, wearing a nawab's cap,' said the prince.

Rachael gave an embarrassed grin and took off the cap.

'May I be so bold to ask whether you work for the theatre, ma'am?' the prince's companion asked, looking down.

'For heaven's sake, no. Pray, whatever gave you the idea?' replied Rachael.

The young man looked at the prince then cleared his throat. 'Well, the first time we saw you, you were in a burqa, the second time you were in a dress and now ... or perhaps you work for a costume company?'

Laughing, Rachael picked up her stick and began making patterns on the ground with it.

'Myself called Ahmed,' the rotund young man continued. He touched his cap lightly as Rachael nodded her head. 'I hope everything's all right?' he asked.

'How could any—' Rachael was about to hurl a tirade of abuse at the prince, but stopped short. She gathered her hair and twisted it into a knot at the top of her head. Turning to the prince she asked, 'Are the nabob's hunting parties similar to this?'

'Not at all,' the prince replied. 'This was an emergency hunt. No frills. You ought to have seen Nawab Asaf-ud-Daula's hunting parties. He was the . . .' The prince paused and rubbed his chin. 'Yes, he was the fourth nawab of Avadh. His hunting parties had no fewer than eight hundred elephants. One elephant was used simply for carrying all his rifles. There'd be dancing girls, singers, musicians and hawkers selling all kinds of wares. It looked more like a caravan than a hunting party.'

'And Nabob Wajid Ali Shah's?' asked Rachael.

'He's not keen on hunting . . . It's no longer what it used to be. Anyway, breakfast will be served soon. Do let me know if you need anything,' said the prince.

Then the two men touched their caps slightly, bowed and left.

Rachael thanked the servant and sat down on the rug spread out for her. She swallowed as she looked at the breakfast spread before her. She had never imagined breakfast to be so lavish, and that, too, in the forest. There were cakes, biscuits, fried fish, boiled fish, different types of curry, parathas, rogni rotis, pickled salmon, sausages, tea, coffee, wine. This was a feast! She felt full just looking at it.

The servants were fussing over the prince. They called him Chote Nawab. She wondered what it meant. He smiled at her as he took a bite of the rogni roti.

'What took you to Chowk the other day?' he asked.

'How can you be so sure it was me?'

The prince looked her straight in the eye, then glanced at her hands and replied quietly, 'I'm sure!'

Rachael pecked at her paratha, wiped her lips with the serviette then answered, 'I'd gone to ask Bade Miyan whether he knows someone who can teach me Hindustani music.'

'You want to learn Hindustani music? Why?'

'Because . . . I don't know. I suppose because I love it.'

She shifted uncomfortably and wished he would not stare at her like that.

He collected himself and, looking at his food, said, 'I could teach you.'

'You could? But where?'

'At my palace, of course.'

'Father would never give me his permission.'

'I will teach you on one condition.'

'What?' Rachael asked suspiciously.

'That you teach me how to play the piano.' His face was serious as he spoke. But his smouldering eyes – they were teasing her, baiting her, goading her to accept the challenge.

A couple of hours had elapsed since Rachael had finished her breakfast. Although it was mid morning, it felt like dawn, as the trees shut out most of the sunlight. Rachael watched with interest as the men tied the tigress to either ends of the pole. It was such a beautiful creature. Even in death it looked regal and awe-inspiring. Once the tiger had been secured and lifted onto the shoulders of six sturdy men, the party was ready to move back to Lucknow.

She smiled as a servant trotted up to her with a horse. So Chestnut had been found. She patted her horse lovingly and thanked the servant. As she mounted Chestnut, she glanced at the prince. He was explaining something to the man who rode right in front. Perhaps explaining a shorter way to reach Lucknow, she hoped. Even though it was still morning, it was already warm. Mother must have made sure all the windows had been shut and the khus mats sprinkled with water. Rachael watched the prince as he took one last look at the victorious hunting party, then trotted back to ride beside her.

'Where did you learn to ride so well?' he asked.

'I spent many a summer with my grandparents. They live in a little village on the foothills of the Himalayas. I would spend all day just riding.' She stopped speaking, as she remembered the hills, the undulating terrain, the evergreen foliage.

'Why did you kill that tiger?' she suddenly asked.

'I beg your pardon?'

'You killed a beautiful majestic beast like that for mere sport? Or was it to prove your manliness?'

'I—'

'I can understand if one kills to fill one's belly. But you can't possibly eat a tiger, so pray what was the need to kill him?'

'Well, if I didn't, *we* might have been *its* dinner,' he replied and rode off in a huff.

Five minutes later he was back. He came dangerously close to her. She wondered at the thrust of his chin.

Did his chin naturally jut out like that or was it plain arrogance?

'Her,' he said.

'What?'

'It was a tigress.'

With that he galloped away to join Ahmed in front of the hunting party.

Chapter Seven

SALIM

Salim entered the main hall of Parikhana, the Academy of Music and Fine Arts, quietly. He always felt a little unnerved when visiting Parikhana. This was where you could find the best talents of Avadh, honing their dancing and singing abilities. It was no wonder Abba Huzoor was so fond of the place.

Abba Huzoor looked at Salim and nodded. Salim bowed and raised his right hand to his forehead in reply and sat down. He looked around. Chand Pari, dressed in a white kurta with delicate silver embroidery, was enacting Krishna Leela through dance form. She was accompanied on the sitar by two musicians while Ustad Burhan Mian played the tabla and Ustad Ali Khan provided the vocals.

Why had Abba Huzoor summoned him, Salim wondered. Of course, he was ecstatic. He hardly ever got to see him, much less spend time with him. He looked at him now as he took a puff from his hookah. He was engrossed in watching Chand Pari. His expressions and hand movements echoed those of the dancer. It seemed even his heart beat in time to music.

Chand Pari was performing one of the stories from the childhood of Lord Krishna. Salim watched with interest as the movements of Chand Pari's hands indicated she was churning butter. Once the butter was made, she hung it from the ceiling in an earthenware pot. Her expressions changed. She was now enacting Little Krishna who loved butter and came toddling along. He could not reach the butter however hard he tried. It was much too high. Suddenly an idea struck him. He picked up a stone and threw it at the pitcher holding the butter. The pitcher broke and Krishna happily scooped all the butter . . .

Salim's thoughts flew to Hazrat Ammi. He had heard she had come to the Parikhana when she was just sixteen. Her father had died when she was little and she used to live with her phuphi and phupha. Her phupha was a renowned designer and embroider of caps. Once, when commissioned to do some work for the regal household, he incurred the wrath of Abba Huzoor and his men were sent to imprison him and bring him to court.

The men could not find him but instead chanced upon his niece Hazrat Ammi. So entranced were they by her charm and wit that they went back to the palace singing her praises, her uncle forgotten. She was soon made a part of the Parikhana. Abba Huzoor, too, fell under her sway. So charmed was he by her beauty, grace and intelligence that he bestowed upon her the title of

Mahak Pari, a fairy that spreads fragrance wherever she goes. That was before he married her and she became a mother to Birjis Qadir. Thereafter she came to be known as Begum Hazrat Mahal. But for Salim she'd always be Hazrat Ammi.

The music picked up crescendo, as did Chand Pari's fall of the feet and movement of the hands. She swirled around faster and faster in time with the beat and finished with a flourish.

'That was beautiful, you have made us happy today,' Abba Huzoor remarked, before dismissing all those present in the room with a wave of his hand and turning to Salim.

Salim performed the taslim. Straightening up, he said, 'I believe you sent for me, Abba Huzoor?'

'We heard you killed that tigress.'

'Yes, Huzoor.' Salim inclined his head respectfully.

Abba Huzoor came close to him and patted his head lovingly. 'We are pleased, my son. Inshah Allah may you always make us proud.'

'I'll try my best,' Salim replied, his Adam's apple moving.

'We shall have a celebration in your honour tomorrow.'

Salim's eyes shone as he exclaimed, 'Ya Ali! Thank you so much Abba Huzoor.'

Sitting in the shade of the long veranda of the palace, Salim looked across the Gomti at the park. A circular portion of the park had been enclosed with bamboo fences and iron railings. That was where the elephant fight was soon to commence. A crowd had begun to gather along the fence and on the verandas, balconies and rooftops of houses that overlooked the park. There were even some enthusiasts who were perched on trees.

Salim thought of how he had shot the tigress. He felt a cold tingle of fear as he recalled how close he'd been to getting killed. Then he remembered Miss Bristow. What an affront – a woman in breeches! She ought to have been a man. She was far too haughty and emancipated for a woman!

And yet he could not deny he found her attractive, even in a man's clothes. The way her hips filled the lean trousers and the way the taut shirt moved whenever she breathed. And her blue eyes, her honest, laughing eyes – neither too big nor too small, just perfect.

What was wrong with him? Why the hell was he thinking about that English woman? And what was he thinking – offering to teach her music? What if she took his offer seriously?

The bugle sounded, announcing the arrival of Abba Huzoor. He entered the veranda with fanfare, accompanied by the peacock fan-bearers. Everyone stood still with folded arms and bowed heads.

Abba Huzoor sat down and signalled for the fight to commence, with a wave of his hand. Salim watched him as he sat there, his hands moving as though he were composing a piece of music in his head. It was true – Abba Huzoor's entire being was submerged in music. He had heard that even when he slept, his hands and feet moved about as though dancing.

He turned his attention to the two elephants, tied with a rope, at opposite ends of the arena. Both of them were in rut, which was done on purpose. Elephants were peace-loving creatures and would not be inclined to fight unless they were ruttish. A foul-smelling, greasy liquid was oozing out of their temples.

As soon as the bugle sounded again, the ropes were cut loose. The two elephants raised their trunks and tails and, trumpeting loudly, charged towards each other. As their heads collided with an enormous impact, a loud roar went up from the crowd. The mahouts kept goading the two animals on with their spiked red-hot iron spears.

Salim watched the elephants jostling each other with disinterest. 'You killed that majestic beast for mere sport? Or was it to prove your manliness?' Miss Bristow had taunted. Someone else had said something similar when he was sixteen. 'Only cowards kill dumb animals that cannot retaliate. If you want to prove your royal blood, go and fight against injustice instead of killing innocent beasts.' Even today, after all these years, he had not forgotten the look of contempt on that woodcutter's face – it was almost as if he had spat on him.

Grimacing, Salim looked in Abba Huzoor's direction. He had left. One of the elephants had fallen to the ground. The other elephant was about to rip open its belly with its tusks, when Salim raised his hand and shouted, 'Stop it!'

All eyes in the arena turned on him.

'Are you all right, Salim mia? You look as though you've just seen a maneater,' Ahmed tried to joke. He began to wipe the beads of perspiration that had broken out on Salim's face.

Salim looked at the elephants. Blood ran from their foreheads, down their trunks and mingled with the mud. He pushed Ahmed's hand away from his forehead impatiently and turned to the mahouts. 'Take your elephants to the vet and treat their injuries.'

Then turning to the audience he announced, 'Let this be known throughout Avadh – no more fights are ever to be held in my honour again.' With that he strode off.

It was exactly seven days since the elephant fight. Salim stared moodily at the painting that hung on the wall of his parlour. He did not know what had made him halt the fight. All he knew was, as long as that Englishwoman's words kept haunting him, he would never be able to kill another animal again.

He turned slightly when Chilmann walked up to him, bowed, raised his hand to his forehead and whispered, 'Chote Nawab.'

'Yes?'

Chilmann handed him a piece of paper. 'A servant gave this to the gatekeeper and asked him to give it to you.'

Salim looked at the paper quizzically before reading it. It was a short missive. His brows creased as he read it:

It is my pleasure to accept you as my teacher. My parents attend afternoon mass on Sundays at two o'clock. Pray tell me if I should come then. My companion Sudha shall do the needful.

Miss R. Bristow.

That was all it said. Salim began pacing the room, hands behind his back. He spoke after a long time, ordering Chilmann to call Daima. Then he walked over to the window. Lifting the khus mat, he looked out. The late afternoon sun came streaming into the room, burning everything it touched.

'You called me, Chote Nawab?'

Salim turned around to face Daima. 'Yes, Daima. I need your help.'

'Anything for you, Chote Nawab,' Daima answered.

'That's why I sent for you, Daima. I need you to arrange for an English girl to be brought to my apartments without being seen.'

Daima's jaw fell open as she exclaimed, 'Hai Ram, what are you saying, Chote Nawab?'

Touching Daima's arms lightly, Salim said, 'It's not what you think, Daima. She's a respectable woman. I will teach her music, that's all.'

'But an *angrez*?' Daima asked incredulously.

Salim did not say anything. Merely walked over to his desk and read Miss Bristow's note again.

'I'm sorry, Chote Nawab . . . I cannot do it,' said Daima.

Letting out a heavy sigh, Salim looked at her unrelenting form. Her mind seemed to have been made up. Kicking off his uncomfortable khurd nau, he padded barefoot towards her. Ah! The marble floor felt cool. He held her arms and pleaded once again. 'Please, Daima.'

'There's no way I'm going to let a cow-eating white-skin to enter this palace as long as I live.'

Salim raised his voice, 'Don't cross your limits,

Daima. I won't tolerate anyone speaking about my acquaintance in that manner.'

Daima glared at Salim. Neither of them spoke. Picking up the silver spittoon, she spat out some betel juice. Then, pursing her chapped orange lips, she said quietly, 'Thank you for showing me my place, Prince Salim . . . I had forgotten that I'm a mere servant.'

'Ya Ali!' Salim closed his eyes for a split second in sheer exasperation. 'I didn't mean that, Daima. Go away, I don't need you,' he shouted irritably at the fan-bearers who were following him as he paced the room. He walked over to the surahi which stood in a corner of the room and gulped down some water noisily. Turning back to Daima, he made her sit down on the takhat. He knelt before her and looked her in the eye. 'Look, Daima, you know very well that you're all I have. Amma left me soon after birth. Abba Huzoor never has time for me.'

He got up and walked over to his desk. He twirled the quill pen that lay on it, before returning to Daima. 'I would never go against your wishes, Daima. If you don't want her to come here, so be it. But just consider this – I gave my word to that woman and I'm honour-bound to keep it. You know as well as anyone that in all these years I've never broken a promise.'

Daima's face softened. 'What do I have to do?' she asked quietly.

Salim gave her a tight hug. 'Thank you, Daima.'

Shrugging out of his embrace, Daima replied, 'Now tell me what you want me to do.'

'Miss Bristow's parents will leave for church on

Sunday at two o'clock. You must reach her house at ten past two. Just go up to the gatekeeper and tell him you need to speak to Sudha. She will take care of the rest.'

'I hope Ramji will forgive me for committing this crime,' Daima said, shaking her head.

Salim smiled at her remark but chose not to say anything lest she change her mind. As the call for the evening prayers wafted in through the window, he knelt down facing Mecca. He raised his arms, muttering the holy verses under his breath. Then he lowered his forehead to the ground as he finished his prayers.

Chapter Eight

RACHAEL

As the carriage trundled down the street, Rachael looked at the older woman seated across from her. 'Pray tell me, what I should call you?' she asked.

'Everyone in the palace calls me Daima,' Daima replied curtly, revealing crooked yellowing teeth. Her breath smelt of betel nuts and betel leaves.

An awkward silence ensued as Daima turned her back towards Rachael and looked out of the window. She must have been beautiful when young, Rachael thought, what with her oval face, broad forehead and sharp nose. She wondered what Papa would say if he discovered she had again gone out without permission. Her thoughts flew back to the afternoon when she had just got back from the forest.

'Tea laid out in garden, missy baba. Sahib waiting,' Ram Singh had announced.

Swallowing, Rachael made her way slowly towards

the garden. She stopped by the eucalyptus tree. She rested her palm against its smooth straight trunk as she watched her father. He sat alone, stirring his coffee. As he stirred, his anger brewed, or so she imagined. She took a deep breath in, then breathed out.

'Good afternoon, Papa,' she said, as Ram Singh held out a chair for her.

Papa pulled out his watch from his pocket, looked at it and then at her. 'Good *evening*, Rachael. Did you have a good day?' he asked pointedly.

'Yes, Papa, I . . .' she cleared her throat. He didn't look angry. Maybe he didn't know that she had gone riding by herself to the forest and been escorted back by the nabob's son.

'Oh yes, I know,' he said, reading her face, a twisted smile marring his sculpted features. 'How old are you?'

'Umm . . . eighteen?'

'Exactly. You're now an adult, Rachael, and I've decided not to treat you as a child anymore. Even though you insist on acting like one.'

Crinkling up her nose, Rachael looked out of the carriage window. She had managed to wriggle out of mass and tea at the Wilsons' that afternoon by feigning a headache. So she had done something childish again. But how could she have said 'no' to such an exhilarating prospect? Besides, she'd do anything for music. Even if it meant invoking Papa's wrath. Or suffering the presence of that arrogant prince.

She watched as the carriage passed through the Kaiserbagh gateway. It was intricately sculpted with mermaids and fishes. She marvelled at how the tiles placed on the low wall and the wavy lines on the parapet made it appear as though the mermaids were frolicking in the sea. The entire complex looked like a tent city.

'Pray tell me, what is it called?' she asked Daima, as they passed a building which looked like an airy tent in concrete. Its eight towers looked like pegs holding the tent to the ground.

'Lanka,' Daima replied. 'It's a theatre.'

Rachael was speechless. She had never seen such elegant structures, not even in England. The carriage soon halted. With Daima's help, she wrapped the long silk chador around her, before stepping out of the carriage. She followed the elderly woman excitedly as she led her down a long corridor. She had never been inside a palace before. It was very quiet. Except for the occasional beating of the long khus mats that hung over the archways, against the walls, in the hot summer breeze.

She stopped to look through one of the small arched windows on the outer wall and gasped in disbelief – she could see for over a hundred yards through that little peephole, beyond the courtyard and the palace gates, right into the marketplace. It was like looking through a pair of binoculars.

Daima tapped her shoulder and gestured they had better be moving. They passed a door to what seemed like a hall. Two female guards stood at the door in a state of lethargy. Rachael looked at Daima questioningly.

'Zenana,' Daima replied. 'We better not be seen here . . . Otherwise lot of questions getting asked.'

Footsteps echoed through the corridors as someone

called out to Daima. 'Don't stop . . . Keep walking,' she whispered to Rachael in clipped tones.

Rachael tripped over the chador and had to stop to wrap it around herself. She bit her lip as Daima gave her an exasperated look. A flight of high, narrow stone steps led them into a spacious front room. The floor was covered with white marble. There were small latticed windows along the walls.

'Thank you, Daima.' Rachael heard a voice behind her. It was the prince. She could recognise that deep authoritative voice anywhere.

'I shall take your leave now, Chote Nawab.' Daima bowed slightly and left the room.

Rachael turned towards the prince. She played with the soft ends of the chador before taking it off and shaking her hair. 'Thank you for your magnanimous offer to teach me Hindustani music,' she said.

'I did not expect to hear from you. Not after vexing you by killing that tigress,' Salim replied, watching her.

'Sir, who am I to question what you choose to do in your spare time? I have come here to learn music, that's all.' She looked around, noticing the low wooden platform covered with white sheets, the oblong pillows with red silk pillow covers, the chandelier, the silver lamps, the qatat hanging on the wall and the pitcher that stood in a corner. Biting her forefinger, she asked, 'May I be so bold as to enquire whether this is your apartment?'

'So it is. If it's not up to her ladyship's standards, we can go to another room, or maybe another palace?' Salim taunted.

'Pray, will the others not wonder why a woman is in your apartments and not in the zenana?'

'They'll simply assume you're someone I've taken a fancy to.' He grinned and winked at her, twirling the quill pen that he held in his hand, his eyes noting every detail of her body.

Rachael was taken aback by his impertinence. 'Is that what they think? That I'm a nautch girl?'

The prince came close to her and whispered huskily, 'Does it matter what they think?' Again those eyes – teasing, mocking, weighing, challenging.

Lowering her gaze, Rachael played with a lock of hair that had come loose, fuming inwardly. The arrogance! Papa would have his head for speaking to his daughter like that.

'Shall we, then?' the prince asked, holding a door open for her. He bowed slightly and added, 'After you, ma'am.'

Rachael sauntered into a hall – it was a music room. Her eyes lit up like Mother's did whenever a parcel of her favourite ham arrived from back home in England. She covered her mouth with her hands as she exclaimed, 'Oh my goodness!'

The room was full of every plausible Hindustani, as well as Western, musical instrument that she could think of. There was the sarod, sitar, veena, harmonium, tabla, sarangi, rebab, dhol, santoor . . . Why, there was even an old piano that stood by itself, a little conspicuously, in the west end of the room.

'Our small collection,' the prince said humbly, the tone and the look on his face belying modesty. 'Is there any particular instrument that you wish to learn?'

Rachael strummed the strings on the sitar, then the veena. Then she picked up a trumpet and blew hard into it.

'Oh please, it sounds like a donkey being strangulated.' The prince covered his ears, lines creasing his forehead.

Laughing, Rachael turned to face him, then blew into the trumpet again.

'Ma'am, kindly desist molesting the qurna,' he said as he snatched the trumpet from her hand and put it down.

Rachael licked her lips. 'I fear I have no idea where to start.'

'Since you play the piano – and very well, if I may add – I think we should start with the harmonium. Please be seated.'

She sat down on the Persian carpet, playing with the tassel of an oblong pillow.

'The octave do-re-me-fa . . . becomes sa-re-ga-ma . . . in Hindustani. Now listen.'

Rachael watched as the prince's right hand moved elegantly over the keys of the harmonium while the left hand pumped the bellows.

'You play with perfection!'

'When you have Ustad Junaid Ali Khan as your teacher, you cannot but play perfectly. He once threw the tabla at me when I was out of tune.'

'No! Pray tell me it did not hurt?'

'Not really,' the prince grinned. 'I ducked just in time. But the poor tabla broke into pi—' He stopped speaking as he heard footsteps outside the hall. 'I hope it's not Abba Huzoor,' he whispered.

Rachael looked towards the door. It was a servant. He placed two silver bowls containing melons before them, bowed and swayed out of the room.

The prince picked one bowl and handed it to her. As she slowly ate the cool refreshing fruit, he started strumming a sitar. 'I composed a new tune yesterday. Let me play it for you.'

Rachael watched him play. She noticed his fingernails were square, practical, unlike her thin, tapering, artistic ones, with all the moons visible. 'Play the last stanza a scale higher,' she said after a while.

'All right, let's try doing that . . . Ya Ali, you're right, ma'am. It heightens the climax.' Salim put down the sitar with a satisfied smile.

'Not "ma'am" – Rachael.'

'Ray . . . Chal,' Salim drawled.

Rachael smiled. She liked the way he said her name – Ray Chal, like two separate words; two happy notes of a lilting song. Or the sound of a brook bubbling over pebbles. Ray Chal Ray Chal . . .

'All right, your turn now,' said the prince.

'I don't understand.'

'May I remind you of your promise? To teach the piano?'

Walking over to the piano, Rachael tried to play, but it was in vain. Some of the keys were dead, others were off-key.

'Well, in that case, you can teach me in your home.'

'Home?' She looked hastily at the clock that stood

along the wall. 'Oh goodness, it's four o'clock. I had better leave if I wish to sneak back before Mother and Papa get back home.'

She hurriedly wrapped the chador around her.

Salim was on his feet in a trice and sprang before her. 'Wait, you cannot leave so soon. We'd only just started.'

'I must. I don't have my parents' permission. But do not vex yourself. I'm going to coax Papa to let you teach me Hindustani music. I'm sure he'll say yes. He has a soft spot for me, you know.'

'Who wouldn't?' Salim mumbled.

Scrunching up her nose, Rachael looked at him, not sure she had heard right. He looked back at her with a straight face but his eyes were laughing.

She thanked him and hastened through the hall and down the stairs. In her hurry, she did not realise she had dropped the bracelet that Christopher had given her last Christmas.

Papa was strolling through the front garden, speaking intently to a sepoy, when Rachael alighted from the carriage. Her teeth sparkled as she flashed him a quick smile and tried to look demure. Papa dismissed the sepoy and turned towards her. He did not say anything. Merely took the pipe out from his mouth and raised a single brow questioningly. He looked funny whenever he did that. He had thick eyebrows – straight rather than curved. And when he raised them, they looked like caterpillars marching up a hill.

Be serious, Rachael, she chided herself as she flashed

him another smile and covered the distance between them. 'Papa, don't worry,' she said as she straightened the creases on her dress. 'I've been responsible. I didn't go to Chowk or any such place.'

A hint of a smile flitted across Papa's face. 'But you went out without a chaperone. Where's Sudha?'

Rachael gave a sigh of relief. Papa seemed a little distracted. He had forgotten she was supposed to be home nursing a headache. 'I have some good news,' she piped as she put her arm through his.

'Yes?'

'I've found my music teacher.'

'And she is?'

'He's . . . he's good.' She clutched his sleeve and looked him in the eye. 'Oh Papa, pray do let him teach me. He's a perfect gentleman.'

Papa looked at her thoughtfully as he put the pipe back in his mouth. 'Oh well . . . as long as it stops you from gallivanting off to places like the Chowk. But the lessons must take place here, and only after I have spoken to . . .' He waved the pipe in the air looking for the right word. 'Your . . . err . . . teacher. And approved of him.'

'Oh thank you, thank you, my sweet Papa,' Rachael exclaimed and planted a kiss on his cheek before running off indoors, the footman running after her with the chador.

Chapter Nine

SALIM

Salim followed Ram Singh as he led him to Colonel Felix Bristow's study. The door was open. He entered the room apprehensively as Ram Singh stepped aside to let him pass. He wondered why the colonel wanted to see him. Did it have something to do with RayChal coming to his palace yesterday without permission?

He squared his shoulders as he looked at the colonel. He was seated behind a huge oak desk immersed in some papers. Not a single hair on the top of his head was out of place. Each hair stood exactly as the other – like a row of soldiers standing at attention. Salim swallowed. There was something about that man that made his nerves rattle. He coughed slightly. Colonel Bristow looked up. 'Good morning, sir,' Salim said, extending his hand to the colonel.

The colonel ignored his hand and brusquely replied, 'Morning. Do be seated.'

The chair made a scraping sound as Salim pulled it back and sat down gingerly.

'So you want to teach my daughter music?' the colonel asked as he lit his pipe.

Oh, so that's why he wanted to see him, Salim thought with a sigh of relief. 'Sir, with your kind permission,' he replied.

He shifted uncomfortably as the colonel looked him over. The smell of tobacco made him yearn for his hookah. He turned his gaze to the bookcases that lined three walls of the room. They were made of dark wood and lent a sombre atmosphere to the room.

The colonel finally spoke. 'I was expecting someone older. What instruments can you play?'

'Sir, I can play most Hindustani instruments – tabla, dhol, sarod, sitar, harmoni—'

'That'll do. You speak good English for a native.'

'I was sent to Calcutta when I was little, for my education.'

'Who's your father?'

Just then the swishing of skirts distracted Salim and he looked towards the door. It was Rachael. She was frantically waving her finger and mouthing the word 'no'.

Puzzled, Salim turned back to the colonel and said, 'Umm . . . my father . . .' He again looked at Rachael. She shook her head from side to side and mouthed 'no'.

The colonel raised his brow. 'It takes you that long to remember your father's name?'

'H-he's,' Salim stammered as perspiration ran down his face. 'Ustad Junaid Ali Khan,' he concluded as relief spread over his face. 'He taught me all I know about music.'

'That settles it, then,' said the colonel, putting his pipe in his mouth. 'You can start after two months, when we get back from Mussorie. I shall buy whatever instruments you need.'

'How you spoil her, Mr Bristow,' said a thin sharp voice. Salim almost jumped. He had not noticed the frail woman sitting upright behind him, near the window. It was Mrs Bristow.

'She's all I have,' the colonel said dryly. 'If I had sons . . .' He looked at Mrs Bristow with a cynical smile.

Mrs Bristow pushed back her chair, her lips a straight thin line, and left the room.

A little perplexed by this strange exchange of conversation, Salim stared at her receding back, then at the colonel. The colonel had gone back to his papers. 'I shall take your leave now,' Salim said hastily as he sprang to his feet. Bowing slightly, he left the room.

Outside the study, he leant back against the rough wall and let out a loud sigh. He looked up at the sound of giggling. It was Rachael. 'Ya Ali, why did you stop me from mentioning my father?' he asked in a low voice, glancing anxiously towards the study as he spoke.

Rachael put her chin in the air. 'Papa doesn't like him. He might have withheld his permission. Come now, let me show you the way out.'

'What d'you mean?' he asked, following her. 'And what if your father comes to know?'

'We'll deal with it when we have to,' she replied, as they reached the front garden, almost tripping over

Brutus who was running between her heels, one ear standing upright and the other drooping woefully.

Salim didn't say anything but looked over the fence at the nearby field. He could discern some English boys playing cricket. An occasional shout of 'catch it', or 'six', could be heard, followed by grumbling or cheers.

'Your father tells me you're leaving for the hills for two months?' he asked as he unfettered Afreen from the eucalyptus tree.

'Yes. Mother's feeling miserable in this heat,' Rachael replied as she stroked Afreen's hairy muzzle.

'I shall wait for your return,' Salim said as he swung his legs over the horse. He touched his cap lightly and bowed slightly.

Rachael put up a hand to shade her eyes, smiled up at him, her nose crinkling up as she did so.

He smiled back at her and was soon flying towards Kaiserbagh.

It was late afternoon in September. Salim sat down at the piano. He could scarcely believe he was seated at the same piano he had seen RayChal play for the first time about three months ago. Yes, it was just three months since he first set his eyes on her and only his second visit to her home in the cantonment. Yet he felt as though he had known her all his life.

'Chute Nabob?' said Rachael.

Salim suppressed his laugh and said, 'You can call me Salim.'

'Salim, that's a nice name. Pray tell me, does it mean anything?'

'Salim was the son of the Mughal Emperor Akbar.'

'Akbar – I know him,' Rachael announced proudly, 'but I never heard of Salim, I fear. Was he as famous as his father?'

'He was more famous for his love affairs than affairs of the state,' Salim chuckled. He ran his fingers over the keyboard, before turning to Rachael. 'He fell in love with a tawaif called Anarkali. Almost threw away his empire because of her. He even went to war against his own father, the mighty Akbar, all for the sake of his love.'

'How romantic. What happened then? Were they finally betrothed?'

'No, they drugged Salim, and while he lay asleep, Emperor Akbar ordered his men to bury Anarkali alive.'

'What? What d'you mean?'

'A wall was built around her, brick by brick.'

'No!' Rachael covered her mouth in horror.

'That's what they say, anyway. No one knows for sure what exactly happened. But they say Anarkali was never seen again.'

'I would willingly die a thousand deaths if someone loved me like that,' Rachael said softly.

Salim closed the distance between them and put his forefinger over her lips. 'Shh, you mustn't speak of dying.' Then with mock urgency, he cupped her yielding face in his hands and drawled, 'Have you ever thought what would become of me if you were no more, my Anarkali?'

Covering her head with a scarf, Rachael got into the act. 'Oh, Salim!'

Salim pressed a key forcefully on the piano, then looking Rachael straight in the eye, whispered hoarsely, 'Oh Anarkali! I pray to Allah that all the years left of my life may get added to yours.'

Rachael quickly slid the scarf off, exclaiming, 'Oh no, God forbid, I don't want to spend the rest of my life in a widow's garb. I love colours.' As she spoke, she held the edges of her dress and twirled around. Just then Brutus came yapping into the room, getting caught up in the excitement. Rachael picked him up and gave him a twirl as well.

'Masha Allah!' Salim whispered under his breath, as he watched her, mesmerised. Her long magenta skirt swirled and billowed. Her hair swayed. A shaft of the setting sun came in through the window, caught her golden hair and set it ablaze. Anarkali could not have been more beautiful. He was sure of that.

'Phew, sir, you smell!' Rachael said as she put Brutus down. 'I think it's time for your bath.'

'Have you had him long?' Salim asked as he attempted to straighten the dog's tail. Brutus was not amused and tried to bite his hand.

'No. I was out riding, about four months previously, when I came across a puppy. He was crying most pathetically. I tried to find his mother, but alas, she was nowhere to be seen.'

'And so, of course, you brought him home?'

'I hid him in my room. The next thing I knew mother was holding Brutus by the scruff of his neck. Dangling him before me, she screamed, "Now Rachael, was it you who brought this brat into the house? He has chewed my new shoes, the ones Amy sent last week from Paris."'

'Just then Papa came into the room. "I don't remember giving anyone permission to bring a dog into this house," he said, looking at me sternly. Mother glared at me, hands on her hips. I opened my dry mouth and was about to speak when Brutus started barking at me accusingly. I looked at him in disbelief and exclaimed, "You too, Brutus?" Everyone started laughing then and Papa gave me permission to keep him.' Rachael fondled Brutus's furry ears as she concluded her story. 'And so it came to pass that he was named Brutus.'

Salim smiled and tried to pat him. 'He doesn't like me much, does he?' he said as Brutus barked at him yet again.

'I think he's a little jealous,' Rachael replied.

'Ya Ali, it's getting late. I'd better leave,' said Salim.

But Rachael was too busy tickling Brutus's stomach to hear him. He smiled indulgently as he looked at her, shook his head and left the room.

'Salaam, sahib,' the gatekeeper saluted Salim as he opened the gate for him. He knew him well by now and did not quiz him anymore. He had been coming to Rachael's house for over a fortnight. Even Brutus did not bother with him anymore. He gave him a cursory glance, rolled over and went back to sleep.

Salim sat down on the stool, his back straight. He positioned his hands over the keyboard and looked at Rachael. She nodded her approval. He looked at the black notes before him with full concentration, then ran his fingers over the keys.

'Ouch, that hurt!' he yelped as Rachael picked up the metal rod that stood near the fireplace and rapped it sharply across his knuckles.

'It was supposed to hurt,' she said. 'How many times have I said that you must keep your hands raised while playing?'

Salim pulled a face. 'You're a hard taskmaster,' he said.

'Back to your lessons, sir. Let's not dally. Play that piece for me again.'

From the corner of his eye Salim looked at Rachael as he played the little jig by Haydn again. She was pushing back a lock of hair that had fallen over her forehead as she listened to him play.

'Gently, gently,' she said. 'Don't bang and don't stop at the end of each bar. One note should flow into the next like this . . . . . .' Rachael's fingers waltzed across the keyboard faster than a magician shuffling a deck of cards. Then she turned the page of her music book. 'Now, this next tune is an exquisite piece. It is a sad song; the lover is yearning for his lost love. So play it softly – gently – pianissimo.'

Salim watched in fascination as her deft fingers danced over the keys. He had never seen anyone immerse themselves in music like this, other than Abba Huzoor. And for the first time in his life he found himself wishing time would stand still. Somehow he knew this moment of magic and serenity would always stay with him, and give him succour and redress in the turbulent times to come.

Rachael stopped playing the piano abruptly and looked towards the door. Salim followed her gaze as the sound of footsteps echoed through the hallway. He stared at her, then leapt to his feet and sat down in front of the tabla and began beating the two drums. Rachael, too, hastened to the harmonium.

Salim continued to play the tabla, his head shaking and eyes half-closed as Colonel Bristow peered into the room. The colonel looked at Rachael, who was seated primly before the harmonium pumping its bellows. He caught her eye, nodded slightly and quietly left the room.

It was Jamghat, the traditional kite-flying festival, one of the few times in the year when Salim was up early. The sky was chequered with colours that morning. As though Allah Mia, getting bored with the pale blue when looking out of His window, decided to do some spray painting.

Salim stood on the terraced roof of his palace. He concentrated hard as the thread of his kite got enmeshed with that of his opponent's.

'I wonder what they're cooking for lunch,' said Ahmed as he sniffed the air appreciatively and looked down from the palace rooftop towards the kitchen.

Salim shot him an angry glare, then turned his attention back to the kite. 'Ahmed, stop thinking about food for once and give me some more thread . . . fast . . .'

Ahmed spun the spool hastily, but it was too late.

'Ya Ali, it's been cut!' Salim exclaimed as he watched the kite spiralling towards the ground. He grimaced as a handful of street urchins swooped down on it. They gave a whoop and a jiggle of delight as they grabbed the little silver purse attached to it.

'I wonder what would happen if you sent a message

to your English mem through your kite,' said Ahmed, as he narrowed his eyes to study Salim's face.

Chuckling, Salim tied another kite to the spool. 'And what if the letter got intercepted by her mother and she thought it was from Abba Huzoor? Then I'll be sitting and twiddling my thumbs while she and Abbu have an affair.'

Ahmed threw back his head and laughed. 'So you're having an affair with her.'

'No, we're simply teaching each other music, that's all.'

'Enjoy, Salim mia, enjoy. But don't make the mistake of falling in love; otherwise remember what happened to your namesake's Anarkali.'

'RayChal's not a tawaif.'

'No, she's worse. She's English, a firangi!'

Squaring his jaw, Salim rubbed his fingers where the fine glass pieces on the thread had cut them. He did not like what Ahmed had said, and certainly not what he had implied. Humbug. RayChal and he shared a special kinship owing to their mutual love for music. That's all. What did Ahmed know about women and relationships? For that matter, how much did *he* know about women?

He walked to the edge of the terrace and looked down. All he could see were some maids replacing the long khus mats that hung over the archways with thick padded curtains, a sign that winter was approaching. Salim bent down and picked up another kite. Bah! He'd best forget women and concentrate on his kite. He was supposed to be one of the best kite-flyers in the land. Wouldn't do his reputation any good if he lost this one as well.

Chapter Ten

RACHAEL

Holding her hands over the fire, Rachael rubbed them together to warm them. It was late January. Winter was in no hurry to leave. Mother had pulled her armchair close to the hearth and was waiting patiently for her to begin. It was strange how the furniture, the curtains, the upholstery in the room did not match. What was stranger was that it never bothered Mother. She was so particular about everything else that it came as a surprise. But then Mother never did look upon this house as her home. For her, home was England. This stay in Lucknow was a pilgrimage she had to undertake before returning to her real home.

Rachael pulled up a stool. Sitting down on it, she opened her book and began reading. At the sound of footsteps she stopped and looked up. 'Papa, won't you join us?' she asked.

'Ah well . . . perhaps,' he said, as he sat down heavily on a chair.

'Pray tell me, is something the matter?' Rachael asked as he let out a long sigh.

'Not really,' Papa replied. 'It's just that I have to leave for Calcutta tomorrow.'

'How come? And so suddenly?' Mother asked.

'Oh, I don't know for certain,' Papa replied. 'But some major changes are going to take place in Oudh soon. Dalhousie's army has reached Cawnpore.'

'What? An army? What for?' Rachael asked.

Just then Ram Singh arrived, bowed slightly and gave Papa his pipe. Papa lit it and breathed out a curl of smoke.

Mother waved the air before her irritably. 'Mr Bristow, you know how this smoke bothers me . . .'

'There might be war,' Papa said. He looked at Rachael. 'I want you to discontinue your music lessons immediately. Is that clear?'

'But why, Papa?'

'Do as you're told, girl,' said Mother. 'It never was a good idea to let our daughter be tutored by a native.'

'Yes, Mother,' Rachael replied morosely.

'Good,' said Papa as he slapped his thighs and got up. He turned to look at Rachael when he reached the door. 'I hope I've made myself clear – I don't want to see your teacher here again.'

Nodding her head slowly, Rachael walked over to the window. It was a moonless night and the garden was plunged in darkness. War? Whatever could that mean? Rachael could not comprehend. All she felt was an inherent sense of loss at ending the music lessons. She so looked forward to them each day. Why must they be stopped? It filled her with an inner rage. What did war have to do with music?

Rachael looked around the music hall. It looked different in winter. The khus mats had been replaced with thick padded curtains. Red Persian carpets woven with silk and gold threads covered the floor. Several charcoal braziers kept the room warm. She looked at Salim. He too looked different. He was wearing a colourful coat of brocade instead of the angarkha that he normally wore.

'How did you manage to get permission to come to the palace today?' Salim asked.

'I didn't.' Rachael lowered her gaze as Salim looked at her. 'Papa's gone to Calcutta.' She paused and licked her lips. 'He thinks there might be war.'

'That's ridiculous. Rumours, that's all.'

'He doesn't think it's a good idea to be in touch with a . . . umm . . . Indians at this time.'

'I see.' Salim picked up a sarod and began tinkering with its strings.

'Aren't you going to say something?'

Salim kept quiet and continued tuning the sarod.

She looked at him, then spread her palm over the strings of the instrument so he could not play it anymore.

He looked at her.

'Don't be upset, Salim. Papa is away for a week. Let's make the most of it.'

A small smile lifted the edges of his lips. He covered her hand with his and whispered, 'You're right.'

Rachael got up and rubbed the carpet with her bare

big toe. 'Pray tell me, are all the rooms in the palace as opulent as this one?' she asked.

'Come; let me take you around some of our palaces. Then you can see for yourself,' Salim replied.

'Umm . . . what if someone espied us?'

'Don't worry. They're taking a siesta.'

'How many palaces does your father own?' Rachael asked.

'Ninety. Maybe a hundred. Who knows? Never counted them,' Salim answered with a shrug.

Her eyes twinkled as he gave her a mock salute and said, 'After you, ma'am . . . err . . . RayChal.'

The carriage entered a fortified enclosure through a gateway and stopped before an imposing rectangular building. Rachael alighted and followed Salim to what looked like the balcony of a long vaulted hall.

'This is one of the largest arched ceilings in the world, with no pillars to support it,' he said as she looked up in amazement. He then asked her to wait as he walked the sixty yards to the other end of the hall. He looked across at her and clicked his finger. She was astounded. It sounded as clear as though he had clicked his finger right next to her ear. Then he gestured to her to put her ear to the wall. He put his lips near the wall across the hall and whispered, 'I like you better when you don't tie your hair.' Rachael blushed, then looked at him in fascination. She could clearly hear what he had whispered sixty yards away!

'Our walls have ears, you know,' he said with a grin as he walked up to her and led her up a flight of stairs.

'Crinoline dresses were not meant for walking up steep

and narrow steps,' Rachael muttered under her breath, as she gathered her skirts. Now where is he? she wondered in frustration, as she reached the top of the stairs and found herself facing three narrow passageways.

'I'm sorry, milady, I had forgotten you weren't wearing breeches today,' Salim mocked, leaning against one of the doorless archways. 'Try not to wear a tent next time you come to the palace,' he added as he watched her trying not to trip over her dress.

Rachael glared at him. Again those eyes were laughing at her. Teasing, mocking, provoking.

'Don't worry about me. I'm sure I would have found my way.'

'I'm sure you wouldn't. This part of the palace complex is not called Bhul Bhulaiya for nothing.'

'What's that?'

'It's a labyrinth of hundreds of narrow stairway passages. Anyone who's not familiar with the palace is bound to get lost in this maze. But those who know the place well, for them there is a hidden passage here that leads to the River Gomti.'

'I fear I don't understand.'

'See, if the palace is under attack, we can make our escape to the Gomti, while the enemy loses its way in the labyrinth.'

'That's ingenious.'

Salim held out his hand as they came upon some more steep narrow stairs. Rachael hesitated.

'Trust me, you'll find it easier.'

Rachael gingerly gave him her hand. His hands were callused, from holding the bridle too often. The stairs led them into another hall. There was a long pool with coloured fountains running across the centre of the room. On the walls hung pictures of all the nabobs of Oudh, Salim's ancestors.

Looking at Nabob Wajid Ali Shah's portrait, Rachael remarked, 'You look nothing like your father . . . except your hair, perhaps.'

'True, I take after my mother.'

'Heavens!' she suddenly exclaimed. 'I fear we shall have to cut short this tour. I'm getting late for my class.'

'Class?'

'I teach some native children English. Every Wednesday.'

'Oh, so you're also busy converting us heathens into civilised little Christians, I presume?'

'Of course not! I'm not a missionary. And anyway, what, pray, is wrong with being a missionary? They are simply spreading the word of Christ.'

'Who the hell are they to decide that their religion is right and ours is blasphemous?'

Rachael was taken aback by the vehemence with which he spoke. 'Look, I teach simply because I enjoy the company of children.' She picked at her pagoda sleeve. 'Perhaps because I never had a sibling to play with. I lost my three-year-old brother when I was born.'

'I'm sorry.'

She looked at him. He did look repentant. Her face softened. 'Do not vex yourself. I was too little to be affected.'

'You can borrow some of mine. I have over forty brothers and sisters.'

112

Touching her right cheek theatrically, Rachael exclaimed, 'Ya Ali,' with mock horror.

Salim threw back his head and laughed. Still shaking with laughter, he looked at her. He stopped laughing abruptly. He was gazing at her lips, now her eyes. Rachael lowered her gaze and wished he would not stare at her like that. She felt he could look right into the core of her heart, into her very soul, and she found it disconcerting.

Rachael wondered gloomily where Salim was. The last six days had flown so fast. Papa would be back home tomorrow. Then she would not be able to see Salim again – for how long, she could not tell. She looked out of the window of the music hall at the high wall that surrounded the zenana. How time had flown. Why, it was just yesterday that Salim had led her into this room for the first time. She thought of all the unique structures he had shown her since then. The darbar hall, the vaulted ceilings, the portraits, the little balconies from where the begums could sit behind a purdah and watch the court proceedings. But there was a section of the palace that was still a mystery for her. The zenana.

Daima entered the room. 'Chote Nawab will be here soon . . . can I get you anything?'

'Daima, pray can you take me to the zenana?' She clutched her hands urgently. 'Please, Daima?'

'I'm not sure Chote Nawab would approve.'

'I'm sure he won't mind.'

'Ah well, follow me.'

'Oh thank you, thank you, Daima.' Rachael hugged the old woman and was about to kiss her cheek, but then, seeing the sombre look on her face, she kissed her hand instead. Daima tilted her head slightly like she often did when admonishing someone, but her face had the slightest flicker of a smile.

Rachael adjusted the hijaab that Daima had tied over her head, before entering an inner courtyard. It was deserted, perhaps because of the heat of the sun. Even though it was still winter, the afternoon sun was scorching hot.

The courtyard was flanked on all sides by long corridors. The corridors on the left and right led to several doors which in turn led to the rooms of the begums. The doors right in front opened on to a splendid hall which was packed at the moment.

A strong smell of ittar greeted Rachael as she entered this hall. Mother always wore a perfume from back home. It had a light, flowery fragrance, as light as a butterfly alighting on a petal. So unlike the perfume these natives wore. It clung to you and filled your nostrils with a smell so strong it ceased to be fragrant at all.

Rachael looked about her with undisguised interest. Some of the begums sat gossiping; some were playing chaupad, some chess. There was a small stage at one end of the hall. A small group had gathered there and were listening to the domnis narrating tales of yore. Loud voices made her turn. The two begums playing chaupad were squabbling.

'I refuse to put up with your cheating anymore,' shouted the fair begum with long hooped earrings, as she angrily took a puff on the hookah.

'Oh yes? Don't try to play the innocent with me,' spat out the other begum. She paused, chewed her paan furiously before continuing. 'Shakina found some chillies and lemon under my mattress this morning. Don't I know who's trying to do voodoo on me! And then she pretends to be an angel!'

Rachael looked at her with interest. Her paan-stained lips were the same colour as her dress.

'I should have married a grass-cutter,' said the begum with the hooped earrings. 'I would have been the only wife and I wouldn't have had to put up with you!' She then yanked the chaupad sheet and threw it on the floor.

The other begum grabbed some of the counters and threw them at her.

Daima rushed to the scene. 'You two should be ashamed of yourselves, quarrelling like a bunch of unruly children . . . Is this behaviour worthy of a begum?'

She pulled Rachael away and took her to a begum who sat on a rug, doing calligraphy.

'See how well she writes? It's her ambition to write the entire Koran single-handedly,' Daima explained.

Rachael watched in fascination as she weaved out Urdu letters one after the other. 'Daima, can I try?' She tried to lean closer to the begum, when her left hand knocked over the silver inkstand. 'Oh dear me,' she muttered, her hand covering her mouth as rivers of black ink began to run over the begum's handiwork.

Daima smacked Rachael lightly on her head. 'Hai Ram . . . This girl is useless.'

Sticking out her tongue, Rachael looked across the hall. She saw Salim standing in the doorway. He did not look pleased. She swallowed and plucked at her sleeves. Why, oh why, was she always in trouble?

Chapter Eleven

SALIM

It was a cold morning on 1ˢᵗ February 1856. Salim stood on the balcony of his palace watching Daima feeding the pigeons. They were busy pecking at the seeds, making a low guttural sound as they did so. He snuggled his chin into his qaba as he read the lines again:

> *Restless and troubled*
> *Passed the sleepless night,*
> *My love has departed*
> *To what land I know not.*

Abba Huzoor was a fine poet, no doubt. Salim wished he could write like him. But whenever he sat down to write, he ended up staring at the paper. Words failed him. Ah well, he may never get into his good books because of his writing, but at least Abba Huzoor was pleased with his hunting abilities. He had called him one of his able sons.

But what would he think of his able son if he came to know he had been teaching an English girl Hindustani music in his own palace? Abba Huzoor hated the English. Unlike his predecessor Nawab Nasir-ud-Din Haider, who admired English dress, mores and mannerisms, he shunned everything English. And that girl – RayChal – why did she have to go to the zenana yesterday? What if one of the begums had mentioned it to Abba Huzoor? He would have been dead by now.

He had stormed into the zenana when Chilmann had informed him of her whereabouts. But when he had seen her squatting in the centre of the room with the other begums, he felt as though she had always been a part of his family. And then when he saw Daima chiding her for something, just as she always scolded him, he watched her stick out her tongue and grin shamefacedly at Daima. After that he could not bring himself to scold her.

He had been brought up in a zenana full of women. Yet in his entire life of twenty-two years, he had never come across a woman like her before. Ya Ali, he was again thinking about her. What was wrong with him? What was it about her that held him thus captive? Was he in love with her? No. This was not love. He simply enjoyed her company and loved flirting with her. It was all in good fun, that's all.

Then why was he always thinking about her? The way she talked, the way she laughed, the way she played the piano, the harmonium, her fingers light and feathery, the way she walked, the way she said his name. The way her eyes shone when she smiled, the way she crinkled her little nose. Why, he could even recall what she smelt of – lavender and roses. And why, oh why, did he feel depressed simply because he could not give her music lessons anymore?

And what was that about the war? True, Dalhousie's army had reached Cawnpore but that didn't mean the forces would be turned on Avadh. Why, just last night he had attended one of Abba Huzoor's kavi samelan. Abbu looked unperturbed.

Salim smiled a small wry smile and looked down at the garden below. The blades of grass were bent double by the strong northerly wind and were whispering to each other the rumours that were rife throughout the city.

'Salim mia.' It was Ahmed. He came rushing to the balcony. 'Salim mia, have you heard?'

'Heard what, Ahmed?'

'The Resident has presented a treaty to His Majesty from the Governor General of India, Lord Dalhousie, asking him to abdicate the throne.'

Turning his back to Ahmed, Salim looked again at the blades of grass. His heart sank. So the rumours were true.

Salim strode into the Zard Kothi Palace. Abba Huzoor was pacing the black and white tiled floor and muttering, 'What have we done to deserve this?'

His brother Sikandar Hasmat, his minister, the Residency lawyer Muhsee-ud-Daula, the deputy Saheb-ud-Daula, the finance minister – all of them stood still with lowered heads.

Abba Huzoor ordered Saheb-ud-Daula to read the

treaty aloud – the treaty that had been sent by Lord Dalhousie. That firangi had managed to gobble up the states of Punjab, Burma, Nagpur, Satara and Jhansi in the last ten years. Now he wanted to swallow Avadh, the bloody glutton.

Saheb-ud-Daula touched his cap lightly and started reading. Abba Huzoor stood with his back to the rest, leaning against a pillar. Saheb-ud-Daula read two lines, broke out in a cold sweat, got a lump in his throat and could not continue. Abba Huzoor snatched the papers from him and commenced reading it himself.

Salim's hands curled into fists. Why didn't Saheb-ud-Daula throw those papers in the Resident's face when he gave them to him? Putting Abba Huzoor through this humiliation!

Abba turned to Saheb-ud-Daula and angrily waved the treaty papers at him. 'Why this new treaty? What happened to the old one?'

'Your Majesty, the Resident feels the administration of Avadh has grown slack.'

'What utter nonsense,' Salim muttered under his breath. Of all the allegations levied against Abba Huzoor, this was the most outrageous. Avadh was at the height of its glory, there was no doubt about it. The land was fertile, trade was booming and taxes were low. Why, with all the poets, musicians and artists flocking daily to its courts, it had even become the centre of cultural integration and etiquette.

Abba Huzoor's nostrils flared. He was trying to get a hold on his temper. Salim had never seen Abba fly into a rage.

'How dare he say that? Are the people in our land not happy and flourishing?' Abba finally spoke through gritted teeth.

'Yes, Your Majesty,' answered Saheb-ud-Daula.

'The Company has no right to dispense of the old treaty which clearly states that it can govern Avadh but cannot dethrone us.'

'I agree, Your Majesty.'

Abba stopped pacing and stroked the lion carved on either side of his throne. 'Our ancestors have already given half of Avadh to the British. Now they want to swallow the rest.' He looked at the mermaids carved on the wall, the royal insignia of the Naishapur dynasty. A dynasty that had ruled over Avadh since 1722. He absent-mindedly felt the velvet softness of the oblong pillow, before sitting down on the throne. Nobody spoke. Everyone stood silently with heads hung low. The only sound that could be heard was the sound of breathing. A stale, sweetish smell pervaded the hall. It came from the vase that stood in a corner. The tuberoses it held were half-dead.

Abba Huzoor finally spoke. 'Go and tell the Resident that we will not renounce the throne without a fight.'

Salim sat alone in the music hall trying to play the sitar. But he could not concentrate. He kept thinking of all that had transpired in the Zard Kothi that morning. He tried again. The strings of the sitar were tight and sounded harsh. It was no use trying to hide behind his music. Abba Huzoor needed him. He should go to him.

He put on his cap and made his way towards Abba's

parlour. As he passed the kitchen, he could smell biryani being cooked. Bland white rice with rich juicy chunks of meat. Like the friendship between the English and the nawabs that had lasted eighty years. But the biryani had begun to boil over now. He doubted anyone would be eating in the palace that night.

This corridor was much too dark. Once all this was behind them, he would ask Daima to get the servants to place a couple of candles at the two ends.

Just then, the Queen Mother, Janab-e-Alia, rushed past him. Salim's mouth fell open. It seemed she had come running from her palace barefoot, without her veil and without waiting for her attendants, as soon as she had heard the news of the new treaty.

Salim followed her quietly to the parlour and stood trembling at the door.

'Ammi,' Abba Huzoor exclaimed as Janab-e-Alia entered his parlour, shocked at her appearance.

'We're lost, you have destroyed us,' she shouted without preamble.

'Ammi, please sit down.'

Abba led her to the takhat and gestured to the servants to leave them alone.

'How many times did we tell you to forget your begums and Parikhana and pay attention to the administration of the country?' she accused.

Abba averted his gaze and pulled at his hookah instead. 'Ammi, no matter what we did, they would have still annexed Avadh under some or the other pretext. Look at how they swallowed the other kingdoms. Ours was the only one left.'

'We should never have stopped you from conducting those parades,' the Queen Mother replied with deep regret.

'Do you remember, Ammi, how we used to watch our army parade for hours on end? What eloquent names we had given the regiments – Banka, Tircha, Ghanghor. We even had a regiment of women soldiers. Why, oh why, Ammi, did you make us stop?'

'Your hakim told us your health was deteriorating from standing too long in the sun.'

'And you believed him? If only you knew he was a spy planted in our court by the English. They said to me, "Why do you want to waste money maintaining an army when our army is there to fight for you?" . . . You see, Ammi, we played right into their hands.'

Salim stood rooted in the doorway. He felt guilty eavesdropping like this, but found himself unable to move. He wanted to go and embrace Abba, console him, but knew he mustn't.

'And the irony is, the bravest and the strongest soldiers in the Company's army are from Avadh,' said Abba Huzoor.

Begum Janab-e-Alia walked over to the window, lifted the curtain and looked out. 'That's another reason we can't fight,' she said.

'Meaning?'

Begum Janab-e-Alia dropped the curtain and looked at her son. 'Nothing would be gained by asking our sepoys to fire on their own brothers.'

'But we can't just give up.'

'We won't. We'll fight for justice in Queen Victoria's court.'

Salim's jaw dropped and his forehead creased. He stared at Janab-e-Alia. What the hell did she mean? Then he looked at Abba Huzoor. Abbu, don't pay any heed to her. Queen Victoria's court, indeed. Abba Huzoor would have to go to England for that. It would take him months. What would become of Avadh meanwhile? Of Lucknow? Of the people? What kind of advice was that?

Salim could not believe what was happening. This whole day had been one long nightmare. He dragged his feet to his room. Yes, it was a nightmare. He would wake up any minute now. Any minute.

Chapter Twelve

SALIM

It was not a nightmare. Two days later Salim found himself smiling contemptuously as Major General Outram, the English Resident, marched into the hall of Zard Kothi Palace, his heels clicking on the tiled floor. He walked briskly up to Abba Huzoor and embraced him. He clearly meant business.

Frowning, Salim tried to remember the name of the first resident to be appointed to the Court of Avadh. It was something Middleton. He was supposed to strengthen the friendship between the Company and the nawab. Friendship indeed! Salim smirked. What Middleton and his successors actually did was extort huge sums of money from the nawab and stealthily dig away his power.

Unfolding his arms, Salim put them behind his back and stared grimly at the Resident. Why in Allah's name had Abba Huzoor met the Resident's expenses all these years? For this? In the beginning the Residents merely had a secretary. Now they employed an entire retinue running into thousands, and the poor nawabs not only paid their salaries, but provided and maintained their accommodation as well. And the temerity of that firangi! Did he have no shame? After feeding on Abba's mercy all his life, he was now talking about deposing him? How could he? How dare he?

The two men could not have looked more different. Abba in his silk brocaded angarkha, his neck covered in pearls, wide-bottomed silk pyjamas and pointy velvet shoes. The Resident dressed smartly in his uniform – red jacket displaying all his medals, and black trousers which tapered down to the ankles.

He bowed slightly before Abba Huzoor and said, 'May I remind His Majesty the terms of the new treaty are generous and it would be in his best interest to sign it.'

The nerve of the firangi! Asking Abba to give up his throne, his entire kingdom, for a meagre twelve lakhs an annum and calling it generous! He must be jesting! Salim continued to watch, fuming.

'We don't want your money, we want justice,' Abba Huzoor replied quietly.

Major General Outram ran his fingers over his head and again began to extol the generosity of the British Government. Salim unfolded and folded his arms again as he stared at him. The bloody viper. Ya Ali, he could cut off his tongue right there and then.

'Treaties are signed between equals. Who are we to sign a treaty with the mighty British Government?' Abba Huzoor said evenly.

Salim noticed a vein twitch near Abba's left eye and his jaw tighten as he spoke. He was finding it difficult to keep a rein on his temper. There was no need for that Abbu, Salim thought. Just pick up your rifle and shoot the bloody angrez.

'I think it would be in Your Majesty's interest to sign the treaty,' Ali Naqi Khan, who was Abbu's minister as well as father-in-law, interjected. His head was lowered and his eyes were intent on studying the black and white tiles of the floor.

Abbu's brother General Sahib roared. 'Did you not hear? The king is not independent. His hands have been tied. How can he sign the treaty?'

Abba Huzoor took off his crown and, handing it to the Resident, said, 'Now that we have lost our rank as well as our title, we are in no position to negotiate.'

Salim looked at Abba Huzoor in dismay. What was he thinking – handing his crown like that to that firangi? It seemed so unreal. It could not be happening. He was watching one of Abbu's performances – based on the eternal love story of Lord Krishna and Radha, or the drama where he wore the garb of a Jogi and went around in search of his lost love Gijala. Ya Ali, if only!

A shaft of sunlight came in through the window and the jewels on the crown sparkled for a brief moment before a cloud covered the sun. Abba Huzoor walked to the window and looked out at the grey skies, his back to the Resident. A pigeon flew in and perched itself on Abba's arm, cooing soothingly. Salim saw a flicker of a smile on Abbu's face as he lovingly stroked the bird's soft head.

'Your Majesty,' said the Resident, 'if you do not sign the treaty within three days, I will have no choice but to take over the reins of the Kingdom of Oudh.' With that, the Resident left the palace.

Abba Huzoor left Lucknow on 13th March 1856, in the quiet of the night. He was seated in one of the Cawnpore mail coaches. It was followed closely by the coach with three of his begums and children, Queen Mother Begum Janab-e-Alia, General Sahib and the heir apparent Nawab Munawar-ud-Daula. There were about three hundred courtiers, including ministers and officials. Some of them were in coaches while the rest were on horseback. They would be spending a few days in Cawnpore, before proceeding to Calcutta. From there, Abba Huzoor and Janab-e-Alia would leave for London. Abbu had been told he could not take more than five hundred people with him. Hence some of his begums and children had to stay behind.

Salim watched the retinue leave. It seemed strange. Earlier, all such processions were accompanied with a din of bugles, trumpets, drums and a lot of shouting and cheering. Today, all that could be heard was shuffling and whispers and coughs. Even Abba Huzoor looked peculiar without his crown and velvet robe. He reminded Salim of his torn kite. 'King of the skies' the shopkeeper had said.

The train of attendants following Abba Huzoor became smaller and smaller until all that was visible was the flying dust. Salim stormed into his room.

'Should I get your hookah, Chote Nawab?' Chilmann asked as soon as he entered.

'I don't need anything. Leave me alone.'

He sat down and threw his cap and waistband on the takhat. Chilmann hastened to remove his shoes. 'I said leave me alone.'

Chilmann and the other servants hurriedly left the room.

Salim walked to his desk and slammed his fist on it. With a swipe of his arm, he sent everything on the desk crashing to the floor. Ya Ali, how could the British do this to Abba Huzoor? He felt enraged, cheated. And how could Abba Huzoor abdicate without a fight? How could he? Salim kicked the table.

'Chote Nawab.' It was Daima.

'Daima, all is lost.'

'Don't lose heart so soon, my son,' she said, stroking his head.

'How could Abba Huzoor give up just like that? Like a coward?'

'If he was a coward, he would have signed the treaty . . . He's merely leaving for England to plead his case before Queen Victoria.'

'But we could have won, Daima, thrown those firangis out of Avadh for good. Leaders of all communities had approached Abba Huzoor and pledged to lay down their lives for him. He shouldn't have left without a fight.'

Daima handed him a glass of water. 'Why spill blood when matters can be resolved amicably, huh?' she said.

'I guess,' Salim muttered as he slowly drank the water. He thought of the lines Abba Huzoor had uttered as he left Lucknow.

Daro deewar par hasrat ki nazar karte hein,
Khus raho ahle watan hum to safar karte hein.
(I look at the door and walls of my palace with
longing and despair,
Be happy my people for whom I undertake this
journey.)

Covering his eyes with his hands, Salim wondered how long that journey would be. Would it take him to Cawnpore, Calcutta, London and back to Lucknow? He hoped so.

Salim stood under a jamun tree in front of the Dilaram Kothi. The ground under the tree looked like a purple rash. Some birds were pecking at the fallen fruit. It was just a few weeks since Abba Huzoor had left Lucknow. Navroz and Holi had fallen on the same day that year, but neither of the two festivals had been celebrated. The entire city was in mourning for its king.

Salim watched, bored, as the auctioneer banged the hammer on the table and said 'going, going, gone,' for the umpteenth time that day. He was barely audible above the trumpeting, neighing, roaring and chattering. The air was heavy with the smell of animal sweat and dung. As if that wasn't enough, there was dust everywhere. It had filled his nostrils, was making his eyes burn and had covered his angarkha like garnish. He looked around at the people bidding. Some of them had come from as far as Delhi and Lahore. Each eager to get hold of a regal animal and thus enhance his social status, Salim thought bitterly.

He watched sadly as Sambhu was led away by its new owner. Sambhu – Abba Huzoor's favourite elephant. How often had he watched Abba sitting on his golden howdah on top of Sambhu and swelled with pride. He wondered if Sambhu's new owner would be able to take as good care of him as they had done in the palace. Or would he merely be used for bragging?

Then it was the turn of the rhinoceros. Another exotic beast sold at a bargain price. The Company claimed that it was selling the animals as it could not afford to feed them. But then why sell them so cheap? It made no sense.

But then nothing made sense anymore, not since the day that cursed Resident Outram set his foot in the palace premises. The new treaty made no sense, neither did the way Abba Huzoor left Avadh without a fight. Nothing made any sense or mattered anymore.

He remembered the story Daima had told him when he was little about his forefather, Nawab Nasir-ud-Din Haider. He used to take great pride in collecting animals from all over the world. He had a black stallion that was so strong that it was made to fight a tiger. It threw the tiger off its back with such force and kicked it so hard that its jaw broke. The poor frightened tiger ran away. What would the king say if he saw the plight of all the great beasts now?

Salim looked at the remaining animals. Some elephants were trumpeting and throwing dust on their backs. One of them was trying to tear off a jackfruit from the tree. The horses were swishing their tails to shoo away the flies. Of the two hundred elephants, one hundred and seven camels, two thousand horses, seven hundred other animals like lions, cheetahs, antelopes, rhinoceros and two lakhs of pigeons, just a handful remained. The exotic birds were one of the first to go. Abba Huzoor was so proud of his rare collection. There were talking parrots and mynahs that sang. All gone. Within minutes. Ya Ali, he hadn't realised until now how transient life could be.

The kotwal who had just bought several hundred pigeons approached him. 'Chote Nawab, I've bought them to give them back to His Majesty when he returns.'

Salim's eyes turned moist. He could merely nod his head in gratitude.

'You're here, Salim mia? Do you know what is happening in your beloved music hall?' It was Ahmed.

'What?'

'They are taking away all the instruments. To auc—'

Salim did not wait for him to finish. He had flung himself on Afreen and kicked her hard. He did not stop until he reached Kaiserbagh and strode into the palace.

Chilmann came running after him. 'Chote Nawab, I tried to stop them but they didn't listen to me. I told them how upset you'd be. They said His Majesty should have thought about it before getting in arrears.'

Pushing him aside, Salim entered the music hall. The room was almost empty. All the instruments had been taken away. The few that remained were broken and cast aside. Salim felt as though his heart had been ripped out and thrown into the Gomti. His eyes were red and smarted with unshed tears.

He looked down at a broken dhol. Abba Huzoor

used to play it so well, especially on the seventh day of Muharram. Dressed in black, he would head the procession. He would play the dhol, tied around his neck, beating it faster and faster, in time with the beat, as though in a trance. Now his own city lay ransacked and there was no one to mourn its destruction. Even the dhol lay broken, mute, discarded. For once Salim wished he was a woman so he could find solace in tears.

He picked up a flute. It was slightly chipped at one end. He ran his fingers over the holes then put it to his lips. He remembered Abba Huzoor playing it when enacting the role of Krishna in Rahash, a dance drama based on the eternal love of Radha and Krishna. He could still feel Abbu's breath on it. He kissed it and put it down. Then he started to leave. At the doorway he turned around and took one last look at the room. He grabbed hold of the curtain and yanked it to the floor. 'I hate these firangis,' he muttered through clenched teeth.

A hand touched his shoulder lightly. It was Daima. She handed him a piece of paper. Salim looked at her and then at the note. It was from Rachael. She wanted to see him urgently.

Chapter Thirteen

RACHAEL

Rachael knew it was Salim. She could tell by his footsteps. She had not seen him since her last visit to the palace in January three months ago and yet . . . Why did every part of her being become alert the moment she sensed his presence? He stopped a few paces behind her. She turned and their eyes met. Salim hastily looked away. She did not say anything but watched him quietly as he began to scrape the bark of the neem tree beneath which he was standing. A crow alighted on one of its branches, cawed for a while, then flew away.

'I understand you wished to see me urgently,' he finally said.

'Umm . . . yes.' Rachael fiddled with her ring nervously. She looked at Salim for help as she fumbled for the right words, but he merely stood there with his arms folded, feet apart, his chin jutting out, eyes wary.

'I heard about what happened to our music room and your father's animals,' she said.

'I'm glad you're aware of what your people have been doing to us.'

'East India Company, Salim. I'm not one of them.'

'No?' Salim looked at her pale face, then at her hands and smiled sarcastically.

'No, I'm not. And you cannot even comprehend how sorry I am about all that has happened.'

Rachael felt smoke pricking her eyes and the smell of wood burning. She looked towards the edge of the garden. The gardener was burning some dried leaves and twigs. She turned back to Salim.

'Pray believe me, I'm your friend, and whatever happens, I will always remain one.' She untied the ribbon of her bonnet and gently massaged the red mark it had left under her chin and waited for Salim to say something.

Nothing. He merely bent down and picked up a leaf that had fallen.

Rachael pursed her lips. Fine, if that's how he felt about her, then woe to her if she ever tried to meet him again. She spun on her heels and moved towards her carriage. Salim's hand shot out to stop her. He looked at her then, his eyes intent, as he whispered, 'Thank you.' He lifted her hand to his lips and kissed her ring. 'Thank you for being there for me.'

Rachael pulled the chador further down over her head and looked surreptitiously around the Kaiserbagh gardens. She did not want to be recognised. Since the nabob had left Lucknow, the relationship between the natives and the English had become even more strained. She wondered where Salim was. He was not usually late. She smiled with relief as she saw him trotting towards her.

'I'm sorry to have kept milady waiting,' Salim panted as he got off his horse. 'Just as I was leaving, I got a letter from Abba Huzoor.'

'How is he?' Rachael asked.

'He's better now. Still in Calcutta. He will soon be leaving with Janab-e-Alia for London, to plead his case before Queen Victoria.'

'Does he know about his animals and other effects that have been auctioned off?'

'He has written to the governor general. Told us not to worry.' He took off his cap, ran his fingers through his hair, then put it back on again. 'You know, when Abba Huzoor used to hold court, or when he went out in procession, his men would carry two silver boxes in which anyone could put their petitions and grievances. Complaint boxes used to be placed even on the streets. And Abbu used to address each one of them himself. Now he, the dispenser of justice, has to plead before the queen.'

Rachael walked silently beside Salim for a while. As they reached the banyan tree, she pointed to a marble bench under its shade and asked, 'Shall we?'

'After you,' Salim gestured.

She sat down and turned to him. 'We are leaving for Mussorie tomorrow.'

'To get away from this heat?' Salim asked.

'You know what Mother is like.'

Salim did not say anything but tried to reach one of the many thick string-like structures hanging from the tree.

'Do you know what these are?' he asked. 'These are the aerial roots of the tree. As you know, most trees grow upwards from the seeds planted in the soil.' Salim patted an aerial root of the tree. 'But the banyan tree sprouts from seeds that have been left behind high up on a tree and grows downwards with the help of these aerial roots.'

'That's fascinating,' Rachael replied as she grabbed an aerial root with both her hands and tried to swing.

'And these trees live for hundreds and hundreds of years.'

'You mean to say, if I come back here with my grandchildren, the tree will still be there?' Rachael asked as she let go of the root.

Salim did not answer but grinned instead, his eyes twinkling.

'Pray tell me what you find so amusing?'

'I was just imagining you carrying my child.'

Rachael glared at him, shocked at his insolence, blushed and looked away. A fresh breeze from the Gomti blew her hair across her face. The leaves of the trees shook excitedly in the crisp breeze. She found Salim watching her as she brushed her hair aside with a finger.

'My daughter will have long golden hair like you and I will brush it every morning. I will make her wear beautiful dresses and cry my heart out when she gets married,' he said.

'You Indians are so sentimental.'

'What's wrong with that? We're not ashamed of our emotions. What we feel inside, we show outside. And anyway, what's so great about the English stiff upper lip?'

Rachael thought of her mother and said quietly, 'Nothing, nothing at all. That's why I love . . . Hindustan.'

Salim walked over to the tamarind tree and picked up a couple of dried pods. He came close to Rachael and shook them right next to her ear. They sounded like a baby's rattle. She ran away laughing, then plucked the tree's feathery foliage. It had a peculiar sour smell. She crept back to Salim and tickled his ear from behind. He lowered his ear to his shoulder to stop her tickling him, while his hands grabbed her arms.

Rachael stopped laughing and stared into his eyes. He too had stopped laughing and was looking at her. He lowered his gaze to her lips and muttered, 'Ya Ali.'

Rachael closed her eyes. He smelt of musk, perspiration, tobacco. Not the usual tobacco smell, but tobacco that has been sweetened for the hookah.

Eventually he let her go.

Rachael lay on her bed the next day, staring at the ceiling listlessly. The air was heavy and languid. The fan was moving slowly, rhythmically, lethargically. She could hear a bee buzzing in the garden. The mango tree that stood just outside her window was laden with blossom. Every time the warm wind blew, the scent of mangoes wafted into her room.

It was no ordinary tree, this mango tree, as it bore

fruit twice a year. Once at the start of summer, and once before the rains came. Ayah was sure the tree had been planted by Bhagwan Ram's brother Lakshman, after whom Lucknow had been named. Hence it was twice blessed.

Rachael wondered why she felt so incomplete whenever she was not able to meet Salim. And then it hit her. She was in love. No! It wasn't true. Then why was she thinking about him constantly? Why did she start missing him the moment he left her side? Why did she not get angry when he said he was imagining her carrying his child? Why? No, she could not be in love.

Just then she heard a bird singing on the mango tree. It was the same bird that always seemed to call her – *RayChal RayChal* – the same way Salim called her. She ran to the window and tried to spot it, but it was hidden by the dense foliage. Rachael smiled dreamily and shook her head. Everything reminded her of Salim these days.

She was awoken from her reverie by loud voices coming from the drawing room. She entered the room just as a shoe hit the new servant on the forehead and almost knocked him down.

'Papa!' Rachael exclaimed.

'Son of a pig,' Papa spat out.

'Papa, your language.'

'Rachael, you keep out of it.' He held out a painting for Rachael to see. 'This moron cleaned it with a wet cloth. I had bought it at an auction in London last year. Bloody dim-witted creatures,' he muttered through gritted teeth. He threw the painting aside and stormed out of the room.

138

Rachael looked at the watercolour. It was just a jumble of colours now. She did not know whether to laugh or cry.

The servant stood trembling and wiping the blood from his forehead.

'It's all right. Go inside and ask Ram Singh to put something on it,' Rachael said gently.

The servant looked at her gratefully. 'Yes, memsahib.' He bowed and crept out of the room.

Rachael sighed. No, she mustn't fall in love with Salim. They couldn't possibly have a future together.

Rachael took a bite of her grilled beefsteak. The meat was tough and difficult to chew. As usual, it had a liberal sprinkling of pepper. She sneezed, then groaned inwardly. A heavy breakfast like this on a warm May morning was a recipe for lethargy.

Brutus came yapping into the room and sat down at Mother's feet, tail wagging and tongue salivating expectantly.

'Rachael, make sure your bags are packed before you go to bed tonight,' said Mother. 'We shall be leaving for Mussorie early in the morning.'

'Yes, Mother,' Rachael replied.

'Seems the nabob has backed out. He's not going to London after all. He's sending his mother and brother instead,' chuckled Papa as he took a sip of his coffee.

'I hope the queen gives her verdict in favour of the nabob,' said Rachael.

'Why would you say such a thing, dear?' asked Mother as she patted her lips with the serviette. 'Ram

Singh, close the windows. Flies are coming in,' she added as she tried to shoo the flies with the back of her hand.

'Because East India Company had no business to annex Oudh.'

'Who says so?' asked Papa.

'Any and everyone in their right mind thinks so, Papa.'

Papa raised an eyebrow. Rachael finished her mouthful before replying.

'It's true, Papa. Even the former Resident, Colonel Sleeman, had emphatically stated that the English had no right to confiscate Oudh. To do so would be dishonest as well as dishonourable.'

Papa looked at Sudha and pointed to his empty glass. Sudha hurriedly brought the jug and poured water into it. He then turned his attention back to Rachael. 'Oudh needed better administration than that singing dancing nabob could provide. Why, even his own people wanted to see the back of him.'

'Oh Papa, you're so out of touch with the sentiments of the people,' Rachael cried. 'His people loved him. They resent us. And talking of administration, what improvements have we made in the last two months? All I see is the demolition of buildings, the royal family being forced out of their homes, the destruction and dispersal of the nabob's property and belongings. This is improvement?'

'Two months is too short a time. Give it a year and then Lucknow will run as efficiently as—'

'By then it'll have been reduced to a city without a soul,' Rachael replied and left the table.

* * *

140

Rachael lifted the curtain and looked out of the carriage window as it halted outside the northern gate of the Kaiserbagh Palace. She gave a smile of relief as her eyes rested on Salim. She could scarce believe how happy she felt seeing him again. She had missed him every single day while she was in Mussorie.

He held out his hand to her. Rachael hesitated and furtively looked around.

'Don't worry. They are all my men. They will not dare say anything.' Rachael took Salim's hand and alighted from the carriage.

'Memsahib, I come with you,' said Sudha, as she got off the carriage hurriedly.

'No, I'll be fine. You wait for me in the carriage,' said Rachael.

'You look radiant. I think the crisp mountain air agreed with you,' Salim said as he led her to a row of shops. 'And here I was hoping you would have become lean and haggard, pining for me,' he added with a grin.

Rachael blushed and didn't know what to say. She smiled and nodded her head slightly as Ahmed dawdled towards them and greeted her by raising his right hand to his forehead. 'I had no idea there were shops in Kaiserbagh,' she said as she looked at the stores beneath the vaulted arcade. There were shops selling jewellery, gold and silver, glass bangles, silks, shoes, spices, shawls, utensils, rugs and carpets, and birds in cages. There were even tea stalls and paan shops.

'These shops are for the begums. So they don't have to leave the confines of the palace to do their shopping,' Salim replied.

'Chutki!' Ahmed exclaimed.

Rachael turned. Just ten paces away from her stood a young girl clad in a bright marigold-coloured shirt and a green Gypsy skirt. She was haggling with the shopkeeper. 'If you reduce the price I'll take both the pink and the red lehenga . . .' She turned as she heard Ahmed's voice.

'Salim bhai, salaam. What a surprise.'

Salim hugged her. Then turning to Rachael he said, 'Meet my sister, Chutki, Daima's daughter.'

Rachael extended her hand as she said, 'Hello.'

Chutki let her eyes rest on Rachael. 'Salim bhai, I'm afraid you won't find any foreign goods in Meena Bazaar . . .' she said.

Rachael fiddled with the ribbons of her bonnet, unsure of what to do or say.

'RayChal, our Chutki's going to be married soon,' Salim said. 'She's shopping for her trousseau, I think.' His eyes twinkled as he brought his mouth close to Chutki's ear and lowered his voice. 'Someone told me your fiancé sent you a gift two days back and you sent him a letter in return. The letter smelt of rajnigandha, I'm told.'

Chutki blushed. She covered her face with her hands, and with an 'Oh Salim bhai', ran away giggling.

Rachael looked at Ahmed who had sauntered over to a paan shop. She tugged at Salim's shirt urgently as Ahmed tucked a paan into his mouth. 'I want to try one of those,' she said.

'Are you sure?' Salim asked, his brows raised, as he took a paan from Ahmed and handed it to her.

'Yes,' replied Rachael as she put the green cone in her

mouth. Salim and Ahmed watched her with an amused look.

She bit into it. The betel leaf was easy to chew. But the filling . . . She felt as though she had put a leaf full of juicy pebbles into her mouth. She bit hard but the pebbles were harder. And her mouth was getting filled with this strange orange juice. She tried to swallow it but it dribbled over her lower lip and chin.

She looked at Ahmed, then at Salim. He gave her a devilish grin, and with his hands behind his back, came closer. And closer. Oh no. Her eyes grew wider as he came even closer. What did he have in mind?

Still grinning, he brought his right hand forward and placed a spittoon under her chin. Oh, thank goodness. But what was she supposed to do with that shiny copper utensil? Suddenly she remembered. She had seen a begum spit in one in the zenana.

She lowered her eyes, covered her mouth with her hand and self-consciously spat out the contents of her mouth. As she wiped her mouth with her handkerchief, she stole a glance at Salim. His eyes were still laughing. She crinkled up her nose and smiled, a slow flush creeping up her cheeks.

Oh, how she had missed him in Mussorie. And now that she was back in Lucknow, standing beside him in his own palace grounds, she felt a strange thrill every time he teased her, and wished the day would never end.

Chapter Fourteen

SALIM

Salim patted Afreen's back as she trotted beneath the lofty gateway and made her way through the shrubbery. She stopped before the Khushnuma Palace on the banks of the Gomti. Salim got off and tethered her to an orange tree. He gave a slight nod to the guardsman who stood at the palace door as he saluted him.

As soon as he entered the octagonal hall facing Gomti, he saw chachi, Ahmed's mother, seated on the takhat. 'Aadaab, chachijaan,' he said pleasantly as he raised his right hand to his forehead. 'Is Ahmed home?'

'Aadaab, Salim mia. I'll send for Ahmed in a minute, but sit down beside me for a few minutes,' she said as she patted the takhat.

Salim sat down reluctantly.

'Whenever you come here, you're in a hurry,' she said as she cut a betel nut into little pieces. 'I don't get to see you at all.'

'Cha—' Salim stopped speaking as he heard some loud voices outside.

An English officer called Jackson barged into the hall, followed closely by Ahmed.

'Salim mia, this firangi says we have to leave the palace,' said a ruffled Ahmed.

'What?' Salim asked.

'Gentlemen, I have orders from the Company that this palace needs to be vacated,' Jackson said in clipped tones, waving a set of papers at Salim.

'You've no right to throw us out of our home,' said Ahmed.

'He's right. The Company promised at the time of annexation that it shall have no access to Kaiserbagh, Farhat Baksh, Moti Mahal, Khursheed Manzil and Khushnuma Palace. These palaces are for the sole use of my family. So leave us alone,' Salim ground out through clenched teeth.

'Leave these premises quietly, or I shall have to use force,' the angrez hissed.

'We're not going to budge from here. This is our home,' Ahmed replied and sat down stubbornly on the takhat.

Jackson barked to his men: 'Go and empty all the rooms. Throw out all their belongings on the street.'

Salim and Ahmed drew their swords as the men stormed into the zenana. Four men hastily drew their guns and held them to their heads. Salim pursed his lips and let his sword drop to the floor. He stood helplessly as a sound akin to the clucking of hens when a fox breaks into the henhouse rose from the zenana, followed by a scurrying of feet. Chachi broke down into sobs. He saw Ahmed flinch at the sound of boxes, utensils, portraits being thrown out of the palace and pursed his lips.

Soon he and Ahmed were led into the garden. Jackson shot a sardonic look at him, then locked the palace door.

'I'm going to drink their blood, bloody firangis!' Ahmed shouted as the dust and the galloping horses faded into the distance. He looked at his mother, his sisters, his grandparents, huddled together, too shocked to speak. 'How dare they humiliate us in this manner, Salim mia! How *dare* they!' He kicked a copper vessel lying at his feet. 'My sisters who have never left the confines of our home without purdah. Look at them now.'

Salim put his hand on Ahmed's shoulder. He had never seen him so angry before. 'Ahmed, we'll deal with them later. Right now we need to take care of your family. Let me go to Kaiserbagh and send you a carriage.'

He could not believe what had just happened. He kicked Afreen to make her go faster. As if auctioning Abba Huzoor's animals, taking possession of his rare collection of three hundred thousand books, raiding Macchi Bhawan, turning Qadam Rasul into a storehouse for gunpowder, demolishing gateways and kothis wasn't enough, they had now turned Ahmed and his family out on the streets. Made them homeless in minutes, just like that. The ignominy, the humiliation. If only Abba Huzoor knew. If only he had known this was how the Company was going to treat his family, his Lucknow, he would have never given up the throne without a fight. Never. He was sure of that.

* * *

That evening Salim stood near the pond at the edge of the Kaiserbagh garden. More than half the water of the pond was covered with floating lotus leaves. A cricket landed on one and began chirping by rubbing its wings together. Salim hacked angrily with his sword at the tufts of grass that had grown around the pond. If only it were possible to hack off Jackson's head as easily. A hand touched his shoulder lightly.

'Salim?' It was Rachael.

Salim slowly shrugged the hand off without turning around. He began digging furiously at the roots of some weeds with his sword.

'That's not the way a prince behaves towards a lady,' Rachael playfully quipped.

He clenched his teeth. His chin jutted out. So madam was here to teach him manners, was she? After all, she was one of them. He dropped the sword, spun on his heels and grabbed her forearms. 'No. I don't know how to behave towards a lady as I'm *not* a prince. Don't you know my father has been deposed?'

He let go of her arms abruptly. She fell back, too stunned to speak. Salim raked his fingers through his hair. 'I'm a pagan, a wretch, a sav—,' he shouted, his eyes blazing. He noticed the look of shock on Rachael's face and stopped speaking.

He turned away from her, intently studying the still waters of the pond.

'This is not like you, Salim. Pray tell me what troubles you,' Rachael asked carefully.

'I should have asked you not to come today,' he replied gloomily.

'Why? I thought we were friends? Surely you can tell me? Or do you still regard me as . . . ?' Her voice trailed away as she fidgeted with the diamond on her ring.

'Ahmed lost his home today.'

'What?'

'He and his family were thrown out of their palace by the Company.'

Rachael covered her mouth in horror. 'But how awful. The Company has the right to do that?'

Salim did not answer. He shrugged his shoulders and spread out his hands helplessly, then let them fall limply to his side. He turned away from the pond. Some of the lotus foliage and tubers had turned yellow. They were beginning to rot and were filling the air with a putrid smell. He started walking towards the rotunda.

Rachael walked beside him in silence.

'Ya Ali, what a friend I am. I should be with Ahmed and here I am promenading in the garden . . .'

'Where is he? His family?'

'In the Kaiserbagh Palace. They'll be living with us now.'

'And you say you're not a good friend? You're the kind of friend a person would die for.'

Salim looked at her. She was not joking. She shivered slightly in the light November breeze.

'Memsahib, we must be leaving. It getting dark, you see. Otherwise barre sahib getting angry.' It was Sudha who had hitherto been waiting in the carriage.

'I ought to take my leave now,' Rachael said.

He nodded. 'And I ought to apologise for my behaviour earlier this evening but I don't know how to.'

Rachael looked at him, lines creasing her forehead. 'Apologise? For what? I don't know about Anarkali's Salim but *my* Prince Salim can do no wrong,' she said with a smile.

He smiled back, his eyes soft and moist. A lock of Rachael's hair had come loose and he curbed the desire to tuck it behind her ear. 'Goodbye, RayChal,' he whispered. He watched the carriage trundle away until the gathering darkness swallowed it and he could see no more.

Salim plucked a red rosebud. The petals were tightly shut as though the flower was not yet ready for the onslaught of the bees and butterflies. It held its soft dewy fragrance deep inside. He tucked it in Rachael's hair, just behind her ear.

'I wish we could meet more often. It's almost two months since we last met.'

'We could, if it wasn't for fear of upsetting your father.'

Rachael chuckled. 'Pray, what did you say the name of this garden was?' she asked.

'Vilayati Bagh. Vilayati means "foreigner". See, one of the wives of Nawab Ghazi-ud-Din Haider, my great-great uncle, was English. He built this garden for her, hence the name.'

'Hmm, interesting. So are you also going to name a garden after me?' she asked, an impish smile reaching her eyes.

'Maybe . . . and it'll be more beautiful than anything that man ever laid his eyes on.'

Rachael looked around and said, 'I cannot imagine anything more beautiful than this.'

She was right. Vilayati Bagh was indeed one of the most beautiful gardens in Lucknow. The latticed kiosks, the fountains, the statues, the sheltered walks, the alcoves, the platform for the dancers and the orchestra, the riot of flowers that gave the impression that a painter had run amok on his palette; the tall tamarind and cypress trees standing guard over the orange plantation and the company of one's beloved made the picture complete.

Salim turned to Rachael and drawled, 'It'll be like Jannat, paradise. It'll have every conceivable flower on this planet. We'll call it Dooja Jahaan, the world beyond. A world beyond the reach of ordinary human existence. A world created out of love. And only lovers will be allowed in the garden.'

Rachael laughed.

He watched her as though hypnotised. Subhaan Allah! Why was she so perfect? Even her laughter was so pleasant, like wind chimes.

'Why are you looking at me like this?' Rachael asked.

'Nothing. Just hoarding memories. They'll be useful when you get engaged to someone.'

'Won't you stop me?'

'Do I have the right to?'

'You still have doubts?'

'But your father will never give me the right.'

'I'm sure I could coax him.'

Salim's eyes held hers. He continued to look into her

150

eyes as he lifted her hand and pressed it to his lips.

They were standing close to a fountain consisting of a ripple-carved block of stone. It was placed at an angle of forty-five degrees to give the effect of a waterfall. Salim could taste the moisture in the air. Neither of them spoke for a long time. They listened to the water from the fountain as it pattered on the still waters below. Like the sound of a baby's feet on a tiled floor.

It was Rachael who broke the silence. 'What's that small domed building?'

Salim looked across at the building with a single chamber and a small minar at each end. 'Qadam Rasul.'

'What's Qadam?'

'Qadam means "feet". It's a shrine. It has a stone which bears the footprints of the prophet Mohammad.'

'Oh, it must be a sacred—'

'Not anymore. The Company has turned it into a store for gunpowder.'

'What? But why choose a holy shrine for that? Surely there are other buildings? Aren't they sensitive to the sen—'

Salim gave a derisive laugh. 'Company and sensitive?' He grew sombre and lowering his voice said, 'Let's not spoil this evening. Talk about something else.'

They walked a few paces in silence.

'I wish we had a harmonium or sitar with us. You could continue to teach me then,' said Rachael.

'I can still teach you.'

'How?'

'Singing is as significant a part of Hindustani music

as playing an instrument. To become a good singer, you must master sur and laya. Now, sing after me . . .' Salim closed his eyes, and making movements in the air with his right hand, sang, 'Sa re ga ma pa dha ni sa.'

'Saaa ray—'

'No, listen to me again. Sa re ga ma . . .'

Rachael cleared her throat and tried again. 'Saaaa . . .'

Salim threw back his head and laughed. 'Ya Ali, I've never seen someone make such exquisite music and yet sing so terribly.'

Rachael's face turned red. She reddened easily. Heat, embarrassment, excitement, any emotion whatsoever, made the blood rush to her face, right up to the ears.

He cupped her face in his hands. 'It's all right. You're human. You can't be perfect in everything.'

A small smile lifted the corners of her mouth and slowly spread to her eyes. Her nose crinkled. He took her hand in his and together they ambled out of the park, the sun setting slowly behind them.

Ever since Salim had given shelter to Ahmed and his family in the palace, he had insisted the two friends have their lunch together in his parlour. The two of them were now seated before the dastarkhwan, partaking of their meal in silence.

'Ahmed.' Salim broke the silence.

'What is it, Salim mia?' Ahmed asked, not bothering to look up from his food.

'Umm . . . some more kebabs?'

'Oh, all right, just one more. I've already overeaten.'

Ahmed picked up a gelawati kebab and put it on his plate.

'Ahmed.'

'Yes?'

'Nothing. Can you pass me the chicken?'

'Yes, of course.'

Ahmed handed him the bowl of chicken curry. Salim took his time selecting a piece, then put it on his plate.

'Ahmed.'

'Yes, Salim mia?'

'Umm . . . would you like some more korma?'

'Salim mia, whatever it is you want to get off your chest, say it. Otherwise we'll be here until judgement day.'

'I think I'm in love.'

'Who with? That angrez?'

'Yes, that angrez.'

'Salim mia, you're going to get killed. And get all of us killed as well.'

'Why? Haven't nawabs married Englishwomen before? Have you forgotten Vilayati Begum?'

'It was different then.'

'Ya Ali, what was different? People fell in love then and they fall in love now.'

'Times have changed. The English used to respect us then. They regarded us as the inheritors of profound ancient wisdom. Now they call us heathens, pagans, savages. And we call them pig-eaters. Have you forgotten what happened just two months back in Khushnuma Palace?' Ahmed asked bitterly.

How could he forget? Salim swallowed a morsel.

It tasted bitter like karela. He was filled with renewed anger as he remembered how Ahmed's family had been turned out on the streets by the angrez, without their purdah. Such shame, such indignity. Even prisoners of defeated kingdoms were not treated as harshly as the people of Avadh were being treated.

Daima entered the room. 'Chote Nawab, have you finished? Should I remove the dishes?'

'Yes, Daima, and please ask Chilmann to fill my chillum. The tobacco has finished.'

'I'll do it for you, Chote Nawab . . . Chilmann has been asked to leave.'

'Oh,' Salim muttered. He had forgotten the Company had fired most of the servants last week.

Ahmed shook his head sombrely. 'This is not good. Making so many people who worked for His Majesty unemployed . . .' He paused to place a paan in his mouth. 'Any news from His Majesty?'

'Huh! It's been almost a year since Abba Huzoor left Lucknow and he's still clueless whether he'll get his kingdom back or not,' Salim replied. He nodded to Daima to bring in the jug of water, before continuing. 'It has been four months since Janab-e-Alia reached England. And she has not yet been given an audience with the queen. I always knew it was useless to pin hopes on that Queen Victoria.'

He got up abruptly and washed his hands. 'Believe me; nothing's going to come out of it. We should have fought against these angrez and chased them out of the country.'

'I heard a huge crowd turned up in London to see

them,' Ahmed said as he warmed his cold hands over a coal brazier.

'Who? To see Janab-e-Alia? Yes, I suppose the English think us strange just as we think they're weird – with their hooped dresses and wigs and skin as white as—'

'Balai.'

'You have to bring food into everything?'

'And you still want to marry that angrez?'

'Ahmed, she's one of them, and yet not like them. She's not one of us and yet not unlike us.'

Ahmed shook his head.

Salim looked at his friend and let out a long sigh. He would never understand. It wasn't just her beauty. Nor the love for music they shared. What he admired most about RayChal were her guts. She was a woman and yet she was never afraid. Like Begum Ammi. She was almost like a man in that. And then that fiery passion, her zest for life – he had never seen that in any of the women in the palace. Added to that was her childlike innocence; the pleasure she derived from even the smallest thing.

Salim shook his head again. No, Ahmed would never understand all that. And more.

Chapter Fifteen

SALIM

It was March. Exactly a year since Abba Huzoor had left Lucknow. Salim sat on the takhat in his room, a chapatti in his hand. He turned the chapatti over once more. 'You mean to say thousands of these are circulating throughout Hindustan at the moment?' he asked Nayansukh.

'Yes, Salim bhai,' Nayansukh answered, leaning against the wall.

'And the purpose is?'

'I'm not sure. Some say they contain a hidden message . . .'

'Is that so?' Salim held the chapatti up to the light. 'This one doesn't have any message.'

Nayansukh clicked the heels of his boots together. 'In the basti they're saying they are to appease goddess Durga. But the soldiers in my battalion think the Company ordered their distribution to see how fast a message can be relayed throughout the country. No one knows for sure.' He paused and twirled his moustache thoughtfully. 'Others are saying they're just a symbol. A signal to all chapatti eaters to unite and chase the firangis out of our country.'

Salim was silent. Was it possible there were others who felt like him? He straightened the qatat hanging on the wall. Maybe the time had come to settle matters with the Company.

'Salim bhai, there's widespread unrest in the country. Most Indians hate the firangis. A single match is going to set the entire country aflame.'

Salim walked over to his desk. Tapping his fingers on it thoughtfully, he asked, 'What happened in Berhampur?'

'They were asking the soldiers to bite cartridges greased with pig and cow fat.'

'Ya Ali, that's against our religion.'

'Exactly.' Nayansukh banged his fist on Salim's desk. 'The Company has already taken our lands and property, even our self-respect. Now it wants to take away the only thing we have – religion.'

'So did the soldiers do it?'

He watched Nayansukh cross and uncross his legs. He looked inconspicuous in his boots and dhoti.

'At first they refused. How could they do something so heinous? Then Colonel Mitchell threatened if they did not obey his orders, he would blow them up.' Nayansukh paused, untied his cummerbund and flung it across his neck.

Salim listened to him thoughtfully. He did not say anything for a long moment. The smell of wax made him realise it was getting dark. Daima had started lighting the candles. 'Nayansukh,' Salim spoke slowly. 'If they asked the sepoys in Lucknow to bite those cartridges, would you do it?'

Nayansukh twirled his moustache arrogantly. 'Never. Not in a million years.'

Holi, the day the rainbow left the heavens and walked the earth.

'Holi hai, Holi hai,' Chutki chanted as she covered Salim's face with a pink powder and put a generous helping on his hair as well. Salim smiled as he smeared some red colour on her cheeks.

'Let me get some thandai for you, Salim bhai,' Chutki said as she scurried off.

Salim sat down on the parapet. He watched the others run after one another with handfuls of coloured powder or water syringes full of coloured water. Ahmed sat in a corner stuffing himself with gujias. It had become a tradition to celebrate Holi at Daima's house every year. He missed Abba Huzoor. He used to partake of Holi with full fervour.

Chutki returned with a glass of thandai. Ah, thandai! Made from nuts, seeds, cardamom and saffron and laced with the intoxicant bhang and the fragrance of roses. So cool, so refreshing, so uplifting. He was in another world by the time he had finished the third glass.

Both Ahmed and he were singing boisterously as they made their way home. They stopped as they passed Rachael's house. She was stepping out of her carriage.

'Good morn— good afternoon,' Salim boomed, as

he got off his horse. Rachael stared at his and Ahmed's smeared faces with horror and ran inside.

'RayChal,' Salim called.

He saw her hesitate as she heard his voice and step back out of the house. Warily she walked towards him and searched his face. 'So it *is* you,' she said with a laugh. 'I would have never recognised you if you hadn't said my name.'

Salim smeared some pink powder on her cheeks. 'Holi hai,' he said. Her cheeks were so smooth, like the keys of a piano. She looked surprised.

'Pray tell me why you did that?'

'Holi is incomplete if you do not play it with your sweetheart.'

'What the hell is going on? Who are these ruffians, Rachael?'

Salim scowled. It was Colonel Bristow.

'Oh no, Papa,' said Rachael. 'This is Salim. He's my . . .' She smoothed her hair and licked her lips before continuing. 'My music teacher, remember?'

'Ha, so it is. The ruffian.' He turned back to Rachael. 'Now go inside and wash that off your face.'

Salim's hands curled into fists. How dare he call him a ruffian? If he wasn't RayChal's father, he would have punched his nose. He fidgeted with his cummerbund as Colonel Bristow turned his attention back to him and Ahmed. He stood still, his chin jutting out as the colonel looked him over with disgust.

'Don't you know? A gentleman always dresses up formally before meeting a lady? Be off with you,' the colonel said as he dismissed them with a wave of his hand.

Salim's intoxication evaporated. Ya Ali, this man will be a tough father-in-law, he thought. Would RayChal ever be able to coax him to let him marry her, he wondered gloomily.

As they reached the forest at the edge of Gomti, Salim stared ahead, his jaw dropping as a riot of bright orange blazed before his eyes. 'Fire,' he gasped as he charged ahead. He blinked twice. It wasn't a fire. Just a cluster of rhododendron trees laden with their orangish-red blossoms.

Ahmed shook his head as he caught up with him. As they trotted around the deep end of the Gomti, Salim shouted yet again. 'Ya Ali, blood!' The water was red. Salim stared at it.

'Salim mia, you're drunk. It's not blood, it's Holi colour. You mistake tesu for fire, red colour for blood! Now don't mistake me for a firangi and shoot me!'

But Salim wasn't listening. He kept staring at the swirling waters, at the river as red as blood, a chill numbing his bones. It seemed ominous.

The month was April, the year 1857. Salim looked at the shimmering reflection of the golden domes and minarets of Macchi Bhawan in the Gomti. It felt as though he was looking at the palace of the sea god. Little did he know he would never see that reflection again.

He dived into the river. The water was a little cold for this time of the year. He thought of Rachael. He had not been able to see her since that brief meeting on Holi. He cut the waters and swam faster and faster as he recalled the words of her father. He had called him a ruffian. He dipped his head underwater and remembered how he had mistaken the tesu flowers for fire and the red colour of Gomti for blood. And again a chill of dread shivered down his spine.

'Salim mia.'

Salim's head came above the water. He wiped his face with his hand as he looked at Ahmed.

'Mangal Pandey has been hanged, Salim mia.'

'What? Who's that?'

'The sepoy in Barrackpore. The one who refused to bite the greased cartridges.'

Salim swam to the shore and pulled himself out of the water.

'It was a public hanging, mia,' said Ahmed. 'A warning to the Indian sepoys. This is what awaits them if they don't obey orders.'

Salim did not say anything. He picked up his towel and began to dry himself. Whether the public execution would instil fear in the sepoys or incite them to revolt, only time would tell. Until then he would wait and watch. Watch and wait. And then he would act, when emotions were high and the blood hot.

May 4th 1857. Salim and Ahmed were on their way to Kaiserbagh Palace when they noticed a crowd gathering at the jelo-khana of Macchi Bhawan. They were pouring in from all directions. Salim looked at Ahmed questioningly. Ahmed shrugged his shoulders, equally clueless. Then he looked around and tapped the shoulder of a young lad standing next to him. 'Err . . . what exactly is happening?' he asked.

161

'You don't know? The Company is about to hang Abdul Rehman.'

'Ah! Abdul Rehman Mirza,' Salim exclaimed. Yes, he had heard about the rumpus caused in the city by Abdul Rehman yesterday. He had attacked Major Lincoln with two other men. Then, having escaped unhurt, he had led a procession of thousands of men shouting slogans against the Company and firangi rule. However, as the procession reached Roomi Darwaza, they found Major Lincoln's men waiting for them with bullets and lathis. Abdul Rehman was mortally wounded and finally caught.

Salim stood upright as some redcoats marched into the courtyard and stood in a single file on either side. The crowd became silent. Only the buzz of flies and mosquitoes could be heard. Abdul Rehman Mirza was led into the courtyard, his hands and feet bound in chains. His eyes were half closed and his clothes bloodied. He was flanked on either side by armed soldiers. After taking two steps, he stumbled and fell. Everybody held their breath as he floundered to stand and collapsed yet again. Two sepoys dragged him roughly to the banyan tree in the centre of the courtyard.

A scene from the past flashed through Salim's mind. He remembered the time when he had watched a butcher skin a goat. The butcher had smashed the goat's head with a stone a few times but that had not killed it. It was still conscious and writhed and twitched as the butcher proceeded to skin it. He had watched in horror as the goat's heart continued to beat for a long time after it had been skinned. Salim was only twelve then. He had a nightmare that night and several other nights. And try as he might, he could not erase the sight of the goat, fully skinned, its body covered in blood, its heart pumping rapidly.

And now, as he watched Abdul Rehman, his hand curled into a fist as he curbed the desire to dash into the jelo-khana and free the dying man. The hangman was now putting a noose around Abdul Rehman's neck. Salim looked around at the crowd. Some of the men stood defiantly, chin up in the air. There was fear in the eyes of some, but their faces remained impassive.

An old man standing next to Salim staggered and was about to fall. Helping him to his feet, Salim asked, 'Are you all right?'

'All right?' the old man answered. His arms shook as he pointed a finger at Abdul Rehman. 'Who will perform my last rites now?' he asked as tears flowed down his cheeks.

He was Abdul Rehman's father, Salim realised and he swallowed. His thoughts flew to Abba Huzoor. He wondered how he was, exiled as he had been from his own kingdom.

The old man was again pointing to his son. 'He's half-dead. What was the need?'

Salim did not answer but stared ahead, his eyes blazing, his face contorted in anger. The commanding officer shouted his command and the noose around Abdul Rehman's neck tightened. His feet thrashed momentarily in mid-air, then all was quiet. Everything was still. The buildings, the people, even the leaves of the banyan tree from which the body of Abdul Rehman now swung, were motionless. A single dry leaf fell slowly, sadly, noiselessly to the ground. Salim looked up at the tree. At the dried yellow leaves, holding their breath and clinging onto the branch, knowing that when the next wind blew it would be their turn to fall.

The crowd began to disperse, subdued, quiet, holding their breath. Salim watched them go. How long would it remain silent, subjugated, afraid, he wondered.

Salim knelt down in his room, facing the west, towards Mecca, as the call for the evening prayers rang out from the mosques. He closed his eyes, raised his arms and muttered his prayer. Then he bent forward so his forehead could touch the ground and thus offered his obeisance to Allah, on this twenty-second day of Ramzan.

Then he straightened up and began pacing the floor. Gangaram had been caught and put behind bars. What he had witnessed in Newazganj yesterday, he had never witnessed before. What started as a quiet gathering to mark the mourning day of Ramzan, the night Hazrat Ali, the fourth Muslim caliph, had been assassinated, soon turned into a frenzied crowd. As the night wore on, the mob became angrier and angrier. Their thoughts were not with Hazrat Ali anymore, but with Abdul Rehman and the twenty sepoys who had been hanged the previous day. Each and every man present in Newazganj was livid. Gone was the fear, the timidity, the hesitation that Salim had witnessed during the hanging.

'Down with Company rule. Throw out these firangis,' the crowd had chanted.

Lifting the khus mat, Salim looked out. Not a soul to be seen.

Early this morning, Salim was informed, the same gathering had taken out a silent procession from Newazganj to the Hussainabad Imambara. On the way back, however, some men lost their cool when they saw Major Lincoln. The bloody firangi responsible for all the arrests and hangings. They tried to attack him. They were arrested, beaten and put behind bars. One of them was Gangaram.

Salim lifted the mat again. He could see no movement in the courtyard below. Then he saw Nayansukh and Daima, creeping towards his room. He did not wait but bounded down the stairs to meet them.

'Daima?' he said as he took her hands in his.

Daima's lips quivered. 'Gangaram is no more . . . Chutki's fiancé's dead.'

'What happened?' Salim's voice was barely audible.

Daima did not answer but simply clung to him.

'They shot him,' said Nayansukh. 'After torturing him.'

Closing his eyes, Salim leant against a pillar as Daima's tears ran down his angarkha.

'His whole body was charred,' Daima whispered between sobs. 'We couldn't recognise him at all.'

'Bits of skin hanging . . . skin peeling off . . . blood oozing from everywhere . . . he had been tied to the floor with ropes . . . then pelted with heated brass rods, Salim bh—' said Nayansukh, his voice breaking.

Salim took a few steps away from Daima. He stood still with his back towards her, his feet apart, arms folded behind his back, chin jutting out. His Adam's apple moved as he tried to get a grip on his emotions. He turned back after a few minutes and looked at Daima's anguished face. He thought of Chutki, of Gangaram, of the frenzied crowd at Newazganj. Yes, the time had come.

Chapter Sixteen

RACHAEL

Rachael sat quietly, sipping her sherbet. She looked around. The hall was full of people talking, laughing, eating, dancing. She knew most of them. Or maybe not. What were they like at home? Did they still wear their charming smiles or did they scream at their servants like Papa did?

She took another sip and thought of Salim. She wondered how he was. What must he be doing right now? It was becoming more and more difficult for her to see him these days. Alas, when would she be able to sneak out and meet him again? She had read somewhere – if you crave for something from the core of your heart, you often get it. And there was nothing she wanted more right now than to waltz with Salim. But first she would have to teach him. She giggled inwardly as she imagined herself teaching him how to dance. She could visualise him stepping on her toes and exclaiming 'Ya Ali' every time he did so.

'May I have this dance?' Salim? Rachael's heart skipped a beat as she turned around. Her face fell. It was Christopher. She had been hallucinating. She rose petulantly and gave him her hand as he led her to the dance floor.

His face was sunburnt. If Ahmed saw him like this, he would say he looked like tandoori chicken. The thought made her snicker.

'What's so funny?' Christopher asked.

'Nothing, nothing at all,' Rachael answered as she laughed even louder.

'Where's the bracelet I gave you?'

'Oh, it's in my jewellery box,' Rachael lied. She had no clue where it was.

'But you promised never to take it off.'

'Umm . . . I broke my promise, I fear.'

'But my future wife ought to learn to keep her word.'

'I beg your pardon?' Rachael looked at him incredulously. 'Christopher, whatever Papa might've said to you, I've never thought of you that way. You're a childhood friend and that's how I intend to keep it.' She looked at Christopher's crestfallen face. 'Look—'

'Then why did you lead me on?' he asked, tightening his grip on her hand. Rachael sighed. Perhaps she *had* led him on. She may even have married him eventually. But that was before she had met Salim.

'Will you or won't you marry me?' Christopher demanded.

'No,' she shouted, just as the band stopped playing.

Her word echoed through the room and everyone stared at her and Christopher. She lowered her gaze and murmured, 'No, Christopher, I cannot.'

Christopher spun on his heels and left the room.

Summer had its own charm. It was a time of abundance, when the branches of trees sagged under the weight of ripe fruit – mangoes, lychee, jackfruit, jamun . . . Rachael found herself in a mango orchard that morning, the trees laden with oval orangish-yellow mangoes. She sat down gingerly on a swing. Well, it wasn't exactly a swing. Just a rope with a cushion on it, hanging from the branch of a mango tree. Soon she was enjoying herself as she swung higher and higher. She sniffed inquisitively as the smell of mangoes in the orchard, mingled with the strong smell of sugar cane growing in the nearby fields, reached her.

Raising her right hand over her eyes, she looked at the tree in front. All she could see of Salim was a flash of white and his pointed velvet shoes. He did not seem like himself today. Something was eating him. She couldn't blame him. After all, he had seen much, lost much and suffered much in the last few months. But what she saw in his eyes today was something different. It was as though he had made up his mind about something and was determined to carry it out. What exactly that was, she could not tell.

She watched him jump down from the tree with a thud and squish a mango gently on all sides with his hands. Then he bit a little hole on the top and gave it to her. She looked at him, then at the mango and again at him.

'Go on, sip through the hole.'

Rachael took a small sip, then she sucked really hard. Thick yellowish-orange juice oozed out and ran down her hand. She licked it with a sheepish grin.

'Mmmm, it's delicious. I've never eaten a mango like this before, and that, too, while swinging from a mango tree. Mother would be horrified. She firmly believes ladies ought to eat mangoes and oranges in the privacy of their rooms.'

'And I've never climbed a tree in an angarkha before,' Salim replied, dusting the mud from his clothes. 'Ya Ali, it has been years since I last climbed a tree.' He picked up a raw mango from the ground, swung it in the air and caught it. 'When Ahmed and I were little, we were sitting on one of these trees devouring mangoes one day, when the caretaker arrived out of nowhere and chased us out of the orchard with a cane.'

'Oh dear!'

'You should have seen his face when he came to know that I was Abba Huzoor's son. He sent me a basketful of mangoes as an apology.'

'You must miss him a lot.'

'Not really. I don't remember bumping into him again.'

'I was talking about your father.'

Salim was silent for a moment. 'I don't miss him as much as his presence. The knowledge that he's there, that I've nothing to worry about,' he replied quietly.

Rachael got off the swing and touched his arm lightly. He smiled at her.

'You look like a baby with mango pulp smeared on

the tip of your nose. Wait, don't move.' He took out his handkerchief and gently wiped her nose before tweaking it.

'Ouch.'

'Where were you yesterday? I missed you,' he said.

Rachael looked at the monkeys chattering and swinging by their tails and legs on the trees before answering. A baby monkey lost his balance while jumping from one branch to another and was caught just in time by its mother. 'There was a party at home and I simply couldn't get away. There's this friend of mine called Christopher . . .'

'Christopher? Who's he?'

Rachael noticed his voice had suddenly gone sharp. She snapped a dry twig she had been playing with. KHATACK! 'He's a good-for-nothing. But a brilliant dancer. It was good fun dancing with him last night.'

'Was it, now?'

'Yes, he's a soldier – same regiment as Papa. Papa's fond of him, you know. In fact, if he had his way, he would love to see me betrothed to him.'

Salim's face turned white. He held her elbows in a tight grip. 'And you? Do you also want to marry him?' His tone was clipped, his breathing uneven.

Rachael laughed inwardly. Contrary to the picture Salim was conjuring, she had spent the most unpleasant evening with Christopher. But at least now he knew she had no intention of marrying him.

She looked at Salim, her eyes narrowing into a smile. 'Are you jealous, Salim? Christopher's just a friend. Like you and me?' She raised an eyebrow and looked at him.

'So we're just friends?'

'Aren't we?' Rachael asked, suppressing a grin. She was enjoying this. So Prince Salim was jealous. Ah ha! Surely he must love her then . . .

'I thought it was more . . .'

'More what, Salim?'

'Nothing.' He picked up her shoe that had come off while she was swinging, and slipped it under her foot. 'Come to Lal Barahdari tomorrow after dusk. You'll get your answer.'

Rachael smiled and a myriad little mango blossoms showered down on her.

The next evening Rachael followed Salim into what looked like a huge hall. He pointed to the throne and said, 'This is the coronation hall.'

The hall led into a spacious palace garden. In the centre of the garden was a magnificent pond, surrounded by colourful little fountains and adorned with statues. The statues were lit by colourful lamps. The entire garden looked like a fairy land.

That wasn't all. In the centre of the pond was a pavilion. Rachael followed Salim demurely, as he led her to a boat. She loved the way the water parted as the oars hit it with a chopping sound.

He held out his hand and helped her get off the boat on to the pavilion. They entered the first of the two rooms. It was covered with Persian rugs and smelt of roses. Not the soft demure smell of the shy pink rose but the strong smell of the passionate red rose. Salim led her to a diwan and she sat down in silence. She did not know what to say. She felt like a princess in a magical palace. It was too beautiful to be true.

Salim coughed slightly. 'You know why I've brought you here, don't you?'

'Maybe, but I want to hear it from you.'

'I want to make you a part of my harem.'

Rachael raised a brow. Now that kind of proposal she had not heard before.

'I don't mind, as long as I'm the only woman in it.' She whipped her gaze to his, expecting to see his eyes mocking her. But they were serious today, dead earnest.

He noisily poured two glasses of sherbet and handed her a glass. 'It's not true that all nawabs have millions of wives. Nawab Safdar Jang had only one wife and he was besotted by her. He did not have a single mistress or concubine or—'

'That's all very well – but you'll have to go down on your knees and propose,' Rachael playfully suggested. She sensed he was tense. For some reason he was not his normal self today. It was as though he were a mine, waiting to explode.

'Ya Ali, I can't do that. In all my life I've bowed before just two people – Allah and Abba Huzoor,' he replied haughtily.

'Then I'm afraid you can't have me,' Rachael said, shaking her head and clicking her tongue mischievously.

But he was still tense and his chin jutted out even more than it normally did. She noticed the vein in his forehead tauten. It always did whenever he was stressed.

'I'm sorry,' he said. 'You forget I'm not English. I do not know the Englishman's ways. I'll do it my way.'

So saying, he pulled her to her feet. 'Let's not tarry, it's getting late.'

Rachael looked at him, bewildered.

Neither of them spoke on the way back. Rachael could not understand what had gone wrong.

Rachael sat in the front garden of her bungalow. She took a sip of tea and looked around. This was the only time of the day when the garden could be enjoyed. It was not too warm, the sun having just set. At the same time there was enough light to prevent mosquitoes and other creepy-crawlies from venturing out yet.

It was 17th May 1857, the middle of a scorching summer. The blades of grass had turned yellow. Even the bees seemed weary of the heat and buzzed slowly as they collected honey. Brutus sat by her chair, lazily watching a yellow butterfly, too hot to give it chase. The bluebells were dead, the geraniums had all but vanished and the hibiscus flowers drooped as they panted for respite from the heat. The leaves of her favourite guava tree were caked with dust.

She wondered what was eating Salim. He was not his usual self of late. The other day, when he had taken her to Lal Barahdari, it seemed he wanted to propose to her and yet . . . She had wanted him to propose. She wanted him to make her his. It did not matter anymore that he was a native. In fact, it never had.

She looked across at Papa. He was smoking his pipe and looking at some papers. She nibbled at her sandwich then pushed the plate aside. Everybody was homeward bound. The clippity-clop of carriages and the bells around the cows returning from the meadows could be heard in the distance. The sky was covered with birds flying in all directions. They seemed extra noisy today.

'Hello, Christopher,' said Papa.

Rachael looked in the direction of his gaze. Christopher was sauntering towards them, still in his uniform. His cheeks were still sunburnt and looked a shade deeper than his red jacket. It was a pity, for they detracted from his boyish charm. She gave him a small smile as her father patted the chair next to him. He was the last person she wanted to speak to right now. Christopher nodded at her slightly before taking a seat. They had not spoken much since their row. A wall of cold politeness had replaced their old camaraderie.

Christopher helped himself to a sandwich before turning to Papa. 'I'm afraid I've some disturbing news, sir.'

'Yes?' said Papa.

'The sepoys in Meerut have mutinied.'

'Is this related to the hanging of that Pandey fellow?'

'It's not just that sir. Eighty-five soldiers of the 3rd Light Cavalry refused to fire the cartridges of the Enfield rifles on religious grounds.'

'What a load of superstitious nonsense.'

'Well sir, there were rumours the cartridges the soldiers were required to bite off were greased with cow and pig fat. And religion forbids Hindus and Muslims from touching it.'

'Oh yes, you can't mess with their religion,' said

Rachael. 'They take it seriously.' She remembered how furious Salim had been when he had thought she was a Christian missionary.

'Were they greased with animal fat?' Papa asked.

'I think there was some truth in the rumours, sir. The eighty-five sepoys who refused to even touch the cartridges have now been sentenced to imprisonment with hard labour for ten years. This sentence was read out before all the troops of Meerut, on the infantry parade ground. The sepoys were then stripped of their uniforms and were made to remove their boots. They were then shackled in chains.'

Rachael shook her head slowly. 'They shouldn't have been publicly humiliated like this. After all, they're soldiers, not common criminals.'

'I agree,' replied Christopher. 'Some of those soldiers were old, having served in the army for twenty to thirty years. They were heartbroken and were sobbing like little children.'

'Dear me,' Rachael said. 'Either way they stood to lose. Even if they had obeyed and used those cartridges, they would have been shunned by their own family and village and pronounced outcasts.'

'Now all the native soldiers of Meerut are in full revolt,' Christopher said. 'They've massacred the English and rode through the night towards Delhi. Sir Henry is expecting some trouble in Lucknow as well and feels it would be a good idea to move all the women and children to the Resi—'

'Oh, Lawrence is being overcautious,' interjected Papa. 'There's no need for that. If the people of Oudh

176

didn't raise their arms when their nabob was deposed, they're not going to do so now.'

Rachael looked at Papa. Somehow she did not feel as complacent as he did. Christopher's tidings made her apprehensive.

The skies suddenly darkened and within minutes there was dust flying everywhere.

Rachael sprang to her feet. 'Goodness, it's a dust storm,' she exclaimed.

The three of them ran indoors, coughing and spluttering. Ram Singh and Ayah hurried outdoors to take the tea inside. The sandwiches and the tea were already covered with dust. They then hurried from one room to another closing all the windows, but the beds and furniture were already covered with a layer of grime.

Rachael stood by her window and watched the raging wind as it bent the trees double, the air swirling with dust. It was followed by thunder and lightning and a heavy downpour. A branch of her guava tree broke with a loud crash. She shuddered. Somehow she got the feeling that this was just the beginning. That a bigger storm was yet to come.

Rachael smiled to herself as she looked at the little necklace. She had been going to the orphanage every morning to read to the sick children. Today, just as she was leaving, Kalan had shoved something into her hands. 'For you, madam,' he said. It was a little necklace made of a handful of marigold flowers, stitched clumsily together. She was surprised, as he was the shyest of the lot. She had never heard him utter a single word before.

The carriage entered the gates of the Bristow residence and halted before the main entrance. As Rachael stepped out, she noticed a woman in a white sari. Daima? What was she doing here? And what was she carrying? It was a silver tray covered with a velvet cloth. There were other women as well, each one wearing a colourful dress and carrying an equally colourful tray.

'Daima? What a surprise!'

Daima looked at her, her face grim, her lips a thin straight line. Without saying a word she brushed past her. All the other women followed her in silence.

'What was that?' Rachael asked Papa as she stepped into the house and closed her parasol.

'That was what comes of getting too cosy with the natives.'

'Pray tell me what you mean?'

'The nabob's son . . .'

'Yes?'

'The audacity of that—'

'Why, what'd he do?'

'Apparently he has taken a fancy to you and wants to make you his concubine!'

'What?'

'You heard me.'

Rachael fumed inwardly. So this is what Salim meant when he said he would do it his way. She should have known better. A mistress indeed! And to think she had thought he loved her and was going to propose to her!

* * *

It was 30th May 1857. Rachael looked at the rows of small beds that lined the biggest room of the orphanage. The windows had been closed to avoid invasion by the little black army of flies and mosquitoes. How could the children sleep in this sweltering heat without a fan she wondered.

She removed the strip of cloth from Kalan's forehead. His temperature was coming down. It was a good sign. Mrs Rodriques entered the room.

'I think you better stay the night,' she whispered.

Rachael looked at the sleeping child, then turned her attention to the caretaker of the orphanage. 'Pray tell me why?'

'It's not safe. They're expecting trouble. There are rumours. The firing of the gun at nine o'clock tonight will be a signal for the sepoys to revolt.'

'But I must leave. Papa will be worried sick if I don't get back home.'

Kalan stirred. Rachael patted his head gently. Dilawar, a fair boy with soft golden curls, muttered in his sleep.

'How will you go?' Mrs Rodriques whispered.

'My carriage is waiting outside.'

'Not anymore. I think the driver has deserted.'

'Oh dear, but I must go home.'

'Let me see if Mr Rodriques is able to arrange something.'

Rachael wrung her hands as she paced the room. So now they were expecting a mutiny in Lucknow as well. She felt apprehensive. She wondered how Salim was. *Stop*, she told herself. It was over. She was never to think about him again. Whatever it was they had between them was over. She would have nothing to do with him ever again.

Wrapping the shawl around her head and shoulders, Rachael stepped into the palanquin. Mrs Rodriques turned to the palanquin-bearers.

'If anyone asks, you are to tell them it is Nawab Wajid Ali Shah's begum.'

The palanquin-bearers nodded and were soon huffing down the street.

Rachael peered through the curtain. The streets were deserted. What if the rumours were true? But then it was late. The streets would be deserted at this time of the night anyway.

A loud yelp made her start. One of the two sepoys walking down the street had kicked a stray dog who limped away yowling in pain. They were now coming towards the palanquin.

'HALT!'

The palanquin stopped moving. Rachael held her breath. She covered her nose with her hand. A foul smell was emanating from a nearby drain.

The tall and stout sepoy tapped on the palanquin and asked, 'Who's in there?'

One of the palanquin-bearers stuttered, 'H-His Majesty's begum, Begum . . .' then turned to his companion for help.

'Begum Mahal,' his companion supplied.

'Yesss. Begum Mahal.'

Rachael sat still, her back straight as she pushed a

truant lock of hair back under the shawl.

'How do we know? What if you're hiding an angrez?' He again tapped the palanquin. 'Begum sahiba, show us your hand.'

Rachael swallowed.

The other sepoy now spoke. 'Leave the poor woman alone, Shekhar. Bloody firangis didn't even let His Majesty take all his wives with him.' He patted one of the bearers on the shoulder. 'Go, take her home quickly. This is no time for a lady to be out on the streets.'

Rachael slowly let out her breath. She wiped her moist hands and then her face.

A few moments later, she heard a gunshot. Loud and clear. It must be nine o'clock. She was still a few minutes away from home.

There was a prolonged silence after that gunshot. All she could hear was the laboured breathing of the palanquin-bearers. She looked out of the curtain again. Now there was just one more street to cross. It was then that she heard it. The sound of muskets amidst shouting and drumming. It came from the native cantonments.

The palanquin turned the corner. She could now see her bungalow at the end of the road. It looked exactly as it did every night. A rectangular white house, shrouded in darkness, except for the faint light that could be seen at some of the windows. She almost collapsed with relief.

She sprang out of the palanquin as it stopped near the gate. She opened the gate, a little puzzled. Where was the guard on duty? Why had he not stepped forward to open it for her? She knocked on the door. There was no response. 'Ram Singh,' she called out and knocked again.

Where was Brutus? She walked around to the back of the house. Yes, her window was open. She pulled herself through the window.

She ran from room to room shouting, 'Papa, Brutus, Mother, Ram Singh . . .' but they were nowhere to be seen. 'Papa,' she shouted one last time on a frustrated sob. She then collected herself and went into Papa's study. No, he wasn't there. She opened his drawer and took out his gun. If she was going to be alone at a time like this, she had better equip herself.

Then she went towards the servants' quarters. Ayah's house was empty as well. Hearing some voices, she rushed into Sudha's quarters. She was horrified to see her surrounded by three to four natives. 'Please forgive me. Let me go,' Sudha was pleading, her hands joined.

'Forgive you?' the man bellowed. He slapped her hard across the face and sent her spiralling to the floor. Then he pulled her to her feet by yanking her hair. 'Do you know the entire village is laughing at us since you ran away from your husband's funeral pyre?' He raised his hand to slap her again.

Rachael caught hold of his hand. 'Leave her alone,' she commanded.

The men turned to look at her now. One of them eventually spoke. 'You keep out of this, memsahib. This is family matter. You not interfere.'

'Yes, memsahib, you leave,' Sudha uttered. 'You see, these be my uncles and brothers.'

'I'm not leaving you alone with these brutes, Sudha. Don't any of you dare touch her,' she challenged, as she pulled out Papa's gun.

Sudha's brother instantly caught hold of her hand and twisted it hard. Rachael screamed in pain. Her grip on the gun loosened and it fell to the floor. He pushed her hard. Her head banged against the wall and soon she was plunged in darkness.

Chapter Seventeen

SALIM

Salim stood in the pavilion on the terrace, from where he could see the intricately carved gateways of Kaiserbagh. He was incensed. How dare a firangi insult him like that in his own country! 'He's a native', Colonel Bristow had said. Just a native.

Daima had been agog when Salim had told her he wanted to marry Rachael. She had decorated all the trays herself. One silver tray contained sweets ranging from the juicy syrupy balls of gulab jamun to the dry diamond-shaped barfi made from cashew nuts. A silver platter had a set of ornaments made from fresh flowers. Another had gold jewellery with a gold engagement ring in the centre. All the trays were covered with a red velvet cloth with tassels of gold.

Salim pursed his lips as he recalled what Daima had recounted last night. She had marched proudly to RayChal's house, followed by a colourful train of maids, carrying silver platters and trays, only to be greeted by Colonel Bristow's 'What the hell!' He took his pipe out of his mouth, and pointing it to the silver trays, said, 'If you have come here to sell something, I'm afraid we're not interested.'

Daima grinned. 'No, no, sahib, you're mistaken . . . we come from Nawab Wajid Ali Shah.'

Colonel Bristow raised his brow.

'His son, our Chote Nawab, Salim, is in love with your daughter and wishes to marry her,' Daima continued.

'What? The gall of that fellow!'

'I beg your pardon, sahib?'

'Tell me something . . . You are . . . ?'

'I'm his daima . . . I nursed him as a baby.'

'Tell me, Daima, is there any guarantee that prince of yours will not marry again? After all, his father is said to have over a hundred wives.'

'That's not true, sahib.'

'And where will he keep his wife? Just a few months back the Company threw out all his relatives from Khushnuma Palace. What guarantee is there that he will not be thrown out of his palace tomorrow?'

'Saheb, he's the king's son.'

'He was. Not anymore. The king has been deposed.' He paced up and down before facing Daima again. 'You seriously expect me to give my daughter's hand to the son of a spineless man who could not even protect his own throne?'

He took out a watch from his pocket, looked at the time, then put it back. Looking at Daima irritably, he lowered his voice and said, 'And Daima, even if his father was still the ruler of Oudh, I would never let my daughter marry a mere native. Never.'

Salim's muscles tensed as he flung the engagement ring into the pond with full force. It startled the sleeping goldfish. The waters rippled as they darted to and fro in panic. So he was just a native. So what if he could read and write English and quote Byron and Keats as well as any Englishman? Or compose? Or play Mozart, for that matter? For RayChal's father, as long as the colour of his skin was brown, he was the same as the dhobi or the sweeper.

He folded his arms across his chest and decided to stay outside a little longer. It was too hot to go inside, while here on the terrace, a light summer breeze was blowing, heavily laden with the sweet smell of tuberoses.

Ahmed appeared just then.

'I've been looking everywhere for you. And you're relaxing here! Do you even know what is happening in the city?'

'What?'

'The sepoys have mutinied.'

'It was about time they did,' Salim replied as he took aim with his pistol and fired. The guava fell off the tree with a thud.

'People are afraid, Salim mia, and many of them are leaving the city. I think you should leave as well. Go to Calcutta, to Abba Huzoor. You'll be safe there.'

'You're joking. Ya Ali, please tell me you're joking.'

'No, Salim mia, for once I'm serious. Nothing's going to come out of this revolt. The English are going to crush this uprising.'

'And what about Lucknow? Leave it for the firangis to molest? I was born here, Ahmed. It was here that I took my first steps. And you want me to leave it when it is vulnerable and needs me?'

He fell silent for a moment as he heard the firing of shots from the cantonment. 'No, Ahmed. I'm not going anywhere. I'm going to stay right here and fight the English – every one of them. This is the moment I've been waiting for.'

'I fear for your safety.'

'Look at these gateways, Ahmed, at the mermaids. Aren't they beautiful? Aren't they?'

'Yes, but—' Ahmed slapped his neck sharply and flicked away a little black smudge. 'Bloody mosquito,' he muttered.

'See that spiral staircase?' Salim asked. 'Do you remember how much fun we used to have running up and down those stairs?'

'And we used to spend hours watching the builders build these gateways and palaces. Remember the time I ran across wet concrete and Chote mia wanted to skin me alive?' Ahmed chuckled.

'And you want me to leave all this for the firangis to destroy? Like they tore down the gateways in Hazratganj? Or demolished Begum Khas Mahal's kothis? Haven't they plundered our city enough?'

Ahmed was watching the nightwatchman who was making his rounds. He blew his shrill whistle, followed by the words, 'Jaagte raho'.

'And just think, Ahmed. What if, what if we're able to defeat them after all? Ya Ali, just think. We'll no longer be slaves to the whims of the Englishman. The talukdars will get back their lands, the farmers will have to pay less tax. We'll win back our palaces, our properties.' Salim's Adam's apple moved as he continued, 'And above all our status and dignity. Just think.'

'Hmm. But I'm not sure whether looting and setting fire to the houses in the cantonment is the right way to go about it.'

'What? They've set fire? To the cantonment? Ya Ali!' Salim leapt to his feet and ran towards the stables.

Salim's heart began to sink as he neared the cantonment. He could see some of the houses on fire and hear the crackling of flames. The air was heavy with the smell of sulphur and of wood burning. It was suffocating and way too hot for this time of the night.

The road was deserted. Just then the quiet was broken by an uproar. A throng of sepoys with raised swords and chanting slogans came rushing round the corner and charged into the brigadier's bungalow. A little ahead, Salim witnessed some other Indians come out of another house carrying furniture, draperies, utensils and paintings. One of them threw a lit torch on the roof of the house before leaving it. Salim shook his head in disapproval. They could not be sepoys. They were behaving like thugs.

Allah, please don't let RayChal come to any harm, he silently prayed. He hesitated as he neared her house. What if he walked into her house and found they were fine? What if the colonel threw him out like he had

Daima? But this was no time to think. Besides, what more harm could that man possibly do?

The gate of the colonel's house was open and unguarded. Salim tied Afreen to the post and walked into the garden. The house was on fire. He rushed in through the open front door. It looked deserted. It was full of smoke. His eyes began to smart. Coughing and spluttering he called out 'RayChal' as he went from room to room, looking for the one face that was dearer to him than his own life.

She wasn't there. Nor were her family and servants. Perhaps they had escaped to somewhere safe. He walked past the servants' quarters and was about to unfetter Afreen when he decided to check out the servants' lodgings as well. Nothing. Ram Singh's house was empty. As he passed Sudha's window, he thought he saw a human shape silhouetted against the wall. He ran in. 'RayChal,' he cried as he cradled her head in his arms. As he got used to the dark, he noticed a blood clot at the side of her head. She was unconscious. 'Oh, RayChal,' he groaned, as he held her close to his heart.

He must hurry. The fire would soon block the doorway. He picked her up in his arms, staggered and fell down. 'Ya Ali, you are heavier than you look,' he muttered, then lifted her up again.

As he carried her out, something fell from the ceiling. He lifted an arm to shield her. The burning wood fell on his arm, scorching it. He winced in pain but did not stop. He placed her gently on Afreen's back, then pulled himself up behind her. Then he galloped towards his palace at breakneck speed.

He passed a long noisy procession. Some of the men were carrying large effigies of firangis. Every few minutes the procession would pause and the head of one of the effigies would be struck off with a sword.

Further ahead, Salim noticed the head of a buffalo calf placed upside down near one of the gateways of Kaiserbagh, with a garland of white flowers around its horns. An ominous warning to the firangis that their end was near. But he did not stop until he was inside the palace gates.

Next morning, Daima entered Salim's parlour just as he had finished his breakfast and was washing his hands.

'How is she, Daima?' he asked. 'Has she regained consciousness?'

'She has,' Daima replied curtly. 'And madam is throwing a fit . . . As if being insulted by her father wasn't enough, now I have to put up with her tantrums as well . . . Hai Ram, what is the world coming to!'

'She must be worried about her parents. I'll go and see her right away.'

Daima gestured to the servant to clear the breakfast dishes away, before speaking. 'You did not do right, Chote Nawab . . . bringing the enemy home, that too a woman . . . what war strategy is that?'

Salim ran his right hand up and down his left arm as he paced the room. 'Daima, she's not our enemy. She doesn't even know. All she knows I guess is that some Indian sepoys have revolted against the Company.' He stopped pacing and stood before Daima. 'Ya Ali, she doesn't even know that I'm also involved.' He paused, lifted his chin before looking down at Daima. 'And it is my wish that it stays that way.'

Daima picked up Salim's hookah and placed it before the takhat.

'How long can you hide something like that from her?' she asked as she straightened up.

'Eventually she will come to know. But I want to be the first to tell her.'

'As you wish, Chote Nawab . . . Our lips are sealed.' She bowed slightly and left the room.

Salim sat down on the takhat and took a long puff on the hookah, a frown forming double lines between his brows. He got up slowly, put on his shoes and cap, then walked down the corridors to the zenana and knocked on Rachael's door.

She pounced on him as soon as he entered. 'How dare you bring me here without my consent?'

'You were not conscious.' He noticed her wound had been cleaned and dressing applied to it.

'And you saw that as an excellent opportunity to kidnap me,' Rachael replied as she dabbed at the beads of perspiration on her forehead.

Salim's eyebrows knitted together. What was wrong with her? He put his life at risk to rescue her and here she was accusing him of kidnapping her? It was preposterous. 'What? What did you just say?' he asked, bewildered.

'You heard me. Since you couldn't get your way with Papa, you brought me here by force.'

Salim walked slowly towards her until he was just a breath away. He had a strong inclination to grab her arms and shake her hard. 'Look, I brought you here for your own safety. And I promise you, the moment things settle down and it's safe for you to venture out, I'll take you to your parents, even if I have to risk my own life. But until then you'll stay here, whether you like it or not.'

Rachael waved her hand to shoo a fly away.

'Saira,' Salim called out to the female guard stationed at the doorway.

'Yes, Chote Nawab?'

'Where are the maids with the fans?'

'Chote Nawab, most of them have been sent away by the Company.'

'Send for the eunuchs from my chamber, then. And remember, RayChal is my guest. Make sure she never has to suffer the slightest discomfiture.'

'As you wish, Chote Nawab.' So saying, she bowed and raised her right hand to her forehead. Walking backwards, she left the room.

'I'll run away,' said Rachael.

'What?' Salim sighed, exasperated. 'You'll do nothing of the sort.'

He strode out of the room, paused at the door, looked at Rachael, then spoke to Saira and her companion who stood with folded arms and bowed heads at the door.

'Make sure she doesn't leave this room.' He watched with satisfaction as Rachael's hands curled into fists and curbed an insane desire to kiss her hard.

'As you wish, Chote Nawab,' the two guards replied in unison.

* * *

Salim knocked on the door. A young woman clad in a blue sharara opened it. 'Where's Ray—?' He stopped short. The woman in the blue sharara *was* RayChal. He could not tear his eyes away from her. Was it really his RayChal or a Jannat ki hoor? Or were his eyes playing tricks on him?

She was wearing a sharara, the colour of sapphire, the colour of her eyes. She had covered her head with a matching dupatta. She wore huge silver earrings and blue bangles that clinked every time she moved her hands. She had even applied ittar. The smell was intoxicating.

'I had nothing to wear, so the maid . . .' she trailed off and shyly looked away.

'RayChal, I . . .' He could not continue. He brushed back a lock of hair from his forehead, lost for words.

Rachael stared at his hand as he did so, then clutched it urgently. Salim followed her gaze and looked at his arm. His skin was wrinkled and looked like the layer of cream that forms on hot milk. He looked back at her questioningly.

'Your arm. How did it get burnt?'

He didn't say anything but continued to study her face.

An enlightened look came over it. 'Oh, I see. You got hurt when rescuing me from the flames.'

'No, I kidnapped you, remember? I'm an uncivilised barbarian who lusts after women and has to have them, even if he has to stoop so low as to kidnap them.'

Rachael blushed. 'I'm sorry, I didn't mean what I said the other day.'

Salim came dangerously close to her. 'What did you mean, then?'

Rachael's temper rose slightly. 'What was I supposed to think? After you sent your flatterers to my father. Asking me to become your concubine.'

'Daima's not my flatterer. She's like my mother. Why, she *is* my mother. And I sent her to your house to ask your parents for your hand in marriage. Concubine indeed! Ya Ali, what do you take me for?' He turned away from her and said in a lowered voice, 'Just shows how much you understand me or my love.'

'But that's what Papa sa—'

'You know what?' Salim swung around to face her again. 'You and your papa are the same. He has categorised me by the colour of my skin. For him, all those who have brown skin are the same, whether he's a king or a sweeper.' He ran his fingers through his hair. 'And now you've done the same. You've heard from somewhere that nawabs are sleazy and have concluded that I'm no different.' He held her arms in a vice-like grip. 'Have you ever seen me with another woman? Have you ever heard me going to a tawaif? I don't drink – well, not that much anyway. And yet . . .'

Rachael tried to loosen his grip on her arms and said softly, 'You do have the hookah, you know.'

Salim smiled slightly. 'Yes, well. I'm not exactly a saint either.'

They both stole a glance at each other and smiled softly.

'You look much nicer in Hindustani attire than in those tents of yours,' he said over his shoulder as he left the room.

Chapter Eighteen

Rachael

Rachael turned red with embarrassment as the two maids Salma and Saira helped her undress. She had never undressed in front of anyone other than Ayah and Sudha before. But then Ayah had seen her since she was born and Sudha was just a couple of years older than her. Besides, she was more like a sister.

But as the cool scented water of the hammam engulfed her, she began to relax. She had often wondered what life in the nawab's palace was like, how different the lives of the begums were from that of her own. Most of the English girls she knew in Lucknow whiled away their hours reading books and poetry, writing long letters back home, taking siestas in the afternoons and getting ready for dinner or a ball in the evening. The women in the palace did much the same, albeit a bit differently. 'Decking up' for them meant taking long luxurious baths, letting the maids rub perfumed oils into their bodies, applying henna.

She found it hard to believe sometimes – true, she had often dreamt of living in one of these palaces, but she had never imagined her wish would one day come true . . . and certainly not in this manner. It was strange, unbelievable. And this easy friendship she shared with Salim – they had so little in common, and yet . . . She blushed again as she remembered the look on his face when he saw her in Indian dress. So he had sent Papa a marriage proposal. He had wanted to marry her. She should have known better than to believe Papa's words. He always did have a tendency to exaggeration.

She sighed as she thought of Salim's burnt arm. It had been burnt saving her life. Rachael smiled. He had ridden through the night, through the riots to save her. *Her.* Only her. She dared not believe she held a special place in his heart. And yet, she wanted to believe it was so. He would not have done that for just anybody, would he?

The maids began to giggle as they patted her dry. Rachael blushed deeply as Salma ran her fingers over her arm and exclaimed, 'It's so smooth, like silk.' Saira pointed to her feet and exclaimed, 'Look at her feet. So dainty, so delicate, like doll made of china.'

Snatching the towels from them, Rachael said curtly, 'I can manage. Go get my clothes.' She grimaced as they ran away laughing. She missed Sudha. She understood her wants even without saying. She was so mature, not like these juveniles who did not understand her half the time. She wondered how Sudha was. How her cruel relatives were treating her. She worried about her parents. She wondered how they were, where they were.

Nobody knew. Even Salim was of no help. Whenever she asked him, she got the same curt reply. 'I don't know. I'll tell you as soon as I hear something.'

It was strange. The city was gripped in a revolution and yet in the palace, behind the high walls surrounding it, life carried on as normal. It felt unreal. Like a dream. Except the occasional sound of a gun being fired in the distance.

Crunching up her nose, Rachael looked at the jewellery laid out before her. Having helped her dress, the maids were now insisting she wear some. She chose a dainty pearl necklace with earrings that looked like teardrops. Salma and Saira were disappointed. They wanted her to wear a gold necklace with some gems on it.

As Saira secured the necklace around her nape, she said, 'Memsahib, if I tell you what I know, you will jump for joy.'

Rachael turned around and looked at her. 'What is it?'

Salma nudged Saira with her elbow and hissed, 'Daima said not to tell anyone.'

Rachael's brow furrowed. 'Why? Pray tell me, what is it?'

Saira lowered her head and said nothing. Salma came forward with an earring.

Brushing her hand aside, Rachael looked at Saira. 'Look, don't be afraid. You can tell me. Or else . . .' She stood and looked sternly at the two maids. 'I shall have to complain to Chote Nabob.'

Saira clasped her hands. 'No, memsahib, don't say anything to Chote Nawab. We will be sacked. Chote

Nawab want to give you the good news himself, that's why Daima say no tell.'

'What good news?' Rachael asked.

'That your parents are found. They be in Residency and alive.'

'Really?' Rachael exclaimed, her heartbeat quickening, unable to believe what she had just heard. 'Is it true?'

'Yes, memsahib,' Salma replied quietly. 'But please no tell Daima or Chote Nawab, they dismiss us.'

'Of course I won't tell them.' She took Saira's hands, which were visibly shaking, in hers. 'You've nothing to fear. Thank you so much. You've made me very happy today.'

Saira and Salma exchanged looks and gave a sigh of relief as they continued to help Rachael finish her toilette.

Rachael looked out of the lattice window of her room in Kaiserbagh Palace for the umpteenth time that day. The windows of the zenana did not provide a view beyond the palace gardens. She paced the room restlessly. She had hitherto never stayed cooped up indoors for so long.

It had been two long weeks since Salim had brought her here. She wondered what he did all day. She was living here in his home and yet she saw so little of him. Ever since she had learnt from Saira and Salma about her parents' whereabouts last week, she had asked them when Salim would be back. They had no clue. Either that, or they'd been ordered not to tell her. She pursed her lips. Surely there was something she could do.

And then she grinned. She knew what to do. She

would sneak off to the stables and go riding. Not far. Just a few laps around the palace. Surely that couldn't harm anyone.

She smiled and bowed her head slightly as the female guard stationed at her doorway raised her right hand to her forehead and bowed low at the same time. Screwing up her nose, she covered it with the ends of her hijaab as a strong dank smell emanated from the stables. She looked around surreptitiously and was about to go in when she heard the sound of horse's hoofs. Frightened, she turned around slowly to see who it was. It was Salim. He stared at her sombrely.

He did not take his eyes off her as he sprang down from the horse. After what seemed like a hundred years, he turned his gaze to the stable boy and gestured to him to take Afreen away. Rachael squared her shoulders as he turned back to her.

'Where do you think you were going?' His voice was quiet and smooth.

Bracing herself, Rachael looked at him defiantly. 'I know where my parents are. I want to be with them.'

'Who told you?' he asked through gritted teeth.

'I just know,' she replied. She then turned her back to him and started walking towards the stable door.

Salim's hand shot out to stop her and he pulled her roughly to face him. 'I will not let you go. Do you understand?'

'I'm not your prisoner, Salim,' Rachael shouted back as she struggled to free her arm of his hold.

Letting go of her arm, Salim ran his hand over his face. 'Ya Ali, why don't you understand? It'd be foolhardy to step out of the palace. You'll get killed the moment you do that. I'm not keeping you captive, believe me.'

Rachael looked at him. He was wearing boots. He had a sword tucked into his cummerbund. He was even carrying a rifle behind his back. 'Where have *you* just come from?' she asked.

Looking down at the soft damp earth, Salim began patting it smooth with his right boot. He cleared his throat. 'You know I'm the nawab's son. I have my duties.' He paused, coughed and continued. 'I had to attend the court. Some of the sepoys are getting out of hand. I've to help maintain law and order.' He coughed again.

'Oh. Can't you ask these sepoys to stop this mutiny?'

Salim smiled. Rachael immediately felt foolish asking such a silly question.

'It's not so simple,' Salim answered. 'Thousands of people who have been made jobless – the king's army, the king's servants . . . they have all joined the sepoys in the uprising.'

Rachael did not say anything, merely nodded. Salim touched her cheek lightly with the back of his hand. 'Go back to your room,' he whispered. 'I'm sure it's a matter of days before I'm able to let you go.'

'Are you sure you'll be able to let me go?' Rachael lifted a brow as a smile hovered over her lips.

Salim put his right hand over his heart. 'Maybe not,' he answered as his eyes plunged right into her soul. Rachael crinkled up her nose as she met his gaze. She could feel her ears grow hot and turn scarlet as she blushed.

* * *

That night Rachael flopped down on her four-poster bed, her right leg dangling. Beads of perspiration covered her forehead. She had tried everything to keep herself cool but nothing had worked. She walked over to the window. Both the windows in the room were open but there was no breeze. The air was still. Rachael sighed. She couldn't bear this relentless heat anymore. She would go mad. She turned away from the window as Saira announced Salim's arrival.

He walked in, looking cool and comfortable in a white cotton kurta pyjama, and held out a bunch of flowers.

Rachael looked at him and then at the gift. 'Tuberoses,' she exclaimed as she accepted his gift. 'They're beautiful. You have good choice.'

The edges of Salim's lips lifted into a smile as his eyes swept slowly over her. 'That I have,' he replied.

She was about to retort when he whispered, 'Keep them near your bed. They're supposed to induce passionate dreams.' He winked at her as he said those words.

Astounded, Rachael felt herself redden as she glared at him. But she could not suppress her smile. She inhaled their heady aroma. The fragrance was indeed intoxicating.

'Sweet dreams,' Salim whispered as he waved his fingers at her, his eyes teasing and laughing.

She let out a long sigh.

'Anything the matter?' he asked.

'It's much too warm,' she replied.

'Lie down,' he said.

'What?'

'Do as I say. Lie down.'

Rachael lay down on the bed, painfully conscious of Salim's eyes on her.

'No, not like that. Put your head right next to the basin.'

Rachael looked suspiciously at the exquisitely carved marble basin that stood right next to the head of the bed and put her head beside it.

'That's it. Now let your hair float in the water.'

'You mean like this?' she asked, as she tentatively let her hair into the basin.

'Yes. Now doesn't that feel cooler?'

Rachael closed her eyes. 'Heavenly. I did wonder what that basin was for.'

Salim caressed her forehead gently. 'As long as I live, you will never face any discomfort whatsoever.'

Rachael started to sit up, but he gently pushed her back. 'Don't get up. I came to speak to you about something, but it can wait.'

'What is it?'

'I . . . wanted to tell you where I was all day today. And yesterday. And the day before . . .' He cleared his throat and averted his gaze. 'Ah well, it's nothing that can't wait. It might be a long day tomorrow. Don't know when I'll see you again. I might have to stay at the . . . umm . . . other palace.'

'I understand. Pray do not worry about me.' She looked at him and grinned. 'You'll find me here when you get back.'

Salim smiled. His fingers lingered on her forehead for a moment and then he was gone.

Chapter Nineteen

SALIM

It was 30th June 1857. Exactly one month since the troops in Lucknow had revolted. Salim looked around at his fellow soldiers hiding in the forest near Chinhat, a village about six miles away from Lucknow, then trotted up to Barkat Ahmad, their commander.

'Is everything under control?' he asked.

'Absolutely,' Barkat Ahmad replied.

'I hope they're not more than us,' said Salim.

'Do not you worry, Salim bhai,' piped Nayansukh, twirling the ends of his moustache with his right hand. 'Except a small handful, all the sepoys of Lucknow are with us. Do not you worry; we will outnumber them for sure.'

Ahmed trotted up to them. 'The firangis are not yet here. Do you think they've changed their plans?'

'No, I've information they're heading this way,' said Barkat Ahmad.

Just then a couple of bullock carts passed by.

'Watch how I make sure Raja Jia Lal's strategy works,' Nayansukh said. He cupped his hands over his mouth and shouted: 'Halt! Who goes there?'

The bullock carts stopped in their path. Two men clad in vests and dhotis ambled towards them, their hands joined in supplication.

'Where off to, brother?' Nayansukh asked, twirling his moustache and chewing tobacco.

'Sir, we just going to the city with some supplies.'

'OK, listen carefully. If you pass firangis on way, tell them most Indian sepoys at Chinhat gone back as they think English not coming. Only advance guard is left.' Nayansukh spat out the tobacco on the ground before continuing. 'Have you understood?'

'Yes, yes. We say it. No problem.'

'Good. You can go now. Good day.'

A good one and a half hours elapsed before the 32nd Regiment under the command of Sir Henry Lawrence was finally seen advancing towards Chinhat. As they reached the clearing, Barkat Ahmad gave the command to open fire.

Standing behind a clump of trees with some others, Salim watched the ferocious fight and waited for Barkat Ahmad's signal. It was strange. The firangis wore red coats. Some of his men also wore the same. Sometimes it was difficult to tell who was who. But of one thing he was certain – he would not want to be in the firangis' position right now. They were out in the open and heavily outnumbered by the Indians, who were well hidden behind the trees and bushes.

The Indian sepoys were now retreating. Salim watched the jubilant English. 'There they go, after them!' they were shouting triumphantly. What they didn't know was that the Indian sepoys were merely changing front. Soon they were advancing towards them, en masse, from the right.

Barkat Ahmad now signalled to Salim to lead his troops. Salim broke out in a sweat. He was seized with a sudden panic. He had never killed a man before. An urge to turn back and run away from the battlefield took hold of him. He looked across at Ahmed. He was staring straight ahead, the same fear reflected in his eyes.

Salim recalled the woodcutter's words. 'Only cowards kill dumb animals,' he had said. Cowards. He was only sixteen then and had gone hunting with Ahmed. Espying a spotted deer, he picked up his rifle and fired a shot. The bullet missed the deer but hit a woodcutter nearby who was busy axing a tree. The man had survived, the matter had been hushed, but the woodcutter's words were to haunt Salim for the rest of his life. Salim wiped the perspiration from his forehead. He remembered Colonel Bristow's words. He had called Abba Huzoor a coward. 'A spineless king' he had said. Salim's blood began to boil. 'A good soldier must never carry his emotions with him to the battlefield,' he had heard Daima tell Nayansukh once.

He straightened his back, drew his sword and with a cry of 'Ya Ali' charged at the enemy. As he plunged his sword in a soldier's stomach, blood began to ooze out and a few drops splattered on Salim's clothes. As the sight and smell of warm blood filled his nostrils, he began feeling faint and nauseous. Afreen tottered as he dropped his sword and clutched his head between his hands. 'Ya Ali,' he mumbled as the ground spun before him.

'You alright, Salim mia?' It was Ahmed, who had rushed to his side.

'Yes, I'm fine,' Salim replied, getting a hold on himself.

Ahmed bent down and handed him his sword.

A couple of hours later, in the thick of battle, he heard Ahmed yell, 'Salim mia, watch out!' He turned hastily as a red-hot cannonball came hurtling towards him. He ducked just in time. The cannonball whizzed past him and exploded a couple of paces behind him. The impact knocked Afreen over. Salim sat dazed, blackened from head to toe, Afreen's reins still in his hands, the taste of gunpowder on his palate. His heart was beating rapidly, but he was unhurt. He looked around. A bloodied black body lay where the cannon had exploded. The sepoy's left arm had been torn away. His skull had split open and part of his brain lay on the ground. It could easily have been him, Salim thought, as bile rose in his throat.

The firangis were now retreating. Salim stared at the battlefield for a few moments as they fled. Gun carriages, cannons and dolis stood abandoned. And then he touched his ears with horror. He could see the horses without their riders galloping helter-skelter, but he could not hear their neighing. He could see soldiers mortally wounded, writhing in pain, but he could not hear their groans. The explosion had rendered him deaf. He turned frantically to Ahmed. 'Ahmed, I can't hear,' he shouted.

Ahmed jumped off his horse and rushed to his side. 'Can you hear me?' Salim shouted even louder. Ahmed nodded as he clutched Salim's hands, tears streaming down his cheeks.

It was later that night, as Salim accompanied his men to the palace, that he got his hearing back. His men were in high spirits and shouts of 'Allah-o-Akbar' and 'Har Har Mahadev' suddenly burst on him. He looked heavenward and thanked Allah for restoring his hearing. He should have felt relieved, ecstatic even. On the contrary, he felt an unaccountable sadness. As though he was bereft of something. After what he had seen on the battlefield that day, he would never be the same again. The sound of firing, the sight of the wounded soldiers and horses, the gore – they would haunt him for the rest of his life.

Salim clambered into bed and was about to blow out the candles that stood near his bed when he heard a noise like thunder and the chandeliers began to sway violently. He rushed to the window and looked out. Nothing but darkness. He then ran out on to the terrace. He could see a yellowish-orange glow in the direction of Macchi Bhawan.

He scurried back to his room, threw on an angarkha, and slipping his feet into a pair of khurd nau, rushed towards the stable.

Riding through the darkness, he thought about the noise he had heard a few minutes back. It reminded him of the thunderstorm when he was three. The wind had blown so hard, it had brought the jamun tree crashing to the ground. The sound of the tree as it crashed to the ground was earth-shattering and terrified him even today.

As Afreen neared Macchi Bhawan, he was enveloped in a thick black dust. He coughed and spluttered. Afreen sneezed. He slowly slid off Afreen and gaped in horror at the dust and the smell of gunpowder that hung in the air. The fort that had been built in the style of a chateau was no longer there. Nothing of the brick buttresses, the tall towers or the high wall remained. In its stead stood a pile of bricks and mortar. That's all. The place looked as though it had been uninhabited for years. Not bustling with soldiers and creaking with the weight of guns and ammunition as it had been just a few hours ago.

He leant against a broken pillar as it gradually sunk in. The firangis had evacuated the fort and then blown it up. That was the reason there was no sign of life or dead bodies. They had abandoned the fort and made their escape.

Hearing a low rumble, Salim turned sharply. There, just a few inches away from him, lay a firangi soldier. Salim edged closer. He was alive and snoring and reeked of liquor. Salim shook his head and gave a small smile. He ran his hand over his face. It was covered with dust. He dragged his feet to a well, drew some water and splashed his face.

He looked around at the myriad little fires that were now slowly dying out and shuffled towards the Rumi Darwaza, which still stood erect. It looked like a huge hedgehog with its curved back covered with spikes, a silent witness to the destruction that had just occurred.

Salim looked down as he stumbled upon a slab of stone. It had two fishes engraved on it. The insignia of the Naishapur dynasty. His dynasty. He had often heard Abba Huzoor narrate the incident – when Nawab Saadat Khan Bahadur, the first nawab of Avadh, was coming to Lucknow from Faizabad by boat, a fish had jumped out of the waters onto his lap. As fishes were a sign of aristocracy as well as a good omen, the nawab decided to adopt it as the royal insignia.

Now both the insignia and Macchi Bhawan, the fish house, lay in the dust. Salim shuddered. Was this the end? Or just the beginning?

It was six o'clock in the evening on 5th July 1857. Salim stood uncomfortably in the splendid hall of Chandiwali Barahdari. It had rained all day, making it one of the most humid days of the year.

All Salim wished to do right now was to tear off his nukkedar cap and the emerald angarkha, both of which were heavily embroidered in gold, and dive into the cool waters of the Gomti. He played impatiently with the long string of pearls that hung from his neck. Why did Daima have to insist that he wear some jewellery today?

He looked around the hall. Raja Jia Lal Singh had just arrived with the military officers. Over three thousand sepoys had gathered to witness the coronation of Mirza Birjis Qadir Bahadur, ruler of Avadh. After the defeat of the English forces, the Indians realised they were in need of a single leader at the helm to guide them. After much debate, it was decided the leader would be the son of the last king of Avadh. As he was a minor, his mother Begum Hazrat Mahal would be the acting regent.

The young prince was ushered into the hall with much fanfare. He looked regal in a purple angarkha with golden buttons. Salim smiled sardonically at his brother as he solemnly took his seat. He was thirteen or fourteen years of age, he couldn't remember exactly.

Salim recalled the coronation of Abba Huzoor in the Lal Barahdari. He must have been the same age as Birjis then, or perhaps a year or two younger. He had watched in awe as Abbu had sat down on the throne, in his peacock-blue velvet robe and a crown studded with rubies and diamonds. How his heart had swelled with pride.

He wondered what Birjis must make of all this. What would a boy of thirteen know about a king's responsibilities? Perhaps it was all a game for him. Like Salim used to play when he was little. He would sit on a mound of mud on the banks of the Gomti and proclaim himself king. He would then order Ahmed and his other friends about. Is that how Birjis felt right now?

Salim shot a look at Begum Hazrat Mahal. He had not expected this from Ammi. How could she not have put his name forward for the coronation? Wasn't he older than Birjis Qadir? Or did she not think him capable? No, that was not it. It was his blood. He did not have blue blood flowing through his veins as Birjis did. Just then Ammi looked at him and smiled. Salim hastily looked away.

Raja Jia Lal Singh was reading out the army's document of support for Birjis Qadir. When he finished reading, the document was stamped with the official seal. And just as the sun was about to slip quietly behind the domes and the cupolas, Birjis was led to the throne.

Abba Huzoor's bejewelled crown flashed before Salim's eyes. A few months back it had been stolen by the firangis. Therefore the risaldar had to place an ordinary crown on Birjis's head. Salim stood still as a twenty-one gun salute was given by the Faizabad artillery to the little sovereign. Everyone cheered. 'You are our Kanhaiya,' the sepoys chanted.

Salim smiled sardonically as some of the sepoys waiting outside the palace gates began firing their guns in their excitement. Ammi was now declared the Queen Mother amidst some more cheering. Gold mohurs were offered to her as well as to Birjis. Robes of honour were also distributed. Ammi briefly addressed the crowd. She asked them to make a pledge to drive the firangis out of the country.

Amidst all this celebration and cheering, a mendicant stepped forward. Salim hoped he was not going to cause any trouble. A hush fell in the hall as the holy man clicked his tongue and shook his head. The crowd parted to let him pass. 'The hour of crowning was not auspicious,' he bellowed as he stood before the throne with his feet apart. 'It should have taken place on a premeditated auspicious hour, some other day.' He looked around the room at the stunned audience, his eyes red, his long matted hair flowing. 'This does not bode well for the king or for Avadh,' he prophesied, looking straight at Birjis Qadir and at Ammi's hand which lay protectively on her son's shoulder.

'Such humbug,' Salim muttered under his breath. All these mendicants were a bunch of poseurs, out to wheedle money from whomsoever they could. Yet a shiver ran down his spine at the sinister prophecy.

Chapter Twenty

RACHAEL

Rachael sat on the takhat in the room in her palace, stitching her dress. It had torn in several places during the scuffle with Sudha's relatives. She wondered where she was now and what had become of her. What about Mother and Papa? She hoped they were safe. And Brutus? Was he with her parents? What if they hadn't managed to take him with them? Rachael shook her head. No, she mustn't think like that.

She heard some murmurings and listened, as the smell of incense and sandalwood floated into her room. It was the women in the zenana saying the namaz. They said it five times a day, she had been told. How could these simple, God-fearing people loot and kill the English? They must hate them.

What about Ayah and Ram Singh? And their home? It must have been reduced to ashes, along with her piano. She swallowed the lump in her throat. She remembered how alone and frightened she had felt that day. And the irony of it all was that she was living here, in the home of a native prince.

At least Salim was with her. She wondered where he was right now. She had been foolish to think he would have sent Daima to her parents with anything other than a marriage proposal. Had she lost her mind? He was such a gentleman, her Salim, and he was hers, only hers. She smiled, her face aglow with a soft gentleness, as she thought of him. Such thick long eyelashes he had. Did his upper and lower eyelashes not get entangled when he closed his eyes, she mused.

She wondered how long she would have to stay here. It was already a month and a half. Not that she was complaining. They were all polite to her. Too polite perhaps. All except Daima, who tried her best to avoid her. And when she did have to speak to her, she did so in monosyllables.

Rachael stopped stitching and frowned, her nose crinkling up as she did so. Now, how could she win her over?

Rachael tiptoed into Daima's room and whispered, 'Hello, Daima.'

Daima, who was bent over her work, jumped up with a start. 'You gave me a fright, girl . . . What is it? What do you need?'

'Nothing. I just want to . . . help you.'

Frowning at her, Daima narrowed her eyes in full concentration as she tried to thread the needle. Her mouth fell open as Rachael took the needle and thread from her hand, threaded the needle and handed it back to her without saying a word. 'Thank you,' she said gruffly and started stitching. Rachael sat down on the takhat beside her. Daima did not look up. Her fingers continued to zip up and down over the cloth.

'Pray tell me, Daima, what are you making?'

'Chikan.'

'Chicken?'

'Chikan is embroidery. Very fine and delicate it is.'

'Will you teach me, Daima?'

'You need a lot of patience.'

'I have patience.'

Just then the laundry woman came in with a bundle of clothes. 'Chote Nawab's clothes,' she said.

Daima turned to Rachael. 'Excuse me; I have to put these away . . . Now that most of the servants have been sent packing, I have to do all these jobs myself.'

Rachael got up. 'Let me help you, Daima.'

'Look, girl, if you're still harbouring hopes of marrying our Chote Nawab, you can forget about it . . . There's no way I'm letting him marry you, not after the way your father treated me.'

Rachael looked down, fidgeting with her ring as she asked quietly, 'Must children always have to pay for their parents' sins?'

Daima was silent.

Rachael continued. 'I know not what Papa did or said that day. But if I'd been there, I'm sure it wouldn't have happened.'

Daima kept her silence.

'I'm sorry, for whatever he said,' she whispered. She

took out a silver chain that she always wore around her neck. 'My mother gave this to me when I was a few months old. I want you to have it.'

Daima stared at her for a few moments, then closed Rachael's fingers over the chain. 'No, my child, your mother gave it . . . It must mean a lot to you.'

'You are Salim's mother. That makes you my mother as well.'

'That you should think of parting with something so precious for you, is gift enough for me,' said Daima, her eyes becoming moist. 'Now put it back around your neck before you lose it,' she gently chided and left the room with a bundle of clothes.

Rachael watched the rains from the balcony of the palace. It was astounding how the monsoons transformed the entire country. The grass that had wilted and turned yellow just a couple of days back was now parrot green. The flowers that had drooped under the glare of the sun now smiled gaily like little girls in colourful frocks. As she watched, the rain slid down the domes and minarets of the palace and ricocheted off the waters in the pond below.

She wondered how Mother was coping. Mother could never decide whether she hated the Indian summers more or the monsoons. For the rains had a life of their own. They brought in their wake a swarm of fireflies, cockroaches, bats, lizards, red ants, frogs, white ants, moths, beetles and crickets, none of which Mother was fond of.

But the rains had a magical effect on Rachael. They lifted her heart and made her forget all her worries. As she continued to look out of the window, she noticed some children playing in the garden and ran down the steps to join them. The first few drops hit her hard, but once she got used to it, it felt wonderful. The children were surprised to see her. They went all shy and quiet at first, but seeing her exuberance, recommenced their games. They held hands and danced and skipped while the thunderous rain and her silver anklets sang in unison.

She was soon soaked to the skin and her clothes clung to her. But she didn't care. She was having far too much fun to stop now. She saw some movement in the grass near the pond, and turning to her little friends, put a finger to her lips. Quietly she crept up to whatever it was that was hopping about, and picked it up. It was a frog.

She showed her catch to her new friends who had crowded around her. The frog stared at them with petrified beady eyes. Rachael stroked its slippery back. It was shivering. 'I think he's scared. Let's put him back.' She left it gently where she had found it and watched it hop into the pond croaking. *Ribbit ribbit*. The smell of rain, the smell of moist earth filled her senses. She sat down on the swing while her little friends pushed the swing higher and higher. She laughed and shook the droplets from her hair. She saw a peacock showing off its exquisite fan of feathers. Spreading her dupatta over her arms, she chased the peacock round and round the garden, much to the amusement of the children. Then a loud clap of thunder followed by a sliver of silver thread sent her and her little friends scurrying indoors. She splish-sploshed into her room, still laughing when she heard 'RayChal'.

She swung around, her long hair flying, to find Salim standing at the door.

Chapter Twenty-One

SALIM

Salim stared at Rachael as she swung around to face him, her golden wet hair flying as she did so. As the maid began to light the candles in the chandelier, a thousand Rachaels stared back at him, wet hair caught in midflight.

He gazed at her, then at her reflections in the chandelier, then at her again. 'Subhaan Allah!' he whispered huskily. He waved his hand dismissively at the maid. She bowed and backed out of the room quietly. He walked slowly towards Rachael. She shivered slightly as his breath caressed her. Whether it was his nearness or the cold that made her shiver, he could not tell. A wisp of wet hair clung to her cheek. A drop of water slid from it and stood trembling on her lip. He picked the drop carefully with his finger and kissed it. A soft red glow began to creep up her face.

Smiling, Salim put his finger on his lips, then pointing

to her lips, raised his brow, his eyes seeking permission.

Rachael smiled, her eyes twinkling, her nose crinkling as she whispered, 'No.'

'Just one small kiss?'

She shook her head slowly from side to side. 'No.'

He put his right hand over his heart theatrically, sighed loudly, 'Ya Ali,' and left the room. Reluctantly he crawled towards his room. Was it his imagination or did he feel a dull ache where his heart was? The way RayChal had looked at him, dripping as she was from head to toe, he had wanted to hold her really tight; he loved her with such intensity that it hurt. Ya Ali!

Salim entered the house behind Kaiserbagh Palace, at the northern end of Nagina-wali Baradari. Begum Hazrat Mahal sat on a takhat drawing on her hookah. She was talking to some shadows on the other side of the khus mats. As a hot blast of wind shook the mat on the doorway, the smell of khus wafted into the room.

Raising his right hand to his forehead, he said, 'Aadaab, Ammi.' She raised her right hand in reply, her gold bracelets clinking, and indicated that he be seated. A eunuch, looking ridiculous in a parrot-green kurta, entered the room with an abkhora of water and offered it to Salim.

Salim looked at Ammi as she sat there, leaning back slightly on the oblong pillow, her brows furrowed in concentration. She could not have been more than twenty-six years old. He could see why Abbu had fallen for her and why all the other begums were jealous of her. It wasn't just the beauty and charm she exuded. It was also her intelligence and the courage and conviction with which she spoke. He loved Daima, it was true, but this was the woman he idolised. But apparently she did not think the same of him. Otherwise, would she not have put forward his name for the coronation?

Ammi raised her right hand and the maid requested the men on the other side of the room to stop speaking. 'Begum Sahiba would like to say something,' the maid announced.

'We have listened to your grievances,' said Ammi, her huge gold nose ring swaying as she spoke. 'Now we want to ask you – what should we reward you sepoys for? For plundering our people and destroying their shops and business? Or for murdering innocent babies and women? Or for sleeping at your posts instead of fighting?'

She pulled her soft transparent dupatta, that had slipped slightly, back over her head. 'You should be ashamed of yourselves. It has been days since we surrounded the Residency and you have not yet succeeded in capturing it. The British flag still flies high over the Baillie Guard.' She paused briefly to wipe the perspiration from her forehead and to draw on her hookah. 'Now go away, all of you, and don't come back unless you have proved yourselves to be men.'

Ammi whispered something to the maid.

'Begum Sahiba would like to speak to Raja Jia Lal Singh in private,' the maid announced.

There was much shuffling, whispering and coughing as the men left the room.

'Raja Jia Lal,' said Ammi, after the rest had left.

'Yes, Begum Sahiba, I'm here.'

'Raja Jia Lal Singhji, you will have to speak to these sepoys and tell them to stop bickering about petty matters. If we want to throw the firangis out of our country, we've got to stand united. Otherwise prepare to be their slaves for another two hundred years.'

'Yes, Begum Sahiba, I'll try my best to drill some sense into their heads,' answered Raja Jia Lal, from the other side of the mat.

'Now if you'll excuse me, my son is here and I wish to speak to him,' said Ammi.

'Aadaab, Begum Sahiba,' Raja Jia Lal said as he prepared to leave.

'Aadaab,' Ammi replied.

Salim looked at her. She was tugging at the pearls and rubies that had been embroidered on the pillowcase with gold and silver threads.

'Any problem, Ammi?'

'No. These sepoys should be concentrating their efforts in ousting the Company . . . instead of plundering and looting and creating anarchy in the kingdom.'

'You're right,' Salim replied. He paused, then added, 'You sent for me, Ammi?'

Ammi took a long draw at her hookah. It made a gurgling sound. 'You're upset with us?' she asked eventually.

'Ya Ali, why would I be?' Salim replied, averting his gaze.

'Because Birjis has been crowned and not you.'

Salim fidgeted with the sword tied to his cummerbund. 'I'm sure you had good reason.'

'You know what happened to Nana Saheb, as well

as in Jhansi. The Company refused to acknowledge the adopted son of Laxmibai as the heir apparent. We did not want to take any risks.'

Ah yes, Dalhousie's famous Doctrine of Lapse. Denying Indian rulers the right to adopt an heir. The company had used the doctrine to gobble up Nagpur and Jhansi. No wonder Ammi did not wish to take any chances. Salim felt a little ashamed for doubting her intentions.

'Besides, Birjis's coronation was just a ceremony to establish leadership. The real king is still your Abba Huzoor. Once we have defeated the firangis, we will hand over the kingdom to him,' Ammi continued.

'Of course.'

Ammi got up and walked over to him. She took his right hand in hers and patted it. 'We have a difficult job on our hands. Do we have your support?'

'Ammi, it is there even without the asking.'

She turned away and sighed. 'These men were here today asking to be paid. Now where do I get the money? I had a mere twenty-four thousand rupees. It's all gone.'

'What about the treasury?'

'We cannot touch the king's treasury. It won't be right.'

'We can melt the silver and gold from the thrones and other furnishings and ornaments.'

'That's an excellent idea, Salim. Why didn't we think of it before? That should take care of our problems for a while. We have already set up a foundry to produce arms and ammunition. So that has also been looked into.'

'We can also repair all the guns that were disabled by the Company during annexation.'

'That's right,' said Ammi with a smile.

Salim coughed. 'Ammi, I've heard that some of the begums have been writing to Abba Huzoor against you.'

'Let them. They show their love for him by writing long woeful letters and sending him a lock of their hair. We'll prove our love for him by restoring his kingdom.' She looked at Salim arrogantly, challenging him to oppose what she had said. Salim merely nodded.

She continued speaking, her eyes flashing angrily as she spoke. 'These are the begums who refused to let their sons be crowned for fear of the firangis. We were the only one who had the courage to put our son on the throne.' She sat down on the takhat and pulled at her hookah. 'You know, Salim, we don't care what they say. They are like hyenas who will willingly partake of a lion's kill, but will shy away from the kill itself.'

Salim sat in silence for a while as she angrily smoked the hookah. When she did speak, she was solemn.

'The time has come for us to avenge what the firangis have done to us. The way they deposed your father.' Her voice had risen sharply. 'The way they threw out our family from Farhat Baksh, the way they hung our sepoys for refusing to forsake their religion, the way they've destroyed our places of worship like Qadam Rasul . . .'

Salim looked at her. Her jaw was set and there was a fire smouldering in her eyes. He remembered the destruction of his music hall, the auction of the animals, the bombardment of Macchi Bhawan.

'Yes, Ammi,' he said quietly. 'It's time to avenge their wrongdoings.'

It was evening. A momentary hush had fallen over Lucknow. Salim recalled what Ammi had said to him. 'We'll prove our love for him by restoring his kingdom,' she had said. He walked wistfully to the large mulberry tree and sat down heavily on the circular marble parapet around the tree. He looked at the garden. It was empty except for a handful of men busy at work. The gardener was collecting all the twigs and leaves that had been broken by the downpour that morning. The sweeper was sweeping the water that had collected in puddles into the gutters. A maidservant was picking some marigolds for the evening prayers. It was such a contrast to the hustle-bustle and noise that filled these gardens every year on this day. The day Abba Huzoor celebrated his birthday.

Daima had narrated to Salim how the most learned astrologers in the land had been summoned to the court by Salim's grandfather when Abba Huzoor was born. Their task was to prepare his horoscope. They made exalted predictions for the little prince. However, there was one small hitch. There was a likelihood the prince might renounce the world and become a priest. To prevent that from happening, the astrologers suggested the prince be made to wear the saffron robe of a holy man on his birthday.

And so it came to pass that on every birthday, Abba Huzoor would smear his body with the ash of pearls and don saffron robes. He would sit on this parapet under this very mulberry tree while beautiful damsels danced and musicians played on their shehnais. All his begums would be dressed in saffron as well. The gates of the Kaiserbagh Palace would be thrown open for the public and any and everyone could come and join in the festivities as long as they wore saffron clothes.

Salim rose slowly. He squared his chin as he watched a parrot peck at the mulberries. They had to defeat the firangis. Chase them out of this land and bring Abba Huzoor and those happy days back to Lucknow. Yes, he would do all he could to support Ammi in her endeavours.

Chapter Twenty-Two

SALIM

Salim put down his gun and pulled himself out of the trench. There was a lull in the firing. He was bored. How many more days would he have to spend outside the Residency before it finally fell? He looked at the main building, which was an enormous three-storeyed structure. Built with bricks on a raised piece of land, to the east of Macchi Bhawan, it had spacious rooms, verandas, porticos and countless windows. Salim knew his great-grandfather had built it for the English Resident. But what year was it? He thought hard. Must have been somewhere around 1800, he concluded.

He looked askance as Nayansukh exclaimed, 'Oh no, I think I've fired my last bullet.'

Ahmed looked into his bag. 'I'm also running out of cartridges.'

'Salim bhai, there're a lot of unused cartridges and bullets on the other side of the wall—' said Nayansukh.

226

'Don't even think about it,' interjected Salim. 'You will be shot even before you pull yourself over the wall.'

Nayansukh said nothing but kept looking around. Salim watched him suspiciously as he walked over to some street children playing in a gutter nearby. There were about seven or eight of them. They were trying to catch some tadpoles. 'Madan, hurry, hurry, catch it,' yelled the smallest boy in the group. Madan swung around and did a little jig as he held a tadpole aloft by its tail. He wore a vest, which was torn at several places, over an oversized pair of shorts. His bare feet were caked in mud. But his grin – Salim had never seen anyone so happy in a long time. 'Oye, Billu,' Madan called out to the little boy. Billu shrieked then burst out laughing as Madan swung the tadpole in front of his face.

Salim raised a brow questioningly as Nayansukh crawled back stealthily into the trench a few minutes later with Madan, Billu and another boy. Nayansukh ignored him and turning to the children asked: 'So did you understand? We will keep the firangis busy this side with our firing. And while we do that, you sneak in . . .' He pointed with his right hand. 'You must go over that low wall, all right? Quietly collect as many unused bullets and cartridge—'

'What is cart—?' Billu asked.

'This,' said Ahmed as he held up one for all to see.

'What's all this, Nayansukh?' Salim asked. 'Putting the lives of these children at risk?'

'Exactly, Salim bhai. Children. They're our safest bet. The firangis are not going to fire at children.'

Nayansukh gave Madan a shove. 'Go now and wait

for my signal. Remember, when you get back, I'll give all of you a free meal.'

'Yay,' the boys shouted in unison and ran off to do his bidding.

Salim stared after them, still unsure. Then he bellowed 'Fire!' His men started pelting bullets at the firangis. Through the corner of his eye he saw Nayansukh raise his hand to signal to the kids and watched them scramble over the wall.

A few minutes later some shots were heard at the far end. Salim raised his hand to signal to his men to stop firing. He listened. Silence. A solitary eagle circled the Residency, then flew away screeching. Salim, Nayansukh and Ahmed looked at each other.

Then there was a thud as three bodies were flung over the wall. Salim ran towards the sound, followed by Nayansukh and Ahmed. The three of them stared in stunned silence at the bodies lying in a heap, covered in blood. They were not laughing anymore, their mouths still. Billu's body lay right on top. A wisp of hair had fallen over his forehead, his lips soft and red. He looked even more innocent in death. But his eyes were wide open. They were cold and stony and stared at Salim accusingly.

Salim did not know how long he stood there, gazing at the three crumpled-up bodies. Finally, he looked at Nayansukh, his jaw taut, eyes smouldering. 'They are Hindus,' he said curtly. 'Make sure they get a proper cremation.' Nayansukh slowly nodded. Salim walked back stiffly to where the rest of his troops stood.

* * *

Later that night, Salim entered the room he was sharing with Ahmed. It was in one of the looped houses surrounding the Residency. He ran his fingers through his hair and wondered how many more nights he would have to spend here. As he discarded his wet clothes he remembered the look on the children's faces at the mention of a free meal. And then their dead bodies, heaped on top of each other like rag dolls. He lay down on his makeshift bed, his hands folded behind his head, and stared absently at the ceiling. He thought of all the comforts of the palace, of Daima, Chilmann, all the servants who attended to his every need. He wondered how Abba Huzoor was coping in Calcutta.

'Salim mia?' It was Ahmed.

Salim rolled on his side and looked at Ahmed as he settled down on the adjoining bed.

'Did you tell Rachael?' Ahmed asked.

Salim did not reply immediately. He walked over to the window, then answered softly, 'No. I want to, but I just can't.'

'But this is not right, Salim mia. You're hiding something so huge from her? What if something happens tomorrow? What if her parents get killed? *Then* will you tell her? What'll you say? "I fired the shot that killed them"?'

'What do I do? Should I drop everything? Stop all this fighting and go back to Kaiserbagh?'

He turned his back to Ahmed and looked out of the window. The troops were singing and dancing on the street. Turning back to Ahmed he said, 'Ahmed, I haven't a clue what I should do. On the one hand there's Abba

229

Huzoor, the promise I made to Hazrat Ammi, and on the other . . .' He picked up a surahi and finding it empty smashed it to the ground.

'Why get cross, Salim mia? I was merely giving you advice as a friend. The rest is up to you and up to your . . . your . . . whatever she is of yours,' said Ahmed, pulling a sheet over himself and closing his eyes.

'I don't want to lose her, Ahmed, I don't want to lose her,' Salim whispered hoarsely. He looked at Ahmed when he did not reply and heard him snoring. Salim gave a small smile. So like Ahmed to say something that would keep him awake all night and promptly fall asleep himself.

But Ahmed was right. What was he to do? On the one hand was his father, his men. He could not be unfaithful to them. On the other hand was his love. He felt torn. He could not betray his father, but neither could he his love. She trusted him. Believed everything he told her. Ya Ali. What was he to do?

Salim stood in an eight-foot narrow trench a few yards away from the firangis defending the Residency, with Ahmed and some sepoys. They watched as the last of the twenty-five guns was pushed into position. They had also succeeded in erecting barricades in front of and all around the guns. Now they were waiting patiently for his signal to fire.

Salim waved his hand irritably as a mosquito whirred in his ear. He narrowed his gaze as he spotted an old woman in the garb of a beggar carefully laying mines, just two hundred yards from the firangi defences.

'Is that woman mad? What's she doing here?' Ahmed said.

'Shhh! Just watch,' Salim hissed. He held his breath as a firangi soldier spotted her. She hastily sat down.

'Hey, who are you, what're you doing here?' the firangi asked gruffly.

'I poor beggar,' the woman coughed. 'Just resting me old bones. I go as soon as I get life into them.' She wiped her face with the edge of her tattered sari.

The soldier looked her over and dismissed her. Salim silently rejoiced. But a few minutes later he was holding his head in his hands dejectedly as a drop of rain fell on his forehead. The drizzle turned to thick rain and the sepoys watched in dismay as it washed away the old woman's efforts.

Salim watched with disgust as some sepoys dawdled to their posts just then, after spending a night consuming bhang. That, too, just after Ammi had reprimanded them. With a laid-back attitude like that, how were they ever going to budge the garrison at the Residency? Ya Ali, didn't they realise time was running out? Soon relief would be reaching the English troops from Kanpur. After the victory at Chinhat, Salim had expected Sir Henry and his men at the Residency to surrender within days. Alas! They were more resilient than he had thought.

Life in the Residency could not have been easy, he mused. For one, it was housing way too many more people than it was built to hold. All the women and children who had been evacuated successfully from the Marion cantonment. Not to mention those who had made their escape from neighbouring towns. And what

231

about the injured and the sick? How were they coping?

Pursing his lips, Salim shook his head disapprovingly at the sepoys who were waving their bayonets in the air. They had placed chicken or kebabs at the ends of their bayonets and were waving them at the firangis posted at the Baillie Guard. Yes, food must surely be scarce in the Residency. Most of the traders had stopped selling them food, even at abominable prices.

'I'm already starving,' Ahmed grumbled. He fumbled in his pocket. 'And just two paan left. Those, too, dried up in the heat,' he said as he put a paan in his mouth. 'Salim mia, you know what happened two days back . . .'

'What?'

'The children, Salim mia.' Ahmed stopped speaking to spit out some betel juice. 'What happened shouldn't have happened.'

Closing his eyes, Salim shook his head from side to side. What atrocities man commits in the name of war. Those innocent children. Did they deserve to die in that manner?

The rains finally abated. Salim looked around at his troops and gave the signal. Instantaneously the sound of muskets firing filled the air. Muttering 'Ya Ali', he loaded his gun, only his hand being visible over the trench. He fired. As the cloud of dust settled, he saw the sprawled bodies of the two firangis he had just killed.

A bullet grazed a couple of inches over his shoulder. If he was not in the trench, he would have been shot, he realised, his heart pounding.

A sepoy fired a block of wood at the firangis. Salim shook his head. Chucking wood, copper coins, stinkpots or even stray bullets was not going to make a dent in Sir Henry's defences. What they needed was to blow up the place. Just like the firangis had blown up Macchi Bhawan. But he would never order his men to do that as long as there were women and children in the Residency.

Salim cursed loudly as it started to rain again. He was tired of this rain, tired of standing in the trenches in damp clothes day in and day out. Ya Ali, when was it ever going to stop? The smell of the rain mingled with the smell of gunpowder, and with that fizzled all hopes he had haboured of capturing the Residency that day. The damn bloody rain. It had foiled their plans yet again. And those firangis – they surely did have nerves of iron; he had to give them that.

A sense of panic had gripped the city since the news reached them that firangi troops under General Havelock and Sir James Outram were marching towards Lucknow. Sepoys, as well as civilians, poured into Alambagh to defend their city.

Salim narrowed his eyes. It was raining hard and difficult to discern what was happening ahead. He steadied Afreen and peered through his binoculars. He could now perceive Hazrat Ammi in the thick of battle. She rode the tallest elephant and was charging ahead, her sword raised. On either side of her rode Raja Jia Lal Singh and General Syed Barkat Ahmad. Two French soldiers rode beside them. What a woman, Salim mused, as he watched her slash a firangi's head off with her sword.

But the firangis were ripping them apart. They had captured five guns so far. Salim looked on in dismay as some of his men began to retreat. He put down the binoculars and kicked Afreen hard. Just then something caught his eye.

Bringing Afreen to an abrupt halt, he looked through the binoculars again. Was it Ahmed? He was slumped over the back of his horse. He looked again and blinked. 'Ahmed,' he shouted. But the rain, the clanking of the swords, the groans of the men hurt, the neighing, the trumpeting, the firing of shells and muskets, drowned his cries.

Choking back a lump in his throat, he looked heavenward. Ya Allah, please don't let anything happen to my Ahmed, he silently prayed. Slowly, he inched his way through the fighting men, towards his friend. Jumping off Afreen when he was a couple of yards away from him, he sloshed through the mud to reach his side. 'Ahmed,' he cried again as he dragged him off his horse and onto Afreen's back, then galloped towards the outer walls of Lucknow.

'Salim mia,' Ahmed whispered in a weak voice. Salim gripped the reins tightly and continued to gallop at breakneck speed until he was sure they had left the firangis far behind. Then he patted Afreen's mane and made her slow down. He looked around in desperation through the blinding rain until he spotted a mud house. It looked deserted. Bringing Afreen to a halt, he tied her to a nearby tree. Next he heaved Ahmed over his shoulder and carried him inside the house.

Panting heavily, he looked at Ahmed. Blood was oozing

out of his left arm. There was blood everywhere – on the floor, his clothes, even his boots were caked with blood. But he was lucky. Damn lucky. The bullet had just missed his heart. Salim tore his waistband and tied it tightly around his arm. With the remnant of the waistband, he wiped the mud and perspiration from Ahmed's face.

'Are you all right?'

'Still alive, Salim mia.'

'Isn't this the same arm you broke when we fell off that guava tree? When you were ten?'

'Same one, Salim mia.'

'Can I get you anything?'

'Nihari-kulcha and perhaps some kebabs.'

Salim glared at him. 'Ya Ali! Kulcha and kebabs. And I almost got a fit thinking you were dead.'

Ahmed smiled tiredly. 'Water will do for now.'

Salim smiled at him and shook his head. He must get him to the palace soon and checked by the palace doctor. He was losing too much blood.

'How did we fare in the battle?' Ahmed asked.

'The relieving English forces are moving steadily towards the Residency,' said Salim as he slowly fed Ahmed some water from his cupped hands. 'This is the first time in three months, since the uprising started, that we've been defeated.'

'Don't worry, Salim mia, we'll bounce back.'

'I hope so,' Salim replied gloomily. He spoke slowly. 'Otherwise we're doomed. If the firangis lose, they will simply go back to their motherland. But if *we* lose, we will be hanged, each one of us.'

* * *

Salim walked up the steps of the palace. He was relieved Ahmed was out of danger and in safe hands. But alas. They had lost the battle in Alambagh. The firangi army under Havelock and Outram had succeeded in entering the Residency. But . . . there was still hope. How were the firangis going to leave the Residency? After all, it was still surrounded by thousands of his men. And how was the already heaving Residency going to cope with the additional men?

As he walked down the corridor, deep in thought, he saw Pyaari begum and Dulari begum approaching him. Oh no, not them. If only he could ignore them. He couldn't wait to get out of his muddy wet clothes and go to the hammam.

'Greetings,' Salim said, raising his right hand to his forehead.

'Greetings, Chote Nawab. So what news do you bring from the field of battle?' asked Pyaari begum.

'Not good, I'm afraid. We just suffered our first defeat. But Ammi says we mustn't lose heart.'

'What else can she say?' said Pyaari begum.

'Yes, she doesn't want this struggle to end so she can carry on with her paramour Mammu Jaan,' said Dulari begum.

'Huzoor, what're you saying?' asked Salim, bewildered.

Pyaari begum put a paan in her mouth and said, 'It's not just us. All of Lucknow is talking about her lover.'

'We've even heard Birjis Qadir is his son,' said Dulari begum, as she played with the ends of her dupatta.

'What utter nonsense,' said Salim. 'Stop spreading these rumours, for Allah's sake. She's doing a

236

commendable job of an acting regent. You should be giving her your support instead of slinging mud at her.' He took off his turban and was about to stomp off when he saw Rachael feeding pigeons in the inner courtyard of the zenana. He smiled, the begums' gossip and the defeat in Alambagh momentarily forgotten.

The begums followed the direction of his gaze. 'Go, Chote Nawab, we won't keep you. Go to your guest.'

'Guest or something else?' quipped Dulari begum. The two women giggled.

'Chote Nawab, I know you wouldn't like to hear this. But it's a fact – as long as we've traitors like Begum Hazrat Mahal and spies like your English friend in our midst, we'll never be able to defeat the firangis.'

'That's enough. If we lose, it'll be because of people like you.' Salim plucked at his sleeve to get a grip on his temper. 'Now listen carefully, you two. I don't mean to be rude, but RayChal is my guest and I will not have anyone speak about her in that manner. If I ever catch you indulging in harmful gossip like this, I will have you thrown out of this palace.'

'How many mouths are you going to shut, Chote Nawab?' Pyaari begum asked with a contemptuous smile, then turned on her heel and left.

Chapter Twenty-Three

RACHAEL

Rachael let go of the pigeon she was playing with as soon as she espied Salim. He sounded angry. His voice rose sharply and she heard him say, 'RayChal is my guest and I will not have anyone speak about her in that manner . . .' What had they said about her that made him so angry? But she was pleased he had stuck out his head for her.

She approached him quietly after the two begums left. His clothes were muddy, stained, wet and untidy. He hadn't shaved. But stubble suited him, she decided. He looked ruggedly handsome. 'Salim?'

'What?' he asked sharply. 'I mean, yes RayChal?'

She lowered her gaze and looked at his clothes. She realised with a start that they were not just covered in mud. There was blood on them.

She pointed to a bloodstain and exclaimed, 'That's . . . that's blood.'

'Yes.' Salim hesitated, then conceded, 'It's Ahmed's.'

'What? But how?' Rachael looked him straight in the eye. She could perceive her question had rattled him.

'We were in . . . we were trying to control an angry mob.'

'Pray tell me, is he all right?'

'Yes, he's fine now. His mother and the palace doctor are taking care of him.'

'I'd like to go to *my* mother.'

Rachael watched as Salim quietly sauntered towards the far end of the courtyard, picked up one of the pigeons and stroked its head. Then he turned to her. 'You want to be cut into bits? Do you know the moment you step out of this palace you'll be killed?'

'I'm sure I could disguise myself. You know, don a burqa or something?'

'I suppose we might be able to smuggle you out of the palace safely. But how in Allah's name do you think I'm going to sneak you into the Residency? Do you know there are as many as forty thousand sepoys surrounding it right now, thirsting for English blood?'

'Forty thousand?'

'Maybe even more. Look, I've promised you I will take you to your parents as soon as it's safe. Trust me, will you?'

'How much longer? I've been here for ages. I miss my parents.' Rachael sulked.

Salim let go of the pigeon. For a long moment only the flapping of wings and the soft cooing of the pigeons could be heard. He rubbed the back of his neck and sighed tiredly. 'RayChal, please, not now. I'm wet, I'm tired, I'm hungry. We'll talk about it some other time.'

Rachael screwed up her nose at the smell of pigeon droppings and watched Salim walk away. Something was not right. The way he hung his head, the way he walked, the way his shoulders drooped. He didn't just look tired and hungry. He looked defeated.

Later that evening, Rachael sat hunched before a low mahogany table, her brows furrowed with concentration. She dipped her quill pen into the ornate silver inkpot that stood at the edge of the table. 'Alif,' she said aloud, as she wrote an alphabet on the paper before her. 'Be . . . pe . . . te . . .' She looked at her handiwork dubiously, not pleased with what she had written. Urdu was much more difficult than she had anticipated.

Daima entered the room with a tray of food. She removed the cover. There were some rotis and lentils. 'Hai Ram, I brought the wrong tray,' she exclaimed and hurried back to the kitchen.

Rachael waited for her impatiently. The smell of hot freshly prepared chapattis and yellow lentils cooked in butter ghee and cumin seeds had whetted her appetite.

Daima soon re-emerged and placed the plate on the round, grey, marble-topped table.

'Pray tell me whose plate that was, Daima?'

'What plate?'

'The one you took back?'

'Umm . . . Salim's.'

Rachael's spoon cluttered to the floor. She looked at her food. 'Rice, chapattis, vegetables and chicken curry for me and just chapattis and lentils for Salim?'

Looking down, Daima replied, 'Food and money are both becoming scarce, child . . . we are having to ration.'

'But then why all these extra dishes for me?'

'You are guest . . . we can go to bed on hungry stomach but have to make sure our guest has been fed well.'

Rachael did not know what to say. She had lost her appetite. She ate slowly and quietly. Daima placed a glass of water next to her plate.

'You know, when His Majesty was king, over a hundred dishes used to be cooked every Eid . . . this year we could manage just five.'

'Daima, where does Salim disappear for days?'

'God alone knows what these boys are up to . . . Mind you, Salim is good boy . . . it is that boy Ahmed who leads him astray.' She started fanning herself and Rachael.

Rachael wanted to say it was the contrary but refrained from doing so.

Daima continued speaking. 'Now that most of the servants are gone, I have to attend to everything . . . since morning to night I'm working . . . I'm not complaining but at this age it becomes difficult sometimes.' She put another chapatti on Rachael's plate. 'I feel bad serving daal roti to Chote Nawab . . . when His Majesty was still king, every day was a feast . . . but not once has my boy complained . . . when I gave this plain food to him the first time, he said, "Daima, we need food to appease our hunger . . . And this food's doing just that . . . But make sure our guest has enough to eat."'

Rachael found it impossible to eat now. 'Daima, from tomorrow, pray serve me the same food as Salim.'

'I cannot—'

'Please Daima, I'm not a guest anymore.'

'But—'

'For Salim's sake?'

Daima patted her head lovingly. 'You good girl . . . you'll keep him happy.'

The next morning, Rachael was seated on the carpet of her front room, a chessboard before her. A female attendant stood behind her, head lowered, waving a fan slowly to and fro. Across the board sat Saira, consternation written on her face. She kept nodding her head vigorously as Rachael picked up each piece and explained its move. Rachael stopped speaking and looked at her impatiently, wondering if she had comprehended even a word of what she had said. She sighed with relief as Salim entered the room.

'A game of chess?' he said. 'I didn't know you could play.'

'Well, you'll be surprised to know I'm a champion player,' Rachael answered.

'Oh really?' Salim dismissed Saira with a wave of his hand.

Saira raised her right hand to her forehead, bowed and backed out of the room.

Rachael swallowed as he folded his arms across his chest and walked purposefully towards her. His eyes twinkled as he said, 'In that case I challenge you to a game. If you win, you can ask anything of me. But if I win . . .' He looked at her lips for a long moment before continuing. 'If I win, you will let me give you a kiss.' He looked at her then, his eyes smiling, baiting, challenging.

'Just one?'

'Just one.'

Raising her chin in the air, Rachael looked at him, her eyes unflinching. 'I accept your challenge, Chute Nabob.'

Salim sat down on the carpet. 'You go first,' he offered graciously.

'All right, here comes my soldier.'

'And here's my horse.'

Rachael crinkled up her nose as Salim contemplated his next move.

'Why do you always scrunch up your nose? As it is, your nose is so small . . .'

She leant over and pulled his nose. 'At least when you've got a small nose, nobody can pull it.'

'Ya Ali, that hurt.'

'I know. Your turn.'

Saira entered just then and placed a bowl of fruits on the table. 'Chote Nawab, is there anything else you need?' she asked.

'No, that'll be all. Now leave us in peace.'

'Very well, Chote Nawab.' She bowed respectfully and tiptoed out of the room.

'Pray hurry up and make your move,' Rachael said impatiently, as she played with her silver earring. Not that she was winning. Salim had made some intelligent moves, especially the last one, and now her side of the board was facing the inevitable.

'Check,' he drawled. 'Try and save your wazir, I mean

queen, Miss Champion.' He drew on his hookah and leant back against the oblong pillow. His hand stroked the velvet pillow cover absent-mindedly as he watched Rachael.

Rachael frowned. 'Ah well, I suppose I've lost,' she finally conceded.

Salim's eyes smouldered as he slowly reduced the distance between them. He gradually raised her hand to his lips and kissed it. He was about to lower his lips to hers when she covered his mouth with her hand.

'Wait,' she said. 'The deal was – *one* kiss.' She caressed the spot on her right hand that he had just kissed. 'And you already have.'

She crinkled up her nose and, laughing, ran into her bedroom.

October was the month of festivals, so Rachael had been told by Daima. She sat on her haunches on the rug in a little room in the zenana, surrounded by marigolds. They were making little garlands for the numerous Hindu gods Daima worshipped. Daima put a needle through one of them. 'See, you put the needle through the flower like this, then you pull the thread and—'

'Ma,' Chutki burst into the room. She stopped speaking as soon as she saw Rachael.

Rachael was surprised at her appearance. She wore a white kurti with no jewellery. She had not tied her hair and it looked unkempt. Nor had she put any kohl in her eyes.

'Ma, what is this angrez doing here?' she asked, hands on her hip.

Daima raised a finger to her lip. 'Shhh . . . She's our guest.'

Chutki wrung her hands. 'How can an enemy be a guest? What's she doing in Salim bhai's palace?'

'Her house was burnt down . . . She's just staying here with us till we hear about her folks' whereabouts,' Daima answered quietly.

'If she doesn't have anywhere to stay, why doesn't she go back to England where she belongs?' said Chutki. 'And take the rest of the firangis with her.'

Rachael shifted uncomfortably. She picked up a marigold and tried to push the needle through it.

'What was it you came to talk to me about?' Daima asked as she finished making the garland.

'I'll be reaching home a little late this evening. Tell Nayansukh bhaiya not to worry.'

'What are you so busy with these days? Are you hiding something from me?' asked Daima.

Chutki's eyes shone. 'I'll tell you when the time comes,' she said.

Daima pulled Chutki aside. 'The knowledge that Rachael is in Kaiserbagh mustn't leave the palace grounds, do you understand?' she hissed.

Chutki threw a venomous look at Rachael. 'Yes, I understand,' she spat out and stomped out of the room.

Sighing, Daima patted Rachael's head and said, 'Beta, don't mind what my daughter said . . . Her fiancé was killed by the Company a few months back . . . That's why she's become so bitter.'

'Oh,' Rachael said softly. She remembered the last time she had met Chutki in Meena Bazaar. She had been happily shopping for her trousseau. It must have been devastating for her.

Daima spoke again. 'I have seen much, suffered much over the years and have learnt to keep a rein on my emotions . . . but she's young, her blood is hot, her emotions raw . . . she doesn't know how to control her tongue . . . I don't know where she is all day . . . This is the first time I have seen her in the palace since Gangaram's death . . .'

But Rachael wasn't listening. She was too stunned by what Chutki had said. So much hatred. She had no clue. Did Daima also hate the English? Did all the Indians feel like that? What about Salim?

Chapter Twenty-Four

SALIM

Salim watched from the tower as Colin Campbell's army approached Sikandar Bagh. So this was the second relief sent to Lucknow. When had the first relief come? Was it September? It seemed so long ago. It had been a disaster for the firangis. But this one? Salim swallowed as he watched the army rolling towards him like a huge wave. The outcome could be different this time though, he thought as he pursed his lips.

He held up his binoculars and looked disdainfully at the smartly dressed Sikh regiment. Bloody kafirs all of them. Most of the other regiments wore no uniform at all. Some wore outfits patched with pieces of curtain cloth. They looked ridiculous. Yes, five months of incessant fighting had left both sides handicapped. Why, even he had not washed or changed for almost a week. Daima was sure to box his ears when he got home. He absently rubbed his stubble as he discerned another regiment.

A shiver ran down his spine. They were the Highlanders, the freshly arrived troops that his men had been talking about. They were dressed in kilts, with plumes on their bonnets, and looked formidable. Like the rakshas in Ravana's army that Daima had so often narrated to him as a child.

A young lad in the front line caught his attention. Unlike the rest, he looked small, almost delicate. Why, he must be just sixteen. His cheeks were flushed with excitement as he laughed and talked to his comrade. This must be his first war. Salim remembered the first battle he had engaged in, just five months back. How raw and inexperienced he had been then.

Putting down the binoculars, Salim went around all the rooms, patting a soldier here, praising another one there. Having satisfied himself that every loophole, every single window and door had been covered, he went downstairs to the room at the far end, the one overlooking the inner courtyard, to take up his position. Stationing himself on the window ledge, he looked around the room. This room had been used for dining not so long ago. The soldiers had rolled up the carpets and sheets and bundled them into a corner. A chandelier still hung from the ceiling, looking morosely at the bare floor.

Salim slouched against the wall. The firangis had been firing incessantly at the solid brick wall for over an hour now. That wall was the only barrier that stood between his troops and the foe. How he wished they would give up and go away. No, he wasn't afraid. Not anymore. Just tired. Even his soldiers were exhausted, disillusioned, unwilling. He did not know how to motivate them anymore.

He straightened up as the shouts of 'Long live the Queen' rent the air and looked out of the window. The Highlanders had finally succeeded in making gaps in the wall. They were now charging into the building with a deafening roar. Salim's heartbeat quickened as he held up his musket.

Shouts of 'Har Har Mahadev' and 'Allah-o-Akbar' followed, as they clashed with the enemy. The window ledge over which Salim stood opened on to a corridor, enabling him to fire at the firangis as they came round the corner. Between exchanging shots, he happened to glance at the peepal tree that stood in the centre of the inner courtyard and noticed something curious.

At the bottom of the tree were innumerable jars of water. As soon as a firangi approached the jars to quench his thirst, he was instantly shot. Salim whistled his admiration at the sepoy's aim and tried to spot him atop the tree but couldn't. He was well hidden by the foliage.

Salim fired at the enemy incessantly, stopping only to reload his musket. His men were fighting bravely but they were outnumbered. The floor of the room was gradually getting covered with bodies. Some of the wounded sepoys lay writhing, groaning, trying desperately to crawl out from under the dead bodies that had fallen over them, crushing them. Salim closed his eyes for a split second as the desperate cries of the soldiers thus trapped tore at his heart.

As Salim was reloading his musket, Naseer, who

stood at the adjoining window, pointed excitedly. 'Chote Nawab, look.'

Salim looked out of the window. He saw a group of firangis run frantically out of the building onto the courtyard, then round the back, chased by a black cloud of bees. He smiled faintly. 'If the bees manage to get under those jackets, their backs will be redder than the jackets they have on,' he chuckled.

'I was thinking more about them two men in kilts,' Naseer guffawed.

Salim laughed aloud.

A moment later Naseer had been hit from behind and fell out of the window with a thud.

Turning sharply to see who had shot him, Salim was surprised to see the young Scottish lad he had spotted earlier that day. Salim hastily fired. Missed. The lad pointed his gun at Salim. 'Ya Ali,' Salim shouted in dismay as he realised he had fired his last cartridge. His shout distracted the lad. He hesitated then fired. Salim ducked, then quick as a leopard he threw his musket and drew his sword. With a shout of 'Allah-o-Akbar', he charged towards the lad and plunged his sword into his stomach.

The lad now lay on the floor, covered in blood. Salim shook his head slowly as he looked down at his beautiful face, his smooth cheeks. He had not even begun to shave. Salim closed his eyes momentarily and his Adam's apple moved. What would RayChal say? Would she approve? Why, she threw a fit for killing a mere ant . . . She would never approve. *No*. She would understand. He'd make her understand. She *had* to . . .

He winced as the sound of Scottish pipers reached his ears, over the shouts and agonised screams of the wounded. The next minute he was spluttering and coughing as smoke began to fill the room. His jaw dropped and eyes grew wide as he heard a crackling sound. The building was on fire. Shouts of agony could be heard as sepoys fell victim to the flames. Oh no, what was he to do? They were surrounded by the enemy and now their garrison was in flames. They were doomed, he thought, as he swiped his hand across eyes that were beginning to smart. Covering his nose and mouth with the ends of his turban, he stumbled over the dead bodies, rushing towards the door. Suddenly, something hit him hard. He let out a loud wail as he dropped his sword and clutched his head. He fell to the floor, unconscious.

It was dark when he came around. Except for the red glow of dying embers. He felt a heavy weight on him and realised that dead bodies lay over him. He pushed them aside with all his might. All around him lay piles of bodies, sometimes as high as five feet. The smell of stale blood and burning flesh was overpowering and oppressive. Salim covered his mouth with his hands as bile rose in his throat.

He swayed and wobbled as he took a few steps. He felt weak and dizzy. The lump on his head hurt when he moved his head even slightly. Stumbling out into the garden, he licked his lips. They were parched and tasted of gunpowder. He shivered. At least the air in the open was less stifling. Perceiving a dead body underneath the peepal tree, he walked towards it. It must be the sepoy who had been firing from atop the tree. Salim looked at his still frame now. He wore a red jacket and silk trousers. As Salim bent closer, he realised he was not a sepoy. It was a woman.

'Ya Ali, it's Chutki!' he exclaimed. He stared at her in disbelief. It could not be. His Chutki, his little sister? She had been hit by a bullet in her jaw, which had then passed through her neck. Salim pulled her into his arms and held her close to his heart. Why? He knew she hated the firangis since they had killed her fiancé. But that she would go to war to avenge his death . . .

'So you want me to protect you?' he had asked her as he watched her tying a rakhi on his wrist on Raksha Bandhan.

'Let it be, Salim bhai. I can fight single-handedly against anyone.'

'Oh really? Well, if you're that strong, let's see if you can wrestle your gift from my hand.'

He held out a closed fist. Chutki tried her best to open it but couldn't lift even his little finger.

Salim clicked his tongue, 'Tut, tut.'

'What, bhai?' Chutki sulked.

Salim finally relented and slowly opened his fist. A beautiful pearl necklace with matching earrings sparkled at Chutki.

He smiled as he watched his delighted sister hold the necklace up against her neck and squeal, 'Thank you, thank you, Salim bhai,' before throwing herself in his arms.

'Wear it the day after your wedding when you leave for your in-laws. It'll remind you that, no matter where you are, I'll always be there for you.'

So much had happened since then. Her fiancé had been killed and now . . .

He looked at her still face, his eyes glittering. 'My brave little sister,' he whispered and kissed her forehead tenderly. He had not kept his word. His little sister had needed him and he had not been there for her. He had failed her, failed Daima.

Ya Ali. What was he going to say to Daima? How was he going to face her? She had told him once there was nothing sadder than a mother whose life exceeds that of her child. Salim closed his eyes and let the tears run down his cheeks.

He stood up slowly as a sliver of light appeared on the eastern horizon. He took off his turban. He spread it out and covered Chutki with it. She looked so small now, so frail. Lifting her stiff cold body, he dragged his feet towards the northern gate.

Salim walked all the way to Daima's house, carrying Chutki's dead body in his arms. It was early morning when he reached there. He quietly placed Chutki's body in front of the tulsi plant in the courtyard.

Just then he saw Daima come out of the house carrying a copper lota of water. Her eyes were half closed, her feet were bare and she was muttering her prayers. She turned towards the east, looked at the sun and joined her hands. She then lifted her hands and began pouring out the water from the lota, muttering some prayers under her breath. Her thin cotton sari blew in the morning breeze and she shivered slightly.

She then turned to pour the remaining water on the

tulsi plant. He watched her as she noticed the dead body. Her eyes flew to his face in alarm. She had turned white. She raised an eyebrow questioningly.

Salim lowered his eyes and nodded. Daima shook her head slowly from side to side in disbelief. Dropping the lota with a loud clang, she dragged her feet to where Chutki lay. With trembling hands she lifted Salim's turban cloth away from her face. She covered her ears with her hands and screamed, '*No!*' With tears streaming down her face she touched the wound on Chutki's neck gently, tenderly, as though it still hurt.

Salim lowered his gaze as she came towards him. 'What happened, Chote Nawab?' She spread out her empty hands. 'All my dreams?' Grabbing hold of the front of his angarkha, she started sobbing hysterically. Salim slowly put his arms around her as her body heaved with spasms of sobs.

After a long time she moved out of his embrace and looked at him. 'Her marriage had been fixed for next month,' she sobbed. She sniffed before continuing. 'First her fiancé . . . now her . . .' She again grabbed Salim's angarkha. 'You were supposed to carry her doli, not her funeral bier.'

Salim stood motionless, his feet apart, his hands hanging helplessly by his side. He looked heavenward as he struggled to swallow his tears, his eyes becoming red with the effort. A single tear slid down his cheek and fell noiselessly to the ground.

Salim cursed himself yet again for not staying back at Kaiserbagh. Ahmed had just arrived to tell him there had been intense fighting for the last three days, while here at the Residency the firing had petered out. Salim signalled to his men to stop firing and be quiet. They listened carefully. Yes, there was no sound coming from the Residency. They had stopped firing. Perhaps the firangis were preparing to surrender.

A shout of 'Har Har Mahadev' and 'Allah-o-Akbar' rent the air as the sepoys charged jubilantly into the Residency. As Salim pushed past the Baillie Guard a fetid smell of decaying dead bodies greeted him. He could see bloated bodies of dead horses carelessly pushed into ditches and covered with flies. The garden was in ruin. Trenches ran across the flower beds and the lawn. The neatly arranged flowers and shrubs had been replaced by wild thorny shrubs, tall wild grass and weeds. Not a single living soul could be seen. The Residency was deserted. The firangis had not surrendered. They had made their escape with all the treasure they had looted from Kaiserbagh.

Salim covered his mouth and nose with his hand as he entered the banquet hall. It smelt of vomit, blood and decay. It must have been used as a makeshift hospital, as bandages covered in fresh blood, basins half filled with water, and vomit lay around. Salim gagged. Ahmed staggered outside, retching violently.

With much trepidation Salim entered the Residency. There were clothes, utensils, beddings and some valuables that had been left behind. He picked up a rag doll that lay on its face on the floor. It must have belonged to a little girl. He wondered how much hardship the children must have had to endure. It was not their fault and yet . . .

Most of the windows had been smashed and glass lay everywhere. The walls were covered with holes made by their intermittent firing over the last five months.

The sepoys gave a whoop of delight and went on a rampage, looting the boxes and trunks of their valuables.

A loud explosion made everyone stop in their tracks. A sepoy had stepped onto a hidden mine. His body was blown to smithereens. Salim smiled scornfully as he watched the other sepoys commiserate for a few seconds, then go back to their looting. They looked jubilant. But this was no victory. The firangis had escaped. For five long months they had bravely held out. And now on 19th November 1857, they had made their escape to safety.

'Is RayChal inside?' Salim asked the female attendant.

'Yes, Chote Nawab,' the attendant answered, bowing low, her right hand raised to her forehead. 'She's in bed. I think she not well.'

'I see.'

Salim entered the khwabgah. Rachael lay in bed, her eyes closed. She was wearing the same white dress she had worn when he had brought her to the palace. She looked out of this world in white. Almost ethereal.

Saira was massaging her forehead with a balm which smelt of eucalyptus oil. She opened her mouth to speak as soon as she saw Salim. Salim hastily put his finger on his lips and indicated that she leave the room. Saira bowed low and left the room quietly, walking backwards.

Salim began to massage Rachael's forehead. Her forehead creased into a frown. She felt his hairy masculine hands with her fingers and her frightened eyes fluttered open. She relaxed when she saw it was Salim.

'You gave me a fright,' she said as she started to sit up.

'Don't get up.' Salim held her shoulders lightly and made her lie back. 'You're not well?' he asked as he squatted on the carpet beside the bed.

'I've got a slight headache, that's all.'

She smiled and crumpled up her nose as Salim took her hand in his and stroked the diamond on her ring.

'I feel like a queen, lying on this enormous bed, with a prince sitting at my feet.'

'You *are* a queen,' Salim whispered. 'Queen of my . . .' he left the sentence incomplete as he placed the palm of her hand on his heart.

She looked at him for a long moment. Neither of them spoke.

Salim looked down at his hands. He was engrossed in examining his fingers as he spoke. 'I've some news for you, RayChal. I've learnt the firang - the English have managed to escape from the Residency. They are in Dilkusha at the moment. I think they'll be leaving for Cawnpore tomorrow.'

Rachael sat up and looked at him incredulously.

'Yes, RayChal,' Salim added sadly. 'The time has come to fulfil my promise. I shall take you to your folks tomorrow. We'll have to leave just before the break of dawn, while it's still dark.'

Rachael clapped her hands with glee. 'So finally I'll be able to see my parents again. Oh God, I've waited so long for this day.'

Salim got up, picked up a rose from the posy on the wall, twirled it, then put it back. 'Yes, finally,' he answered as he choked back a lump in his throat. Ya Ali, the time had come to tell her about his involvement in the uprising. He could not put it off anymore. She would understand, he was sure of that.

Chapter Twenty-Five

RACHAEL

Rachael stood beside her bed, looking at Salim playing wistfully with her fingers. She felt a twinge of sadness as the initial excitement at the thought of seeing her parents again died away. This was their last night together. God knows when they would meet again. What if they never met again? No, she mustn't think like that.

She cupped his face in her hands and felt his stubble prick her fingers and palm. Salim looked at her, gently removed her hands and walked abruptly to the earthenware pot. He poured himself a glass of water, which he drank noisily, spilling some on his chin. Wiping his mouth with the back of his hand, he walked back to where she stood, watching his every move. She smiled as he put his hand in his pocket, two lines appearing between his eyebrows. He held out his fist in front of her. She looked at him, questioning.

'Go on, open it.'

Now what game was he playing, she wondered as she slowly opened his fist. He offered no resistance. As she pulled back his fingers, seven rings with seven jewels sparkled cheerily at her. Jade, sapphire, amethyst, diamond, ruby, topaz and emerald.

'A ring to match your every dress,' he said, as he put them on the bed beside her. Then he picked up the sapphire ring.

'And this one to match your eyes.' So saying he knelt down before her. 'RayChal, will you marry me?'

Rachael turned red and clasped her face with her hands. She looked at him. His eyes were hypnotic, imploring. She could not look away.

'Oh Salim, yes I will.'

'I swear to you, by everything I hold sacred, that I will never marry again. You will be the only begum in my harem,' he said, as he slowly slid the ring on her finger.

Rachael looked at the ring, then at his mesmerising gaze and whispered, 'Salim, even if you had asked me to be your one hundred and twenty-first wife, I would have said yes.'

He got up slowly, his eyes not leaving her face even for a moment, and took her in a tight embrace. 'Oh Ray . . .' he whispered passionately, his voice muffled by her hair. He kissed her forehead, her eyes, her nose, her cheeks. He tried to move closer to kiss her lips, but broke off with a curse.

'What *is* this?' he asked in frustration.

Rachael laughed. 'It's the hoops, the crinoline.'

'It seems more like a chas—'

'Like a what?' Rachael raised her eyebrows, smiling mischievously, her nose crinkling.

'Never mind. You're a lady and I mustn't say it in front of you.'

'What must you say, then?' she asked as she tucked a strand of hair behind her ear.

He came closer. 'Your skin is glowing in this candlelight. Just like Noor Jehan's.'

'Who's she?'

'She's this beautiful, graceful woman I met yesterday . . .'

Rachael glared at him. 'What?'

He threw back his head and laughed. 'She was Jahangir's wife. Remember the story I told you about Salim and Anarkali?'

'Oh yes. The one where that poor girl was buried alive?'

'Yes, same prince. Legend has it that when Salim – or Jahangir, as he was later known – when his wife Noor Jehan ate paan, you could see the orange-red juice going down her throat, so clear and transparent was her skin.'

Rachael blushed. She put her head on Salim's shoulder, twirling the ends of her hair with one hand. 'I wonder what we'll look like on our wedding day. You in your angarkha and me in my white bridal—'

'Not white,' Salim interjected.

'Pray tell me why not? You want me to wear red?'

'No.' Salim's voice dropped to a whisper. 'Orange. The colour of fire. Do you know, when the sunlight touches your hair . . .' He paused momentarily as he playfully covered his face with her hair. 'It looks as though it's on fire. You'll look radiant in orange. Like the goddess of fire.'

'Oh Salim,' Rachael sighed as she sat down on the bed. 'Do you think it'll happen?'

Salim sat down beside her. He moved closer, his lips just an inch away from hers.

'Salim.'

'I love you.'

'I love you too, Salim.'

'Don't stop me today, RayChal. Your lips have been made for kissing.'

'Oh Salim,' she groaned as his lips covered hers. Her heart was thumping so loudly, she could scarce hear her own voice.

Rachael stood under the arched doorway and tried to focus. It was a starless, moonless night. Salim was waiting for her at the bottom of the steps beside a carriage. He sprinted up the stairs as soon as he saw her, took her hand in his and led her towards the vehicle that was to take her to her parents. Neither of them spoke. Halfway down the stairs Rachael stopped and looked back. The palace loomed over her. It looked majestic, even though shrouded in darkness. She saw a silhouette against the window upstairs. She waved. The shadow waved back. It was Daima.

She stopped abruptly as she reached the last stair. Someone was tugging her chador. Her face went white as she slowly turned around. She was relieved to find it was just Salim, who had stepped on it. 'Oh dear,' she exclaimed as it slid to the ground.

With a sigh of exasperation Salim picked it up and draped it around her head and shoulders. 'Well, it's not exactly how it's supposed to be, but it's better than what you had done,' he said.

Rachael grinned and stepped into the carriage. They rode in silence for a while, the clippity-clop of the horses' hooves echoing through the still night. She almost fell off her seat as the carriage came to an abrupt halt and she looked questioningly at Salim. He was equally clueless why it had stopped. The coachman was hitting the horse with his whip and coaxing it to move on. Rachael listened. She could hear some voices and footsteps approaching. She looked at Salim anxiously. His forehead was covered with beads of perspiration.

The voices came closer. They were boisterous. Must be drunk. They were now talking to the coachman.

'Where you off to in the middle of the night?' said one of the voices.

'Stolen goods?' asked a second, laughing.

'Or opium?' guffawed a third voice.

Salim let out a sigh of relief. He gestured to her to cover her face with the chador. She did as she was told.

Salim lifted the curtain of his window. 'Anything the matter?' he barked authoritatively.

The sepoys peered at his face in the darkness, then hastily backed away. 'Salaam, Chote Nawab,' they said in unison, raising their right hands to their foreheads in a salute.

'Nothing, Chote Nawab . . . nothing at all,' said one of the sepoys.

'Sorry, Chote Nawab, we didn't know it was you,' said another.

Rachael continued to sit still as she heard the shuffling of feet. Soon the voices died away.

Salim was now looking at the coachman. 'What is the matter?' he asked in a clipped tone.

'Horse not moving, Huzoor,' the coachman replied.

'Don't just sit there,' barked Salim. 'Do something.'

'Yes, My Lord,' the coachman mumbled. He got off the carriage and began tugging at the horse's reins. The horse still didn't move.

Lifting the curtain, Rachael looked out. 'Pray tell me why the coachman is gathering straw?' she asked. Still looking out, she added, 'Oh no, now he's lighting a fire.'

'Don't worry,' Salim replied. 'It's to frighten the horse.'

Sure enough, as soon as the horse felt the heat from the fire, it began to gallop. Rachael took another quick peek from the carriage window. It was still dark.

'Don't lift the curtain again,' Salim chided.

'But these streets don't look familiar.'

'He's taking us through some by-lanes. It's safer.'

Rachael hugged the chador. There was a slight nip in the air. Her muscles tensed as they neared her home. Salim had agreed to take her to the cantonment first but made her promise not to spend more than a few minutes there. She stepped out slowly and took a long look at what had been her home. It looked like the ruins of an ancient monument. Not a house that had been bustling with life just a few months back. She blinked back her tears as Salim pressed her hand reassuringly.

She made her way through the tall wild weeds that had taken over the garden, shouting, 'Brutus! Brutus!' Where was he? She walked back to Salim and clutched his arm, her nails digging into it. 'I think he's—'

Then she heard it, the familiar bark. A second later he was all over her. He knocked her down in his excitement as he licked her face, her nose, her hands. Rachael laughed as tears rolled down her cheeks. She hugged and kissed him over and over again. 'Oh my baby, I'm so glad you're safe. I'm so glad. Thank you, thank you, God.'

'Missy baba?'

'Ram Singh! So good to see you. How is Sudha? How is Ayah? Have you any news of my parents?' She patted Brutus who was now busy playing with her arm as though it were a bone.

'Her relatives took her away. We fear the worst.'

Rachael got up, brushing away the mud and grass from her dress. She turned her back to Salim and Ram Singh, covered her mouth with her right hand as tears rolled down her cheeks. She remembered how brutally Sudha's relatives had treated her the last time she saw her. But, even so, it couldn't be true. No, nothing could happen to Sudha. She was meant to be with her always. God couldn't take her away just like that. They had shared so much. She understood her needs even more than her own mother did.

Rachael felt a hand touch her shoulder. It was Salim. 'I'm sure she's fine,' he whispered. 'We'll look for her.'

'Yes, I'm sure,' Rachael sniffed. She turned to Ram Singh. 'My parents?'

'Don't know, baba. That day they have to leave in hurry. Parvati go with them. I go to look for you. Sudha stay here to look after house.' He paused, staring straight ahead, as though reliving the horrors of that day. 'Sorry, baba. The mob stop me. I can't go to you. When I get back here, house empty, burning. It takes me long time to put out fire. Very long time. But finally I do it.'

Nodding her head quietly, Rachael walked into the house. Salim's arm came around her protectively. She was too full of emotions to protest.

Much of the furniture was charred. All the books, the curtains, the clothes were now ash. She picked up the book from what had been her bedside table. The edges were black, but she could decipher the title. P.B. Shelley it said. She was aware of Salim's eyes on her. She tried to smile and crinkled up her nose to keep those brimming tears at bay.

She yelped as she entered the living room. 'My piano!'

Yes, it was intact. Salim and Ram Singh helped her to remove the rubble that had fallen over it and thus prevented it from getting burnt. She lifted the lid and began playing like a woman possessed. As she played, Brutus put his snout up in the air and let out a loud howl, then another and yet another. All of them burst out laughing.

'I wasn't aware we had a Tansen in our midst,' Salim remarked.

'Tan who?'

'Tansen was one of the greatest singers of Hindustan.'

'Then we shall have to rename Brutus. Tansen Brutus, how's that?'

Brutus liked his new name. He wagged his tail and licked Salim's hand.

'Missy baba, I find Brutus under a pile of debris that fallen over his kennel and knock him unconscious. I have to make muzzle to put over his mouth whenever I hear crowd passing.'

Rachael held his hands. 'Thank you, Ram Singh. Thank you ever so much.'

'RayChal, we ought to leave now. Otherwise we might miss your parents. It'll take us a while to get to Dilkusha.'

'You no worry, baba. You go look for sahib and memsahib. I keep taking care of house and Brutus. I also put all money, gold, jewellery in trunk and bury it in bottom of garden. When riots finish, you come back for them.'

'You are a good man, Ram Singh. Take care of yourself,' Rachael said.

She then bent down and patted Brutus one last time. Sighing, she stepped into the carriage.

Rachael sighed again as she heard Brutus barking and running after the carriage. She was about to lift the curtain but Salim's hand shot out to stop her.

'It's not safe,' he said. 'Daylight is breaking. We must be careful.'

She wished she could take Brutus with her. Salim had said her parents were leaving for Cawnpore. When would they come back to Lucknow? Everything was so uncertain. If only the Company had treated the Indians better. If only the sepoys had not revolted. If only . . .

She looked at Salim. He was looking at the engagement ring that he had put on her finger last night. He rubbed the sapphire with his thumb wistfully.

'I have something to tell you,' he said.

'Yes?'

He cleared his throat and looked at her hesitantly. 'You know this rising. This war between the sepoys and the Company . . .'

'Don't I know! It's kept me away from my family for all these months.'

'You weren't happy in my palace?'

'No, no. That's not what I meant.'

Salim lowered his gaze. 'Well . . .' He started smoothing the folds of his angarkha. 'I'm part of it.'

Rachael stared at him. He did not meet her gaze.

'What?'

'You heard me,' he answered quietly.

'You've been fighting with the rebels against the English?' Rachael asked with disbelief. 'Pray tell me it's not true.'

'I'm afraid it is.'

'I had no idea. So I have been living with the enemy.'

'But Ray—'

'All those rebels firing at the Residency. You were one of them?'

Salim nodded.

'Even after you came to know my parents were there?'

'Ya Ali, it had nothing to do with your parents,

RayChal. We're fighting for a cause, for justice, for what rightly belongs to us. Surely you can understand that.'

Rachael wrung her arms in despair. 'They're my people, Salim, my family. I cannot not support them!'

Salim did not say anything but stared straight ahead.

'And now you're telling me? After you've proposed to me? How could you, Salim, how could you?'

The carriage stopped. Rachael lifted the curtain and looked out of the window. They had reached Dilkusha – the summer palace of the nabob and the imperial hunting grounds. At the moment it looked more like an army camp. She could see the tent doors flapping in the breeze.

She alighted from the carriage and looked around. She saw Papa talking to one of the soldiers and sprinted towards him. 'Papa,' she cried as she embraced him. He looked haggard. He seemed to have aged suddenly.

'Oh heavens, my princess,' he said, as he looked at her for a long moment then hugged her again. 'I can't believe it's you. We thought we'd lost you. How did you reach here? Where were you all these days?'

'Oh Papa, it's a long story. I'll tell you later.' She walked back to where Salim stood.

'I hate you, Salim. I never want to see your face again. You're deplorable.'

Salim gripped her arms urgently. 'But RayChal, let me explain.'

Rachael looked at him and their eyes met. His eyes were beseeching, hurting, repentant. She hastily looked away. Then jerking his hands away from her arms, she turned on her heels and walked away.

She saw the look of concern on Papa's face. He was just a few paces behind her and had witnessed the exchange between her and Salim.

'Rachael, what happened, poppet?' he asked.

'Papa, I don't want to talk about it.'

'Did he harass you?'

'Worse,' she replied as she stomped off towards the group breakfasting under the mango tree.

Yes, what Salim had done was worse than harassment. He had stolen her heart, made love to her and even proposed to her, while knowing there was no way she could marry a rebel.

Chapter Twenty-Six

SALIM

Dilkusha, the royal hunting grounds, looked more like an army barracks that day. The rows of happily growing carrots had been trampled on. There was no sign of the barking deer, the black buck or the sambar. Most of them had been roasted and washed down with alcohol by the English soldiers the previous night. A strange smell of decay and fresh food pervaded the air.

'RayChal, wait,' Salim cried out desperately, raising his hand to stop her. He let it fall limply to his side as one of the soldiers called out to her.

'Rachael.'

'Christopher.'

Salim watched her animated face as she chatted to Christopher. He felt a stab of jealousy as Christopher held her elbow and led her away. He stood transfixed, watching his life walk away. It was as though he were watching his own janaza, his own funeral.

He watched her as she weaved in and out among her own kind. She threw her head back and laughed at something Christopher said. Now she was clasping an old woman's hands and smiling at her gently. Her Indian outfit looked conspicuous amidst the hooped skirts and crinoline dresses. But she was back where she belonged – a world where there was no place for him. He lowered his gaze, then looked back at her again. She was again talking to that Christopher. He felt like an outsider. Yes, she fitted in perfectly with them, he thought with a pang. Not in his harem. But then, she had adjusted so well in the palace as well, as though she had always lived there.

He sighed and licked his parched lips. She was oblivious that he still stood there. In the last few months they had come close to each other and he felt he knew her well. At least that's what he had thought. And now, suddenly, she felt like a stranger again – he knew her no more.

His shoulders slumped as he turned to leave. A hand appeared out of nowhere and caught hold of his collar. It was Colonel Bristow. 'How dare you lay your dirty brown paws on my daughter!' he hissed.

'I only—'

'You're even worse than I thought.'

'I just escorted her here—'

'And that's precisely why I'm sparing your life. Else you'd be dead by now. Now get lost, you miserable wretch.' So saying, he shoved him out of the gate and walked off.

Salim looked at his receding back, astounded. These firangis had a strange way of saying thank you.

Slowly he made his way back to the carriage. He sat hunched, gripping the edge of the seat with both hands, as the lonely carriage trundled over cobblestones. So what if she's gone, he mused. He had a good life before he met her. And it would carry on the same as before. He grimaced. Who was he trying to fool? Life would never be the same again. She had changed it for ever. He swore under his breath. Never again would he get involved with a woman. Especially if she was English. This pain, this loss, this grief, it was simply not worth it.

Salim lowered himself on the cold palace steps. He looked at Daima. She was speaking to the footman. Must be asking about RayChal. He wrapped his shawl tightly about his shoulders. It was a cold morning with a strong south-westerly breeze blowing, bringing with it the fragrance of tuberoses. And with their fragrance, the thought of RayChal. His lips puckered and shook slightly as he tried to shut her out of his mind. He looked at the garden. It was spangled with yellow roses. They were dancing in the breeze and seemed to laugh at him. 'We told you so, we told you so,' they jeered in unison. He covered his ears with the palms of his hands, closed his eyes and screamed, 'I know, I know, I know; I was a fool!'

Daima rushed to his side. 'Chote Nawab? You all right?'

Lowering his hands, Salim replied, 'I'm fine, Daima.' He paused, swallowed. 'Left her with her people. Where she belongs.'

'She must be happy?'

He did not reply but watched the horses as Sulaiman unfastened them from the carriage and led them away. Eventually he spoke. 'Very. She didn't even look back.'

'What else can we expect from a cow eater . . . ? May she get eaten by worms,' said Daima bristling up. She picked up the shawl that had fallen to the ground and put it around Salim's shoulders.

'No, Daima. Don't curse her. It was my fault. I should have told her earlier.'

'Why not? How can she hurt my son like this?'

Looking down, Salim stared at his shoes for a moment before replying, his voice hardly audible. 'Rather me than her, Daima.'

'This is just great . . . my chivalrous son! But who told her?'

'Ya Ali, who can dig their grave better than I do?'

Putting her hand under his chin, Daima turned his face towards her. 'That was brave of you, Chote Nawab,' she said. 'You didn't have to tell her you know . . . maybe she would have never found out.'

'Maybe, and maybe she would have. I don't know whether I did right or wrong. All I know is I've lost her for ever.'

'No . . .'

Grimacing, Salim shut his eyes momentarily. 'The hatred with which she looked at me before walking away . . .' He paused, his Adam's apple moving. 'I'll never be able to forgive myself.'

'Chote Nawab, all I know is she loves you as well . . . she'll come back.'

'They are sending all the women and children to

Cawnpore and finally back to England. Our paths will never cross again.'

'Don't worry . . . there's no dearth of women for our Chote Nawab.'

Salim got up and walked towards the garden. He picked up a broken branch and snapped it into pieces, his jaw set in a grim line. Then he looked back at Daima.

'No,' he whispered, his voice choked with emotion. 'She was the love of my life. No one can love me like she did. What we shared was beyond this world.'

Chapter Twenty-Seven

RACHAEL

Rachael looked around at what must have been a beautiful garden once. Piles of ash lay everywhere – from the fires the soldiers had lit the previous night to roast the deer the Dilkusha forest was so famous for.

Women and children were coming out of the tents and making their way towards a table laid out under the shade of a mango tree. There were whoops of delight at the sight of fresh bread and cold meat.

'Goodness gracious, there are biscuits and jam and coffee with milk and sugar. I haven't had a breakfast like this in months,' Rachael heard Mrs Wilson exclaim as she piled her plate with food.

She watched the soldiers patiently serve the women and children as they devoured their breakfast. They looked famished. She felt guilty she had been well fed and looked after in the palace while her folk had had to endure so much hardship. Even their clothes were bedraggled. Why, she had never seen Papa so unkempt before. His shirt was torn in a couple of places and a patch had been clumsily sewn onto his trousers, just above the left knee. His hair was long and messy. She did not want to admit it, but he smelt as though he hadn't bathed in months.

Her eyes roved once more over the crowd hovering around the breakfast table. Where was Mother?

'Missy baba, Missy baba,' exclaimed Ayah as she tore herself from the crowd and came running up to her. 'I so happy to see you.' Rachael grinned at her as she clutched her hands excitedly.

'How have you been, Ayah? And pray tell me, where's Mother?'

'Memsahib not well, baba. She got the fever,' she replied, as she led her down a long corridor in the palace. A stale smell of sickness and damp walls greeted her as she entered a dark windowless room. It must have belonged to one of the begums. Mother looked so frail and small in the four-poster bed on which she lay.

Rachael irritably pushed aside the muslin drapes that hung around the bed. 'Mother,' she said in a small choked voice as she reached out for her hand. Then, alarmed at how warm it was, hastily touched her forehead.

Mother smiled at her weakly. 'You're here, my child, you're finally here.' She paused as a spasm of coughing took hold of her.

Ayah rushed to her with a glass of water. After taking a small sip, Mother settled back into her pillow. She spoke slowly. 'Now we can all leave for Cawnpore and then home. Finally home to England.'

'But Mother, you're burning. You can't travel like this.'

'She's right,' said Papa as he entered the room. 'You three will have to come with me and the remaining soldiers to Alambagh.' He looked around the room. 'And for heaven's sake, get rid of some of this luggage. We don't have enough men to carry her *and* the baggage.'

'Papa . . . !' Rachael exclaimed, appalled at the manner in which he spoke, but he had already left the room.

'I need my clothes,' wailed Mother.

'Do not vex yourself, Mother, I'll see what I can do,' said Rachael. She opened her mother's pitaras and looked at the contents.

'Kalyaan carry two pitara,' said Ayah. 'I carry two. Last one we leave?'

Rachael sifted through the contents of the tin box. Her face suddenly lit up as an idea struck her. She pulled out one of Mother's skirts and put it on. Then another on top of the previous one. Then another. And another. Soon she was wearing six skirts. She did the same with the bodices. Grinning, she tried to walk and almost toppled over. Steadying herself, she looked triumphantly at Ayah. 'Yes,' she said, pointing to the box she had just emptied. 'We can leave this pitara behind.'

Most of the Englishmen, women and children gathered in Dilkusha had left for Cawnpore. The remaining party waited for darkness to fall before they commenced their march to Alambagh. Rachael watched as the sick, the injured and the aged settled down in dolis and carriages. She looked at Mother's doli and hoped she was comfortable. Nodding briefly at Ayah and Kalyaan, who were walking beside the doli carrying pitaras, she instructed them to keep checking on Mother. They were to inform her if they noticed anything amiss.

She smiled slightly as Christopher walked up to her.

'I'm afraid you'll have to march with the soldiers,' he said. 'There aren't any palanquins or carriages left. Most of them have left with the party for Cawnpore.'

'That's not a problem,' Rachael replied, tottering under the weight of the half a dozen skirts and bodices she had donned.

Soon they were marching towards Alambagh. Rachael waved to Christopher. 'Come and walk beside me,' she said.

'No,' he answered. 'Only the natives walk on the outside.'

Puzzled, Rachael looked around. She realised she was flanked on either side by Indian soldiers. And it wasn't just her. All the English soldiers marching ahead of her were walking between two neat columns of Indian soldiers. And then the horror of it all struck her. The Indian soldiers were being used as human shields. She was aghast but could do nothing about it.

She sighed as it started to rain. A cold, miserable November rain. She waded gloomily through the sodden earth, her skirts covered with mud up to her knees. They became heavier with each step. If only she had known how difficult it would be to walk in them, she would never have worn them. As though that wasn't enough, even her throat and head had begun to hurt.

Nonetheless, she trudged along. They had reached

the far bank of the Gomti and could hear the sound of guns in the distance. As they made their way through a narrow lane between two rows of mud houses, they were suddenly exposed to enemy fire. The natives, hiding behind the mud walls, rained a volley of bullets on them. It sounded like several fireworks going off at once. Terrified, Rachael hastened her pace. However, she slipped, not for the first time that night. She pursed her lips and steadied herself. She had never felt more unladylike before. Just then the Indian soldier marching beside her groaned and fell to the ground. He had been hit. Rachael watched his bloodied body writhing in pain. She covered her mouth as a sob escaped her lips. She frantically pushed past the marching soldiers, walked up to a parapet by the side of the road and retched violently. Nothing came up. Only tears streaking down her cheeks.

She sat down on the parapet. Just two nights previously she had been so happy. She was going to meet her parents soon and she was in the arms of the man she loved. How she hated him now. How could she have been so gullible? When she had walked away from him in Dilkusha, he had stood there for a long time, looking lost and hurt, his eyes glittering. They looked beautiful – his eyes. Intense, hurt, beseeching, forlorn – all at the same time. She had quickly looked away, not wanting to be hypnotised by them. Otherwise her heart would have melted and she would have gone running back to him.

No, she would never go back to him again, never. How could he have protected her on the one hand and shot at her own people on the other? And how dare he propose to her, knowing all the while that he had been lying to her? She would never trust him again. 'I hate you, Salim,' she muttered through gritted teeth as her eyes filled with angry tears. 'Oh, how I hate you.'

Oh Lord, was this night ever going to end? It seemed like one long nightmare. First Salim's betrayal, then the news about Sudha, Mother's illness and now this. She suddenly found herself longing for the warmth and security of Kaiserbagh Palace. And as suddenly she felt ashamed – she was now beginning to fathom what her people must have been through in the last few months, while she herself was cosseted in the palace. What must they have endured? And she couldn't even make it through a single night.

'What do you think you're doing?'

Rachael started at the voice. It was Christopher. 'I can't go any further,' she moaned. 'Pray leave me alone. You go.'

'Are you insane? You'll get yourself killed,' said Christopher.

'That soldier died because of me,' she screamed hysterically. 'Can't you see? If he wasn't shielding me, the bullet would have hit me. I ought to be the one dead, not him.'

'Calm down, Rachael,' said Christopher, offering her his hip flask.

Rachael did not say anything, merely raised her brows.

'Take a sip. It'll calm you down,' Christopher replied.

Rachael hesitated, then took a small sip. Then another.

Christopher held out his hand and whispered, 'You can't give up so easily. Not now, when we're almost there.'

She nodded quietly as he pulled her to her feet. She followed him, dragging her feet, her skirts and boots caked in mud, and wet hair clinging to her forehead. She must look a sight. Never before had she felt more miserable.

It was almost two months since Rachael and her parents had arrived at Alambagh. Rachael sat on the cold kitchen floor, her forehead etched with lines of concentration, as she rolled out a piece of dough.

'Pray tell me if this will do?' she asked as she pointed to the piece of dough on the rolling board. It didn't look circular at all. More like a kite torn at the edges.

Ayah looked at it and stifling a grin answered, 'Yes, it'll do, baba.'

Rachael sighed and pushed back her hair with the back of her hand, peppering her hair with flour as she did so. She had never been to a kitchen before arriving at Alambagh. Nor had she realised how difficult it was to make a simple chapatti. She watched Ayah in fascination as she rolled them out effortlessly, one after the other.

Looking up, she smiled at Mother as she entered the kitchen. She had burnt with the fever for a whole week after their arrival at Alambagh. Rachael had been beside her day and night – and just when they had begun to despair and thought they had lost her, she made a miraculous recovery. Rachael watched her now as she looked at the chapattis, then at the daal bubbling in the

282

pot, and screwed up her nose. 'Brutus wouldn't even sniff at this food,' she said. Rachael shook her head. Mother was still the same. Nothing could ever change her.

'Mother, at least we have Ayah to make these chapattis,' she said. 'Can you imagine what we would have done if she wasn't here?'

Yes, they were fortunate indeed to have Ayah with them. Neither she nor Mother would have known what to do with the flour. They would have had to starve for sure, for food was rationed in Alambagh. Flour and daal was all they got on most days. Sometimes, if they were lucky, they got some meat and maybe even some peas and vegetables. But those occasions were rare and it was more bones than meat. The shortage was due to the refusal of most Indian traders to sell anything to the English, even at exorbitant rates. There were some who did not mind dealing with them, but they were afraid of being regarded as traitors for trading with the enemy.

Rachael looked at Mother again as she sat huddled on the stool, sipping a cup of tea, cupping her hands around the cup to keep them warm. Poor Mother. Papa had always surrounded her with servants and luxuries. It was a trying time for her.

Life in Alambagh was arduous. Food was scarce, water was scarcer. Soaps were a luxury. Baths had become a weekly occasion. And she was loath to admit that she smelt. But at least she had a change of clothes. Unlike some of the soldiers, who did not have any attire, other than the shirt on their back.

There had been days when they'd hear the sound of firing incessantly. Bullets and muskets would whizz over their heads every few minutes. But now they could relax. It was over a week since the firing had stopped. The handful of soldiers in Alambagh did not pose a threat to the natives. They knew a colossal army would soon be marching in from Cawnpore and were now preparing for the onslaught.

'You know, it is so peaceful here, unlike the Residency. The firing over there was relentless,' said Mother, taking another sip of her tea. 'Every day about fifteen Englishmen or women would die. It was painful.'

'What about the natives?' Rachael asked. 'The ones who were still faithful and were with you in the Residency?'

'Oh, we didn't bother counting them. Their deaths didn't make much of a difference.'

Rachael stared at Mother aghast. How could she be so callous? She would have spat on her if she wasn't her mother. 'They fought against their own people for you and you say their deaths were inconsequential?'

'Ah well!' said Mother as she finished her tea. She got up and walked over to the open window. As she did so, a bullet whizzed past her, missed Rachael's head by half an inch and hit the wall behind. The three women turned pallid. They looked at each other, then at the dent in the wall, too terrified to scream.

'Hai Ram!' screeched Ayah when she finally found her voice. 'I die here one day, for sure.'

'Don't worry, Ayah,' said Rachael. 'It'll soon be over.' She tried to sound calm, but was visibly rattled.

Later that night she tossed and turned in bed, unable to sleep. She kept thinking of how the bullet almost

284

killed her that day. She wondered how the children at the orphanage were. Were they safe? Did they have enough hands and supplies to keep them going? Did they also face such dangers every day? It had never occurred to her, while she was cocooned in the palace, what dangers her own people faced daily. What it was like to live in constant fear of being shot.

She threw her blanket aside and made her way towards the hall. It had been used for dining and entertaining by the king – now it served as a makeshift hospital. She winced as the sound of groans greeted her. 'Not sleepy?' she bent down and whispered to Benjamin, a young soldier who had been wounded in the defence of the Residency.

'I'm freezing,' he replied.

'Let me see if I can find another blanket for you,' said Rachael.

She looked across the hall at Mrs Wilson as she dexterously cleaned a soldier's wound and bandaged it. She had never expected such efficiency from her. But then adversity sometimes brought out the best in some people and she was one of them.

Smiling reassuringly at Edmund, Rachael administered some tincture of opium to reduce his pain. Injured during their march from Dilkusha to Alambagh, he had been in agony since his right arm had been amputated that afternoon. She then wrapped an extra blanket around Benjamin and looked around. Most of the other patients were asleep. And Mrs Wilson was tending to the handful that were still awake.

Rachael sank against the door as she took in the dirt,

the squalor, the rows of injured men and women, the fetid smell. She could not take it anymore. Tears began rolling down her cheeks. She left the hall hastily and stood in the corridor looking at the full moon. She remembered how Salim had looked at her in the moonlight once and remarked that her skin glowed like ivory. Oh, dear Lord. Why could she not stop thinking about him? Oh, how she hated him! For making her cry like no one else ever had. But most of all she hated him for making her continue to love him, despite everything. Yes, she still loved him. She could not lie to herself anymore. She was in love with a man she ought to hate. And she despised herself for loving him so. Why couldn't she have fallen in love with someone like Christopher? Life would have been so much simpler.

Wiping her cheeks with the back of her hand, she slowly made her way back to her room. The last couple of months had been harrowing. Her emotions had swung like a yo-yo and now she felt drained. Would it ever end? Would life ever get back to normal again?

Chapter Twenty-Eight

SALIM

A cold wind was blowing from the Himalayas down to the plains of Lucknow. It was a moonless January night in 1858. The Kaiserbagh Palace was plunged in darkness, the strong breeze having blown out most of the candles.

'There's bad news from everywhere,' Salim heard Nayansukh say as he warmed his hands over the coal brazier. 'Emperor Bahadur Shah Zafar has been defeated. Delhi has been recaptured. Nana Sahib's also been beaten.'

Salim ran his hand up and down his arm as he paced his room. He looked at the dark gloomy shadows thrown by the crystal chandeliers and walked up to where Nayansukh and Ahmed sat. 'What are these Englishmen made of? There were over forty thousand of us, *forty thousand*. Yet we couldn't vanquish a handful of firangis from the Residency.' He absent-mindedly rubbed the spot on his head where he had been hit during the fight in Sikanderbagh. 'Since Delhi's recapture, soldiers have been pouring into Lucknow. It'll be a disgrace if we still can't win.'

Ahmed wrapped his qaba tightly around his shoulders. 'Salim mia, it's true we've got all these men. But they're also a problem. How do we feed these extra mouths? And if Her Majesty is unable to pay them, they go about looting and rioting.'

'Hmm. Ammi has already sold all her jewellery to build the wall around the city. Raja Jia Lal has gone out to arrange for some funds. Let's hope he—'

'Just one,' Ahmed said to Nayansukh as he held out a paan to him. 'Even paan has to be rationed these days.'

Salim remembered the time RayChal had insisted on eating paan. He shook his head. Ya Ali. Everything reminded him of her these days.

'Don't worry, Salim bhai, we'll defeat the firangis this time,' said Nayansukh in a muffled voice, his mouth full of betel juice. 'You've seen all the preparations. The digging of the mines . . .'

Yes, that was true. Since the firangis had left Lucknow two months back – well, most of them had left anyway, except for a small band of soldiers under the command of Outram in Alambagh – there had been frantic preparations in the city for the inevitable attack. The entire city had been converted into a battlefield. Mines had been dug in seven key locations including Chattar Manzil, Chaulakhi Palace and Kaiserbagh. Several military posts had been set up at Alamganj, supported by a second line of defence. There were loopholes in most of the houses, from where they could fire at the firangis. All the streets had been barricaded. Trenches had been dug across the roads in Aminabad, Hussainganj and Hazratganj. A deep moat had been dug around Kaiserbagh.

Hazrat Ammi personally supervised the work being done. Salim was amazed at her energy and zeal. Riding her elephant, she would be with the workers one moment then turn up at the talukdars' homes the next. She'd chide them for their indifferent stance, then hold court in Chaulakhi or give an inspiring speech to the sepoys.

Ahmed cut into Salim's thoughts. 'When life gets back to normal again, Salim mia,' he said, 'one of the first things I'm going to have is mutton biryani and siwaiyaan with lots of balai.' He gave a long sigh. 'Just the thought of them makes my mouth water.'

Salim smiled briefly. 'I doubt if life will ever be normal again.' Yes, it had been a long time since he had smelt the pungent smell of garlic being peeled, of onions being fried and mutton roasting on the grill; the hissing sound of the flames as they licked the fat.

He looked out of the window. It was a dark, moonless night and he could see nothing. He could merely hear the footfall of the nightwatchman as he marched across the palace grounds and his familiar chant of 'Stay awake'. They were awake all right.

He turned back to Nayansukh and Ahmed.

Nayansukh twirled the ends of his moustache and spoke solemnly. 'Don't worry, Salim bhai. They killed my brother-in-law, then my sister. We will avenge their deaths. We'll throw these cow-eating firangis out of our country.'

'Inshah Allah we will,' Salim replied.

It was the middle of March, exactly two years since Abba Huzoor had left for Calcutta. Salim had not seen him since. He wondered how he was. He had been imprisoned in Fort William in Calcutta since the outbreak of the war in Lucknow in 1857. Imprisoned when he was in mourning over the death of his mother and brother. Once a sovereign, now a prisoner. The more Salim thought about it, the more frustrated he felt.

He let out a long sigh and tied his cummerbund. His thoughts flew to Rachael and his Adam's apple moved. He remembered the first time he had met her in Bade Miyan's shop and her hand had touched his hand, nay, his very soul. The first time he heard her playing the piano, her fingers doing Kathak on the keyboard and how he'd been enchanted by her music.

He thought of the first time he saw her in a sharara, a blue sharara that matched the glint in her blue eyes. He recalled the monsoons, the way she had swung around when he called her name, her wet hair flying, a few wet strands plastered to her cheek. And as the maid lit the chandeliers a hundred RayChals had stared back at him, lips quivering, raindrops glistening on her ivory skin.

Salim closed his eyes. He could hear her laughter, smell the light lavender perfume she wore. How soft and delicate her skin was, just like muslin. And her lips felt like a lychee dipped in sweet mango chutney. He shook his head. Why, oh why, did these memories keep clinging to him like a shadow?

He bent down to put on his boots. He thought of the last time he saw her in Dilkusha. How her lovely blue eyes had turned cold as she spat out the words, 'I hate you, Salim.' How he had flinched when she said those words, as though she had slapped him.

Grimacing, Salim felt the tip of his sword with his finger, then put it back in its sheath. Today's battle was going to be crucial. In the last two weeks the firangis had managed to capture Dilkusha, Chakar Kothi, Martiniere, Sikandar Bagh, Shah Najaf, Qadam Rasul, Moti Mahal, Tehri Kothi, Farhat Baksh and Begum Kothi. Today they were bound to attack Kaiserbagh. After all, it was the stronghold of Ammi, the queen regent.

Whatever happened, they could not let Kaiserbagh fall into the hands of the firangis. He picked up his rifle, fitted the bayonet and put it firmly on his back, adjusting the strap.

He felt something hard in his pocket and pulled it out. It was a silver bracelet. He smiled as he remembered how RayChal had dropped it when she had come to the palace for the first time to learn music. She was late and was hurrying down the steps when she dropped it. Just like Cinderella. Salim kissed the bracelet and put it back in his pocket.

He put on his turban. Ya Ali, why did he feel as though someone was twisting his stomach in a thousand knots? He had faced enemy fire several times these last few months, so why this fear? Why this chill running down his spine? He looked heavenward before stepping out of his room, raised his arms, closed his eyes and muttered, 'Allah, be with me.'

Salim put his head on Daima's lap and closed his eyes. She gently massaged his forehead and gradually the creases disappeared. He abruptly pulled her hands away from his forehead and looked at them. They looked like a roti left in the open all night – dried, mottled, crumbly. But hands that gave the best massages in all the land. He kissed them, closed his eyes and put his head back on her lap again.

'We've been beaten, Daima. All's lost.' His voice was anguished, defeated, tired. 'The firangis will be here any moment now.'

Daima patted the hair that had fallen over his forehead. He turned his eyes towards the window. He could hear muskets being fired in the distance.

'We fought as hard as we could, Daima. Men and women – every single one of them. There was not a tree in the garden that did not have soldiers hidden among the branches. But it was in vain.'

'You want to cry?'

He got up hastily. 'Ya Ali, no. Remember what you said to me as a child, Daima? Whenever I came crying to you? "You're a man," you'd say. "And a man cannot cry."'

'Salim mia.' Ahmed and Nayansukh rushed into the room, panting. 'They're here. We've got to run.'

'Outram's forces are killing even the innocent civilians, raping girls. They didn't even spare Darsh

Singh's eight-year-old daughter,' Nayansukh said.

Salim drew out his sword.

'No, mia,' said Ahmed, raising his hand. 'They're too many. We've got to escape to safety with Her Majesty and Birjis.'

'Give me a moment,' Salim uttered and went into his khwabgah. He looked at the faded red kite that hung on the wall. Its tail was slightly torn. It was the first kite he had captured from his opponent. Ahmed and he had run over half a mile to retrieve it.

Next to the kite hung the sword that Abba Huzoor had given him when he had turned sixteen. He touched the jewels studded on the hilt. He looked at the silver platter that stood in a corner; the platter on which his dinner had been served when he kept his first fast of Ramzan. He looked around at the room that had been a mute witness to his childhood, his coming of age, his falling in love. He closed his eyes for a split second, swallowed, pushed the curtain aside and walked out.

He looked at Nayansukh. 'Let's go,' he said hoarsely. 'Ahmed and I will leave the palace first. You follow in ten minutes with Daima.'

Nayansukh nodded. 'Yes, Chote Nawab. And we'll meet at our usual place. At the edge of the Gomti.'

As he quietly scrambled towards the stable with Ahmed, he noticed a handful of pink roses blooming in the garden. Not pink – greyish pink. As though the wind blowing from the cemetery had dusted them with a film of ash. He jumped onto Afreen's bare back and shouted, 'Come, sweetheart, run for your life.'

Once they were outside the palace complex, he looked

back at his home, his palace, his Kaiserbagh. He could still hear the firangis revelling over their loot and the sounds of destruction. Like a pack of hyenas fighting over the lion king's leftovers.

They passed bodies of sepoys recently killed. Some of them were holding swords raised over their heads, some held rifles as though about to shoot. They looked alive, as though they had been frozen in time. There were others with severed arms or legs. The putrid smell of death and decay was everywhere. Salim stepped over the body of a sepoy who had been cut into half and almost shrieked. He covered his ears as the agonised screams of sepoys being tortured rent the air.

'Ya Ali, I can't bear this anymore. I'm going back,' he said.

'Don't be foolish, Salim mia,' Ahmed said. 'They'll chop you up like a vegetable. There are hundreds of them. What'll you do alone?' He looked over his shoulder at Salim. 'Let's proceed to the Gomti and wait for Daima and Nayansukh and news of Her Majesty.'

Soon they were on the banks of the Gomti. Salim looked at its waters. They were red. And this time he was sober. It was indeed blood. Numerous bloated dead bodies floated down the river. He covered his face with his hands and sank to the ground. He wept. He could not stop his tears anymore. His body was racked with sobs.

'Salim mia, get a hold on yourself.' Ahmed's arm slid around his shoulder comfortingly. 'Daima will be here any minute.'

'I'm not a man, Ahmed. That woodcutter was right. RayChal's father was right. I'm a coward.'

'No, Salim mia. You fought like a lion. We were simply outnumbered. And outsmarted.'

'This is not what we wanted. I just wanted to win back my father's kingdom. Where did we go wrong?' He swiped the tears from his face with the back of his hand. 'Abba Huzoor knew all along this would happen. He loved Lucknow too much to see it destroyed. That's why he abdicated quietly. If only I'd understood.'

'Sal—'

Ahmed and Salim looked at each other as they heard the sound of approaching horses, then turned slowly in dread to see who it was. They were his own men.

'Have you any news of Ammi?' Salim asked them.

'Yes. We heard she has escaped with His Majesty, Prince Birjis.'

Salim turned to the sepoys, his hand leaning against the trunk of the tree. 'Is that true?'

'Yes, Chote Nawab. She walked all the way to Ghasyari Mandi. The prince had been wrapped in a carpet and sheets. We heard that her father was carrying him. She then went in a palanquin to Ghulam Raja's house.'

Salim did not say anything. He merely looked at the sepoys thoughtfully.

'Don't worry, Chote Nawab. There are still at least a hundred thousand of us. We will defeat the firangis yet.'

'Chote Nawab,' someone called out in a high-pitched voice. It was Daima. She came running to him, crying hysterically, and fell at his feet. 'Chote Nawab, they've taken him . . . Please save my son, I beg of you . . . they'll kill him.'

Chapter Twenty-Nine

RACHAEL

Rachael sat on the windowsill, overlooking the gardens of Alambagh. Well, it couldn't be called a garden anymore; what with all the trenches ripping it apart, and machines and cannons strategically placed, it looked more like a battlefield. Why, it was a battlefield.

Although it was spring, there was still no sign of life. Most of the trees and shrubs had been destroyed. No sparrows' nests or baby mynahs chirping for more food. Not a single green leaf or shoot in sight. Just decaying flesh and broken bones. The smell of mogra and roses had been replaced by the smell of death. No matter how many bodies the soldiers burnt or buried, the smell of rotting bodies just didn't go away. She saw Ayah lighting a fire using cow-dung pancakes. She hastily turned away from the window as smoke and the foul smell of the cow dung fire wafted into the room.

She thought of Salim. She missed him, missed him as

a soldier misses a limb once it's been amputated. She had tried to hate him but she couldn't. No matter what he did, no matter who he was or whose side he fought on, she would continue to love him. He wasn't even aware she was still in Lucknow. She worried about him. She had heard that Kaiserbagh had fallen. And that all the rebels had either been killed or fled. What if he had also been killed? No, no, she mustn't think like that. Oh God, please don't let anything happen to him.

She heard some soldiers talking and laughing in the adjoining room.

'Hush, someone's approaching,' she heard Christopher say.

Then the thud of the cartridge and the sound of rifles being loaded.

'Hey, relax, it's not a rebel. Just a servant,' said another soldier.

'Let's have some fun,' said Christopher.

Some loud shouts and shrieks made her look out of the window again. She watched grimly as a few soldiers hiding behind windows and pillars pelted handfuls of stones and pebbles between the native servant's feet.

The poor servant, thinking he was under fire from the enemy, ran helter-skelter, his arms raised in the air, muttering, 'Jai Shri Ram, God save me, save me. I no sepoy. I humble servant. Please no kill me.' The soldiers guffawed and jeered.

'Why, it's Ram Singh,' Rachael exclaimed under her breath and ran outside.

'Stop it, stop it all of you,' she shouted.

Ram Singh ran to her and fell at her feet. 'Oh, missy

baba, I so glad to see you. I thought I going to die.'

She held his arms and helped him to his feet. He was still shaking. 'Don't worry, Ram Singh. They were just playing a prank on you.'

'Prank? I almost die of fright! You know, baba, I risk my life to come here. I risk my life every day taking care of your house in the cantonment. I sleep hungry but make sure your dog has eaten. Still we treated badly. Parvati tell me one soldier slap her and make her lick his boots clean.'

'What?'

'They say Indian dog spill English blood. As she also Indian, she has to pay for that sin.'

'But she didn't even take part in the revolt.'

'Yes, the reward we get for being loyal.' Shaking his head, Ram Singh sat down on his haunches. 'I never tell you till now, but when you a baby, Parvati nurse you.'

'Yes, Ayah did mention it to me a couple of times.'

'We also have baby. Baby boy. Parvati feed him after feeding you. But not enough milk for two babies.'

'Oh!'

'Yes, not enough milk for Kartik. He die.'

Rachael covered her mouth in disbelief. 'And yet she loves me so much? Not once has she been bitter towards me.' Her voice was thick with emotion. She was horrified. Ayah lost her baby because of her. Her baby died so she could live. And despite all that, Papa and Mother were so rude to her. Treated her and Ram Singh like slaves!

She remembered the story Ayah and Ram Singh had told her when she was little, about Panna Dai, the maidservant of Prince Udai Singh, who was just a baby then. Or maybe she was his wet nurse. Rachael wasn't sure. But she remembered the story clearly. Her eyes had brimmed with tears and disbelief when she first heard it.

Rana Sangram Singh, the ruler of Chittor, had been killed in battle. His brother Banbir wanted to usurp the throne and came charging into the palace to kill baby Udai Singh, the heir to the throne. Panna Dai, hearing the news, quickly put her own baby in the royal cot, and kept Prince Udai Singh in her arms. Thinking the baby in the cot was the prince, Banbir drew his sword and killed him. What agony, what pain must Panna dai have gone through as she watched her own baby being slain!

Rachael's eyes filled with tears. Ayah was her Panna Dai.

'Baba?'

'Yes, Ram Singh?'

'I forget. I come to tell you I finished repairing outhouse. You can come there today. It not comfortable, but better than this.'

'That's excellent news, Ram Singh. Mother and I will come there today itself. Not sure about Papa, though.'

'You don't have to wear these native clothes anymore, you know,' said Mother, as Rachael walked into their makeshift bedroom.

'I know. I wear them because I like them.' And they remind me of Salim, Rachael wanted to add. 'I have some good news for you, Mother. Ram Singh was here. The outhouse is ready and we can move there today itself.'

'Oh, thank the good Lord,' said Mother. 'Finally a

place of my own. You have no idea how I've lived these past few months.' Mother stopped speaking. She walked over to the gilt-edged mirror and fiddled with the lace on her cuffs and collars. 'Ayah,' she called out.

Ayah hurried into the room. 'Yes, memsahib?'

'Help me get dressed and pack. We're going back to the cantonment.'

'Yes, memsahib,' answered Ayah cheerily.

Rachael pulled out a pitara from under the bed.

Mother sat down on a chair as Ayah brushed her hair.

'Although, I have to admit, this place is better than the Residency,' said Mother. 'There were so many of us, crammed in that hellhole.'

'Yes, memsahib,' Ayah humbly agreed and helped her put on her shoes.

Rachael picked up her bodice, petticoat, chemise and stays and put them in the box. She gathered the chador and began folding it. A soft smile flickered over her lips as she remembered how Salim had wrapped it around her.

Mother handed Rachael her skirts to put in the box. 'And you know what the funniest part was, Rachael?' she asked.

'What?' Rachael asked as she pressed down on the clothes. The pitara was almost full.

'We felt bad when we had to leave the Residency. Despite all the hardships, the dangers, we didn't want to leave.'

'Mother, you've told me all this several times. But not once have you asked me what happened to me. Pray tell me, are you not curious to know where I was, how I survived?' Rachael asked, with a tinge of bitterness in her voice.

'You know I fell ill. We couldn't even go to Cawnpore with the rest. They must be well on their way to England while I'm still languishing here.'

'No, Mother,' Rachael said contemptuously, as she watched her tie the ribbons of her bonnet. 'You had plenty of time after you recovered. But you weren't interested.' Her voice dropped to a hoarse whisper. 'You never did care for me, Mother, did you?'

She swallowed her tears as she punched her mother's flannel waistcoats into a bag. Her voice was barely audible now. 'Why have you never told me Ayah lost a son?'

Rachael noticed the look of alarm on Ayah's face as she looked at her, then at Mother, mumbled an excuse and hastily left the room. There was a long silence as Rachael struggled to get a hold on her emotions.

'I lost one too,' Mother replied quietly in a teary voice.

'How did Richard die, Mother?' Rachael asked as she blew her nose.

Mother sat down on the bed. 'Richard was three years old then. He was such a beautiful baby. Red lips, and a head covered with golden locks. His cheeks looked like ripe peaches.'

Rachael looked at Mother. Her face had never looked so warm and soft before.

Mother continued speaking. Her voice was trembling. 'You were in my tummy then. I went into labour one month early. And we got stuck in a mosquito-infested village. Never before had I been in so much pain. It was a prolonged labour. Eighteen hours. Perhaps twenty. Who knows? It felt like forever. The waves of pain kept coming. Faster, stronger, never ceasing.' She paused and took a deep breath.

'Then Richard got the malaria. The native doctor gave him some medicine but his condition worsened. The way his body burnt before it went cold. My son was dying, Rachael – oh, how my baby suffered! He burnt in a high fever for three whole days. His temperature would suddenly plunge, then after a few hours shoot up again. It was horrendous. To watch your own flesh and blood suffer thus. I kept telling myself he would get better, that he'd pull through. But he kept slipping, and by the morning of the third day I knew he would not survive . . . He had a lovely smile. The last time I saw him – despite the fever, despite the pain – the moment he saw me, he flashed me an angelic smile.

Mother broke down in tears. 'If you had waited and come on time, we would have been in Lucknow before you came.'

Rachael looked at Mother with a new enlightenment. She spoke slowly. 'So all these years you've held *me* responsible for Richard's death? All these years?'

'No, I didn't.'

'You've never loved me.'

'That's not true,' said Mother, as she looked at Rachael with tear-filled eyes. '. . . I didn't even get the chance to say goodbye. I was too weak to leave the bed. And it was the height of summer – hottest day of the year. They could not keep his body for too long in that heat. There was no ice available in that village. So they buried him. Buried him quietly when I was sleeping. I was anguished when I was told. I pounced on your Papa. I almost slapped him. I was hysterical.

'In my sorrow I forgot I had given birth to a new baby. I did not see you for two weeks. Whenever Mrs Wilson asked me ever so gently, "Don't you want to see your little angel?" I'd push her away. "No!" I'd scream. "I'm not ready." It wasn't that I wasn't ready. I was afraid to look at you. I was afraid I'd fall in love again. My heart had been ripped apart by Richard's death. I didn't want it to happen ever again.' Mother covered her face with her hands and started sobbing.

'Oh Mother.' Rachael's voice dropped to a whisper. 'You did not lose one child that day. You lost two.'

'I'm sorry, my child,' Mother sobbed.

Rachael looked at Mother. She knew she should hate her for not loving her, for holding her responsible for the death of her brother, but watching her now, bent double with grief, she could not help but feel sorry for her. After all, she was her mother. She sat down on the bed beside her. She took her hand in hers and caressed it as she sniffed back her tears.

'Oh Rachael, I'm sorry,' Mother sobbed and put her head on her shoulder. 'You know, even as a baby, you were independent. You never did need me. The first time I held you in my arms, you kicked and screamed and turned red, until Ayah took you in her arms.'

'I have always needed you; I will always need you. You're my mother,' Rachael whispered slowly as she caressed Mother's hair, tears spilling over her cheeks.

They sat there, holding each other's hands for a long time. Rachael finally spoke. 'I think we ought to get moving if we wish to reach the cantonment before dark. I'll go and inform Papa.'

Rachael remembered the look on Salim's face after his musical instruments had been auctioned. It was the look of a person who had lost the love of his life. She thought of his father – Nabob Wajid Ali Shah. He had abdicated the throne like a gentleman. He had full faith in the English sense of justice. But what had come of that? His mother lay dead, after spending a fortune and some agonising months in England in a vain attempt to seek justice from Queen Victoria. And he lay in a prison in Calcutta. Perhaps the people of Oudh had been right in rising against the Company?

She entered Papa's makeshift office. She ducked as a boot came flying through the air and hit the servant who stood trembling near the door. It was followed by a loud curse. 'Son of a pig.'

Helping the servant to his feet, Rachael nodded at him to leave the room. 'Papa, at least now stop mistreating the natives.'

'You can't trust these vipers, Rachael. Even after we've been their masters for all these years, they dared revolt against us!'

'And still we haven't learnt our lesson. Even after all these years of serving us night and day, they're still struggling to survive. Look at Ram Singh, Papa. He risked his life to take care of our home and belongings, yet he's still as poor as the day he first came to us. All he ever got in return for his hard work and loyalty is abuse! I don't blame the natives for revolting against us.'

Papa stared at her in disbelief. 'Has that son of the singing, dancing nabob been poisoning your mind against us?'

'Of course not,' Rachael snapped. 'And his name is Salim.'

Papa sifted through the papers on his desk as though he hadn't heard her. 'Oh, they'll pay for the mutiny all right. Every one of them. We will torture them to their deaths. Raze all their buildings, mosques and temples to the ground. We'll bring them down on their knees, the bastards. We shall have our revenge.'

'Revenge?' Rachael knew she was shouting but she didn't care if the whole of Alambagh could hear her. 'Aren't we Christians, Papa? Aren't we the worshippers of Christ? The Christ who said if someone slaps you, offer him your other cheek?'

'It's not just revenge. It's atoning for their sins. Retribution.' Papa banged his fist on the table as he said each word.

Rachael could feel her face flame with anger. She was appalled by Papa's strident views. 'I thought the English were known for their justice and fair play,' she ground out through clenched teeth. 'First you snatch away what rightfully belongs to them. And then when they protest you trample them? That's justice? Retribution?' Her arms tautened as she folded them and stared at her father.

'Young lady, are you trying to tell me you support the mutiny?'

Rachael paced to the window and looked out. She walked back to Papa's desk. Gripping the edge of his desk, she stared him straight in the eye and spat out, 'Perhaps I do.'

Papa stared at her as though he could not believe what he had just heard.

'In that case, I have nothing say,' he said quietly, as he sat down on his chair and picked up some papers.

Rachael tried to get a grip on her anger. She took a deep breath and tried to distract herself. She looked around the room. It looked more like a storeroom than an office. There was a huge pile of ammunition and gunpowder against the wall in one corner of the room. Some files and papers were scattered on a low table. A rickety chair and papa's desk were the only furniture in the room that gave it the semblance of an office. A qatat still hung on the wall. Two fans made of peacock feathers stood in a corner. A chandelier made of red glass hung from the ceiling. It looked as strange as an elephant would look in Sherwood Forest.

She wondered what the room had been used for before it had been taken over by the English. Perhaps it was a begum's room. Or one of the princes'. It might even have been Nabob Wajid Ali Shah's room. What would he say if he saw the state of the room right now?

She turned back to Papa as he lit his cigar and screwed up her nose. She hated the smell and wished he would stop smoking. 'I came to tell you that Mother and I are leaving for the cantonment. Ram Singh has repaired the outhouse.'

'Oh, that's good. I'll be there before it gets dark. I think it's time for the English to celebrate. The mutiny has been more or less crushed.'

'Not mutiny, Papa. The natives call it "the war of independence".'

Chapter Thirty

SALIM

Salim looked at Daima. The only other time he had seen her so distraught was when Chutki had died. He pulled her slowly to her feet. 'What happened, Daima?'

'We were just about to escape from the West Gate of Kaiserbagh when some firangis saw us . . . they caught hold of Nayansukh . . . dragged him to the palace.' Daima joined her hands. 'I beg of you, Chote Nawab, please save my son . . . they'll kill him.'

Salim covered Daima's hands with his. 'Daima, don't embarrass me like this. Isn't Nayansukh my brother as well? Don't worry; I won't come back empty-handed.'

'I'll come as well, Salim mia,' Ahmed said.

'No, Ahmed, we can't leave Daima alone. You take care of her,' Salim said as he jumped onto Afreen's back. He was off before Ahmed could even begin to protest.

As Salim rode back towards Kaiserbagh, he realised there was a stillness in the city that had not been there for a long time. The stillness that is found just before dawn is about to break. For the last few months, every single hour, even at night, had been interspersed with intermittent firing. The firing had now stopped. All that could be heard were the groans of the tortured and the wounded and the shouts of glee of the looters.

A huge fire burnt in the garden, consuming broken furniture, shreds of shawls from which the gold and silver threads had been mercilessly plucked, ripped portraits of his ancestors.

That was not all that was offered to the flames. A sepoy had been tied to a pole and was slowly roasting over the fire. A couple of sepoys had been stripped of their clothes and were being branded with hot iron rods. The smell of skin burning, mingled with the coppery smell of blood, was ghastly, the shrieks of the sepoys unbearable.

Salim jumped off his horse, his teeth clenched, his hands curled into fists as he entered the palace. It looked as though a jinni had picked up the palace, given it a good shake, turned it upside down, then put it down again. The marble floors were covered with fragments of broken china, glass, mirrors and crystals. Marble statues had been smashed, as had the lamps and chandeliers. Piles of silk, shawls, dresses, carpets, muslin, garments of gold, embroidered velvet saddles, swords with hilts and scabbards studded with jewels lay everywhere. The ill-fated palace, having been stripped of its curtains and draperies, now stood naked to the glare of foreign eyes.

Salim picked up a piece of a broken statue; the statue of a woman in a pleated dress, her hair tied in a bun, holding a hoop. It used to be Abba Huzoor's favourite. He had been so pleased with the sculptor when he presented the statue to him, he had given him the pearl necklace he was wearing. Salim closed his eyes. The anguish he felt was akin to the pain he felt when walking over red-hot coals on Muharram.

The firangis were everywhere, filling their pockets with gold and jewels and gems. But Nayansukh was nowhere to be seen. Salim rushed from room to room looking for him. Then he saw him, in the courtyard, just as a firangi hit him hard in his stomach with the back of his rifle.

Nayansukh groaned.

'Where are your queen and the prince?' The firangi asked as he raised the rifle again.

'I don't know,' Nayansukh moaned. This time the rifle hit the side of his mouth and sent him spiralling to the floor. Blood oozed out of his mouth.

'Stop it,' Salim shouted as he charged towards Nayansukh's tormentors, his sword in hand. The firangis were surprised by this intrusion and Salim managed to kill one, then another. But they were too many.

Heels clicked on the tiled floor. Salim turned to look at who it was. It was Colonel Bristow.

'Now, now, what do we have here?' he asked, pointing his cigar at Nayansukh and Salim.

'Sir, this fellow here, we caught him escaping from the palace. I'm sure he knows the whereabouts of the queen but refuses to tell us.'

The firangi soldier then pointed to Salim. 'Sir, I think he's one of the nawab's sons.'

'Is he now?' asked the colonel as he lit his cigar. 'Did you just kill two of my men?'

Salim said nothing, his chin jutting out haughtily.

'Down on your hands and feet, you two. I want you to lick every drop of blood that you just spilt on the floor. That'll teach you to value English blood.'

Salim stood with his feet apart, hands behind his back. He looked at Nayansukh. His presence had revived Nayansukh's courage. The two exchanged a brief look but did not budge. The firangis hit the back of their legs with their rifles, bringing them down on their knees. They still refused to obey.

Colonel Bristow took a long puff at his cigar and watched the rings of smoke as they slowly disappeared. 'Bring them outside,' he commanded.

The soldiers dragged Salim and Nayansukh to the garden.

Colonel Bristow turned to Nayansukh. 'Since you will not tell us where the queen is, we have no use of you.'

Salim watched helplessly as they tied Nayansukh to the mouth of a cannon. He shook his head – just like the goats do, shaking and bleating, fear clearly visible in their eyes, before being slaughtered on Eid.

Tears of rage sprang to Salim's eyes as Colonel Bristow ordered, 'Fire!' The cannon boomed. Salim spluttered as black smoke filled the air before him. He writhed and struggled against his captors as the air cleared.

Nayansukh's body had been blown to bits and scattered all over the garden. Only his arms remained tied to the cannon. His head landed with a soft thud on the grass a few inches away from Salim's feet.

The colonel now turned to Salim. 'I will spare you your life as you brought my daughter back to me alive. But I shall punish you for molesting her.'

'I did nothing of the sort.'

'Lower your eyes when you speak to an officer.'

Salim lifted his chin. 'Those that lower their eyes are either ashamed or cowards. I'm neither.'

'Then we shall have to lower them for you. Mike, get me those iron rods and make sure they're hot.'

Salim stood still, his feet apart, his chin jutting out defiantly. For some reason he did not feel afraid. Perhaps the knowledge that he had lost everything – his brother, his sister, his home, his kingdom, his love – and there was nothing else to lose, gave him courage.

He looked heavenward and whispered, 'Ya Ali,' then looked scornfully at Colonel Bristow as a firangi soldier approached him with two iron rods.

Chapter Thirty-One

RACHAEL

It was late in the afternoon when Rachael and Mother reached their home in the cantonment with Ayah and Ram Singh. Rachael now sat sombrely in what had once been a cheerful room, full of different hues of the rainbow. Now it was black and grey. She looked sadly at another book that was hopelessly charred and put it in the box containing objects to be thrown away. She picked up a blackened rod, then realising what it was, hastily wiped the soot covering it with the edge of her dress. Smiling, she put it to her mouth and gave a delighted trill. It was the flute Salim had given her when she had played the harmonium without making a single error.

A crow sitting on top of the roof began cawing continuously.

'Missy baba, crow cawing bad omen,' said Ayah.

'It's just a silly superstition, Ayah,' said Rachael.

Nevertheless, she was gripped with an uneasy fear. She

wondered if Salim was safe. She shouldn't have walked away from him like that, the last time she was with him. Perhaps she should have let him explain. She wondered if she would ever see him again.

She looked around at what remained of her room and remembered her luxurious room in Salim's palace. The four-poster bed with the legs and headrest covered in gold, the wardrobe full of exquisite Indian dresses, the silver lamp that stood in a corner, the large spittoon and betel box. And how could she forget the smooth marble basin of water that stood right next to her bed?

Salim would come to her room whenever he was in the palace to make sure she was comfortable in her new surroundings. He had said to her once that as long as he lived he would never let her face any discomfort whatsoever. He had kept his word. Everyone in the palace treated her like a princess. 'For us, a guest is akin to Allah,' they would say.

It was painful going through her belongings. Most of them had not escaped the flames. Everything was gone, even the music she had composed and all her music books.

She hated Sudha's relatives for torching her home. Why did they have to destroy her abode? All this burning, killing, destroying – it was so wrong.

She wanted to run away. Yes, she would run away with Salim. Far, far away from this hatred and bloodshed. She was tired of all this misery and destruction.

Papa walked in just then, looking pleased.

'So finally you're here. You look happy, Papa.'

'Yes.' He rubbed his hands with glee. 'Lucknow is

finally in our hands once more. The rebellion has been crushed.' He banged his fist on the crumbling wall. 'All we need to do now is to raze the entire city to the ground. Demolish every single palace. Reduce these miserable wretches to nothing. So they never even dream of rebelling again.'

Rachael did not say anything and continued sifting through her belongings.

'Now no one can stop my promotion. It's been long overdue. I even put your tormentor in his place.'

'Who?'

'That prince.'

'Salim? He never tormented me! On the contrary . . .'

'But you said he molested you.'

'I said nothing of the sort, Papa.' Rachael's voice rose sharply. 'And this is not the first time you've misinterpreted what he did or said . . .'

Papa said nothing.

Rachael was edging on becoming hysterical. 'Where is he? Pray tell me what you've done to him.'

Ram Singh entered the room. 'Missy baba, someone here to see you urgently.'

Rachael rushed outside. Ahmed stood at the gate. Rachael walked up to him and looked at him questioningly.

Ahmed coughed and looked down at his shoes. 'Ma'am, Salim is missing.'

'What?' she asked feebly. She had a sinking feeling in the pit of her stomach.

'He went to Kaiserbagh to look for Nayansukh and

hasn't returned. I thought it might be easier to find him if you came with us.'

'Yes, of course.'

'You're not going anywhere with that native, especially not at this hour.' It was Papa. He stood behind her, with his hands in his pockets.

Rachael turned to face him. 'I am, Papa,' she replied in a voice laced with anger.

'Are you going to disobey me?' asked Papa.

'Yes, Papa,' Rachael replied.

She pushed past him before he could stop her. She opened the gate, then looked back at him. 'Papa, if I find that you've done something to my Salim, I'm never coming back to this house again . . . Ram Singh.'

'Yes, missy baba?' Ram Singh answered, joining his hands, his head lowered.

'Come with me,' Rachael ordered and hurriedly got into the carriage. Ahmed and Ram Singh followed. She looked out of the window as the carriage trundled along. People were fleeing in all directions. Some palanquin-bearers were running alongside her carriage. As soon as they saw a group of English soldiers appear around the corner, they dropped their doli abruptly and ran to save their lives. A hapless begum crawled out of the palanquin and looked around in terror. She had no clue how to save her life and honour, never having stepped out of her home before.

Rachael felt sorry for her. She ought to stop and help her, but no, first she must find Salim. She shuddered as they passed hundreds of men hanging from trees, necks broken, eyes popping out. She bit her thumbnail. No sound could be heard now, except the wheels of the carriage and the horses' feet.

'Don't you worry, baba. We find him. He be all right,' Ram Singh said.

'I hope you'll forgive him, ma'am. Salim mia, he's . . . umm . . . very fond of you. He would've told you the truth if he hadn't feared losing you.'

Rachael gave a small smile. 'You're a good friend, Ahmed,' she said.

Ahmed dimpled, blushed, reddened.

Rachael stood before the palace gate, speechless. She could not recognise Kaiserbagh. The glistening white palace buildings did not look grand anymore. Rather, they stood huddled together like widows, mourning the death of their city.

It was twilight. The garden was covered with dead bodies. The three of them began searching for Salim frantically as the light began to diminish. Rachael looked at the banyan tree. It was the same tree under which she had sat with Salim, oh so long ago. They had talked about their children and grandchildren.

'If I come back here with my grandchildren, would the tree still be there?' she had asked.

Salim had not replied but had grinned at her instead, as he imagined how she would look when she was carrying his child.

Rachael felt numb as she looked at the dead bodies hanging from the tree. The fetid stench of death and decay was overpowering. She covered her mouth as bile rose in her throat. The only signs of life in the entire garden were the vultures picking on the dead bodies. Fattened on the ever-increasing carrion, they felt too slothful to budge at the approach of three lone living beings and continued feasting.

She gasped as a vulture scooped down and started pulling at the remains of a sepoy just a few paces away from her. Suppressing a scream, she took a hasty step back, and stumbled over a body with his face down. A glint of silver caught her eye. His hand was clutching what looked like a bracelet. Her bracelet. The one she had lost. Yes, it must be Salim.

Rachael turned deathly pale. She neither wept nor spoke. She simply stood and stared at Salim's body and the bracelet. After a long moment she looked at Ahmed and Ram Singh. They nodded their heads. She bent down and gently rolled Salim over onto his back. It was almost dark and she could not see his face clearly. As she grew used to the dark and her eyes began to focus, she looked at his face tenderly. Her hands flew to her face and she screamed.

She stared at his face. His dark passionate eyes, eyes that often teased her, spoke to her, made love to her, were no more.

Rachael sank to the ground. Her sobs echoed through the eerie silence. Oh why, oh why did she say to him that she hated him? Why did she not try to see him again? Why did she not give him a chance to explain?

Ahmed walked over to the other side of the tree. She could not see his face. He leant against its huge trunk. His entire body shook as he broke down.

'Missy baba,' shouted Ram Singh. 'He breathing. He still alive.'

Chapter Thirty-Two

SALIM

Salim touched the ground beneath him. It was not mud that met his fingers but bed sheets. He was on a bed. He strained but could not hear a single sound. He wondered where he was and who had brought him here. How long had he lain here?

He felt a hand touch his forehead lightly, then brush back his hair. Clutching the hand, he asked incredulously, 'RayChal?' He heard a movement, but no other sound. He groped urgently for her diamond ring. 'Ya Ali, it is you. I could recognise these hands anywhere.'

She did not answer. He felt her tremble. Suddenly he felt a wetness on his cheeks. Her tears. He did not attempt to wipe them. They felt like balm. He started to sit up, winced as pain shot through him and touched the swathes of cloth covering his eyes. The memory of two hot iron rods coming towards him flashed before his mind. His entire body went taut and beads of perspiration covered his forehead. He felt Rachael's hands on his shoulders and gradually relaxed.

'Don't get up,' she whispered.

Salim drew her into his embrace. Slowly, gently, she wrapped her arms tightly about him as he clung to her. His Adam's apple moved as her body curved to fit snugly into his. Time stood still as neither moved nor spoke.

'RayChal, where exactly am I?' he finally asked.

'This is a small country house a few miles south of Lucknow. It belonged to a friend of mine. Don't worry, you're safe here.'

Salim nodded as Rachael gently wiped the perspiration from his forehead.

'You came back,' he whispered as his fingers lightly touched her cheek, still not believing she was there.

'I was here all along.'

'And I thought you were in England. Had forgotten me.'

'I tried. I couldn't.'

Salim sighed and ran his fingers through her hair. 'You must,' he said slowly.

'Why?'

'When I asked your father for your hand, he was worried how I would support you. Now I have even less.' Salim clutched his bedsheets till his knuckles turned white. Even the thought of that firangi made his blood boil. He was going to kill him one day. Run his sword through each of his eyes.

Get a hold on yourself, Salim, he chided himself. Not in front of RayChal. It seemed she had nursed him back to health. The last thing she deserved was his anger.

'My father is no more,' Rachael said through gritted teeth.

'What?'

'He destroyed . . .' She hesitated, struggling for the right words. 'Something close to my heart. Do you know how it pains me every time I look at you?'

Salim heard her sniffing and blowing her nose.

'I'm sorry,' she said. 'You must hurt so much more.'

'Maybe not,' he replied gently. 'At least I don't have to look at it . . .' he said, pointing to his face. 'Do I look that hideous?'

Rachael caressed his hand. 'They say people in love always look beautiful. Their faces glow with an inner light.'

'In that case I don't think we need candles anymore.'

Rachael laughed. It sounded more like a sob. She pressed his hand firmly. 'We'll pull through, Salim,' she sniffed. 'I don't know how, but God knows we will. I'll make sure we do.'

Salim nodded and gently kissed her hand. 'Yes,' he replied. 'As long as you're there.'

Salim got out of bed early the next morning. He felt a lot better today. But his head still hurt, especially when he moved. He had only walked a couple of paces when he stumbled over a stool. The candle stand that stood on it crashed to the floor.

'Ya Ali! I won't leave that Colonel Bristow. He reduced me to this. I will take my revenge,' Salim muttered through clenched teeth.

'Salim mia, who are you planning to avenge?'

'Ahmed, how is Ammi? Is she safe? Where is she?'

'Sit down first.' So saying, Ahmed made Salim sit on the bed and sat down next to him. 'She's in Bundi. She's carrying on her struggle against the firangis from there.'

'We should go there and join her.'

'We will, Salim mia. Don't get agitated. We'll discuss this later.'

'Why later? I'm fine now. So what if I can't see. I'm sure I can make myself useful. Plan out the strategy, organise . . . You know, Ahmed, day and night there's just one face I see. Colonel Felix Bristow! I want my revenge, Ahmed. I feel like scooping out the eyes of every single firangi with my bare hands. That fiend took my sight. I want to take away something from him that will make him pine for the rest of his life.' He clutched the sheets in a tight grip. His knuckles turned white as he did so.

'You've already done that, Salim mia.'

'What do you mean?'

'Rachael has sworn never to speak to him again. And you know how much he loved her.'

'Wh—?' Salim heard the rustle of skirts and stopped speaking.

'Did someone say my name?' Rachael queried.

'Y-yes, Ahmed was just saying that RayChal is going to be here soon, so he better be going.'

'No, Salim mia, I just ca—'

'You were going, Ahmed,' Salim said smoothly, pushing him off the bed.

'All right, I'm leaving. Good day, Rachael ma'am.'

'Goodbye, Ahmed,' Rachael replied. Salim could hear the amusement in her voice.

'I'm glad you're here. I wanted to speak to you about something,' Salim said.

'Yes?'

Salim cleared his throat. 'Can I have some water please?'

Rachael handed him an abkhora. The water was cool and smelt of the moist clay of which the earthenware vessel was made.

'I know I proposed to you . . .' He took her hand in his and touched the ring on her ring finger. 'I can see you're wearing it. But . . .' He paused, struggling for the right words. 'I want my ring back.'

'What?'

'You don't want to marry a blind man.'

'You can walk, can't you?'

'Yes, of course.'

'You can hear, speak?'

'Ya Ali, I'm blind, not deaf and dumb.'

'Exactly. Everyone has a flaw. You can't see, I can't sing. Nobody's perfect, remember?'

Salim shook his head slowly as a small smile lifted the corners of his mouth. 'How easily you have said this, RayChal. Have you any idea how difficult it's going to be for you?'

'Pray tell me what I have to do to convince you? Should I tie a cloth over my eyes like Gandhari?'

'How do you know about Gandhari?'

'Ayah and Ram Singh used to tell me stories from

323

the *Ramayana* and *Mahabharata* when I was little.'

'But I'll feel—'

Rachael put a finger on his lips. 'Hush. I will either marry you or none at all.'

It was almost three months since Salim had come round and he hadn't felt better in a long time. He lifted his sword high and brought it down with a clang on Ahmed's sword.

'Not bad, Chote Nawab, not bad at all,' said Daima as she entered the living room with a tray of food. She put her hand lovingly on his cheek. 'How are you feeling today, my son?'

He sniffed the air appreciatively.

Daima laughed. 'I've made all your favourite dishes and am going to feed you myself.'

As she put a morsel of rumali roti and kebab in Salim's mouth, Ahmed chirped, 'Daima, for me?'

'Go away, you glutton . . . this is only for my son,' said Daima.

'Let him also eat, Daima. Otherwise he'll cast an evil eye on me and I won't be able be digest the food,' said Salim.

'Aah!' Ahmed opened his mouth wide.

'Eat it yourself,' scoffed Daima.

She fed Salim a morsel. 'Those brutes! As though taking my son and daughter wasn't enough, they had to leave you blind as well.' She began to sniff.

'Who said I can't see?' Salim said. 'As long as you're there, Ahmed is there, RayChal is there, how can I not see?'

Daima hugged Salim and started crying even more loudly. 'Chote Nawab?'

'Yes, Daima?'

'I have always been like a mother to you?'

'Ya Ali, you *are* my mother. Why do you ask?'

'And I have never asked you for anything . . . If I ask you for something today, will you do it for me?'

'Can I ever say no to you, Daima?'

'Leave this country . . . Go and settle down somewhere with Rachael . . . Where these brutal firangis can never reach you.'

'You're right, Daima. This war, this enmity, this bloodshed is not for us.' It was Rachael.

Now when did she come in? How long had she been there? Had she seen Daima feeding him? Salim felt a little embarrassed at the thought.

'Besides . . .' Rachael paused and sat down on the bed next to Salim, adding shyly, 'I don't want our baby to grow up here.'

'Why, what's wro—?' Salim stopped speaking, his mouth falling open. 'What did you say? Our baby? Our *baby*, RayChal?'

'Congratulations, Salim mia. I'm going to become an uncle,' Ahmed gushed.

'Hai Ram, I shall have to get you two married soon,' said a worried Daima.

A slow smile spread over Salim's face. He found Rachael's hand and pressed it hard. He knew Rachael was smiling and blushing, her face turning red. Suddenly the pain, the hopelessness he had been feeling since he had lost his sight seemed far away. A baby, his baby, his own flesh.

'But what do you mean? Why can't our son grow up here? Both his parents did?' he asked.

'It's not the same,' replied Rachael.

Salim did not say anything.

'It's not the city we grew up in,' she continued. 'It's a dead city. Kaiserbagh has been demolished. I have never seen anything so beautiful so ruthlessly destroyed before. Each time I remember what Lucknow was and what it has now become, my heart weeps. We have to go, Salim, we must.' She grabbed Salim's hand with both her hands and shook it hard. 'I cannot bear this grief anymore. I don't want my child to grow up playing with skeletons and bones. Do you remember what you had promised me in Vilayati Bagh? That you would make a Dooja Jahaan, another world for me?'

Salim's Adam's apple moved, but his face betrayed no emotions. He nodded quietly.

'Let's take him to another world, to a world beyond the reach of hatred and brutality,' Rachael added.

Salim took Rachael's hand in his and kissed it tenderly. He looked up when he heard the shuffling of feet near the door.

'Have the others left?' he asked softly.

'Yes,' Rachael whispered.

A soft smile spread across his face as his thoughts turned once more to his baby.

Salim knew it was a bright sunny day. He could sense an orange glow through his vacant eyes as he entered the church. He fidgeted with his collar as he waited in front of the altar, with Ahmed beside him. It was cool inside the church. He could smell incense, candles burning and fresh roses and lilies. The church bells began to ring and someone started playing the organ.

'She's here,' Ahmed whispered as he nudged Salim with his elbow.

'What's she doing?' Salim asked.

'She's entering the church slowly, on Ram Singh's arm. He's feeling ill at ease in a suit,' he chortled.

Salim wiped the sweat from his brow.

'Nervous, Salim mia?'

'Ya Ali, why should I be nervous? I'm not a girl,' he muttered under his breath. 'Tell me, how's she looking?'

'Like a lovely orange jalebi, dipped in lots of syrup,' Ahmed gushed.

Salim shook his head in exasperation. 'Ya Ali, tell me the colour of the dress she's wearing.'

'It's orange, the colour of kesar . . .'

Salim covered his mouth. 'Yes! I knew it. She must look like the sun at dawn, slowly rising in the east, to start a new day, a new life.'

Chapter Thirty-Three

RACHAEL

Rachael looked around the church pensively. It was a small deserted church. Two candles burnt at the altar. All except the first row of pews were empty. Since she was a little girl she had imagined walking into a packed church on Papa's arms, a large banquet and lots of dancing.

'My Rachael's wedding's going to be so grand the whole of Lucknow will be talking about it for days. Even the nabob,' Papa used to say.

She fidgeted with her veil as she heard Salim ask Ahmed what she was wearing. Today, more than ever, she wished he could see. She wanted him to see his bride. *Why, oh why, Papa, did you do it?* And what was worse, he didn't regret it. 'I could have done worse. I could have killed him. After all, he was a rebel,' he had said.

She stole a look at Salim. He looked charming in a cream angarkha with fine gold embroidery and cream wide-bottomed pyjamas. His cap and pointed shoes were the same colour and were also embroidered in gold. He had tied a black cloth over his eyes, which gave him a mysterious charm.

Rachael looked at Mother. She had promised she would come for the wedding when she went to invite her. Since her outburst that day in Alambagh, Mother was making an effort to reach out to her daughter. She still wasn't able to display her affections much, but the ice that had gathered around her heart all those years ago was slowly melting. She did not approve of her marrying a native, and him an invalid too, but agreed to go with whatever Rachael wanted. Earlier Rachael would have put it down to indifference. But now she knew it was her way of saying that in Rachael's happiness lay her happiness.

Mother looked at her just then and their eyes met. She smiled and gesticulated that Rachael was looking lovely. Rachael smiled back at her. The priest commenced the sermon and she turned back to look at the altar.

He was now reading the marriage vows. Rachael's hands shook a little as she put the ring on Salim's finger.

After they were pronounced man and wife, the small party traipsed back to the country house.

Rachael walked over to the basin. The room used to be a guest bedroom. Now it was being used as a changing room for the bride. She splashed some cold water on her face. She hoped the nikaahnama would be over soon so she could slip into some light cotton garments.

'The moulvi is here . . . are you ready?' said Daima, coming into the room.

Rachael blushed as Daima looked her over from head to toe.

'My, how lovely you look . . . I'm sure Chote Nawab couldn't take his eyes off you,' said Daima. Then realising what she had just said, she became sober. She gave her a box carved intricately in silver and lined with velvet. 'Open it . . . It's yours.'

Rachael opened the box. There was a magnificent gold necklace inlaid with rubies and diamonds with matching earrings and bracelets.

'This is beautiful, Daima. But I can't accept it.'

'You can't say no, as it belongs to you . . . It has merely been in my safe keeping for the last eighteen-odd years.'

'I don't understand.'

Daima smiled. 'When Salim was about five, he saw me getting dressed on Eid . . . my husband was alive then . . . Salim saw this necklace . . . Janab-e-Alia had given it to me as a wedding present . . . I was about to put it on when he said, "I want to wear it." I said to him, "This is a girl's necklace . . . everyone will tease you and call you a girl if you wear it." He pouted . . . I could not see him sad . . . so I said to him, "I'll give this necklace to your wife, all right, Chote Nawab?" He nodded . . . A few days later, when I wore the same necklace for a wedding, he scolded me: "Daima, why are you wearing my wife's necklace?" . . . After that I never wore it again.'

Rachael hugged the old woman. 'I don't know what to say. Thank you. Thank you ever so much.'

Daima led her into the living room. The room had been divided into two by curtains. Rachael sat down demurely on the takhat with Daima. The moulvi was seated with Salim and Ahmed on the other side of the curtain. He began reading the nikaahnama. She couldn't comprehend a word of what he was saying. She looked at Daima bewildered.

'Don't worry . . . just imitate me,' said Daima.

Daima lowered her head. Rachael lowered hers. Daima nodded. Rachael nodded as well.

Just then the moulvi's daughter appeared at the door and gestured to Daima. Daima nodded, then waved at her. Rachael nodded and waved. Daima smacked her head lightly. Rachael stuck out her tongue and grinned.

The nikaah was soon over and food was served. Rachael was still eating when Mother approached her. 'I ought to leave now or your papa will get suspicious.' She clutched her hands. 'You must leave Lucknow soon. Tomorrow night. Somebody whispered to your father that you're planning to marry Salim. He's been looking for him since.'

'Yes, Mother, we'll leave tomorrow.'

'I shall be here at midnight.'

'Yes, Mother.'

Later that night, Rachael looked at Salim as he sat back against the oblong pillow and locked his hands behind his head. She put her head on his lap. Salim placed his hand gently, then firmly, on her belly. 'My son,' he said possessively. 'We'll call him Rahim. "Ra" from RayChal and "im" from Salim.'

'What about the "h"?'

'Ya Ali, let the poor child have at least one letter that he can call his own.'

Rachael laughed. 'And pray tell me, what is *my* say in the matter?'

He caught hold of a tendril of her hair and twirled it around his finger. 'My love, you will get to fill his life with a ray of sunshine, the sound of music and the fragrance of love.'

Rachael smiled. Rahim. Son of *Ra*chael and Sal*im*. She liked the name. Walking over to the mirror, she looked at her reflection. Her stomach was still flat. She could not feel him at all. But she knew he was there, growing steadily. Soon she would feel him move, feel him hiccuping, feel his kicks, which would become stronger with each passing day.

'I think we'd better get some sleep tonight. I know not how long it'll be before we're able to get a good night's sleep again.'

He clasped her hands. 'A groom is supposed to give his wife a present on this special night. But I have nothing.'

'But you already have,' she replied as she placed his hand on the necklace she wore.

Salim felt the gold, the smoothness of the rubies, the diamonds. 'Is it? Ya Ali, it's the necklace. Daima remembered? She still had it?'

Rachael ruffled his hair. 'You were just five! How sweet. You're blushing. You're actually blushing.' She placed something in his hands. 'I've something for you as well.' She watched him as he ran his fingers over the holes.

'It's the flute I gave you,' he said.

332

'Play it,' she said softly. 'It's been so long since we heard the sound of music. Pray bring it back into our lives.'

Salim put the flute to his lips. She watched him, fascinated. She had not seen him so serene for a long time. It was as though he was in a trance. There was so much pain, so much passion and longing in the tune he played. Tears sprang to her eyes and flowed down her cheeks.

The room went quiet as he finished playing. 'That was heart-wrenching, Salim,' she said. He merely patted her hand and put down the flute.

Rachael walked over to the window and opened it. The crescent moon hung low in the sky. A refreshing breeze wafted in. So too did the sound of hyenas howling in the distance. The smell of leftover food emanated from the kitchen. She wondered what it must feel like to sleep outside.

As though reading her mind, Salim said, 'You know, when I was about four or five, I'd often sleep on the terrace with Daima on nights like this. It used to be heavenly. The moist breeze from the Gomti lulled us to sleep and the sweet call of the peacocks woke us up. I'd lie there until late at night, counting the stars. Daima would point to the brightest of the lot. "See that star," she'd say. "She's your princess. You'll marry her some day." I would look at her perplexed and say, "What? Marry a star?" And she'd reply, "Don't worry, she'll come down to earth when the time is right."'

Rachael laughed and turned away from the window. 'So I'm a star?'

'Yes,' Salim whispered. 'My guiding star.'

'Oh Salim, I love you,' she said as she slipped her arms around him.

He cupped her face in his hands. 'I can't live without you, RayChal. I don't think I would have survived without you.'

Rachael stepped out of the country house, a bag in hand. Salim, Ahmed and Mother were already there. Ayah was helping Daima put the pitaras and bags in the carriage. Rachael glanced at Mother – how frail and white she looked in the moonlight. Dropping her bag, she went and hugged her.

'It's a pity you've got to leave like this. Without saying goodbye to your father. He loves you, you know,' said Mother.

'I know. But I also love Salim,' Rachael replied.

Mother fidgeted with the lace on her collars, then licked her lips. 'I, too, love you. Always have . . . Just wasn't good at expressing it.'

Rachael took her hands in hers. She pursed her lips and held back her tears. It was a pity – just when she was beginning to know her mother's love, they had to part. 'I know, Mother,' she said, pressing her hands. 'I can feel it. Pray do not worry about me. I shall write to you once we settle down.'

She hugged her hard. Mother held her for a long moment, sobbing softly. Finally she kissed her forehead and let her go.

Rachael swallowed the lump that had risen in her throat and turned towards Ayah who had stepped forward to touch her feet. She pulled her up and embraced her. Mother coughed uncomfortably and walked away a few paces.

'I'll miss you, Ayah, I'll miss you so,' she sobbed.

'Hush, baba,' Ayah whispered in a hoarse voice. 'You mustn't cry. You starting new life. You start it with happy thoughts. No tears.'

Rachael nodded. 'Give my love to Ram Singh and Brutus. I wish I could see them before going.'

'You no worry, baba. I tell them. We be fine.' She touched Rachael's belly gently. 'You write letter when baby coming. I come to help.'

Rachael smiled and nodded as she walked over to the carriage. She climbed into it, followed by Daima. She watched Salim hug Ahmed and thump his back.

'Take care, Salim mia. Inshah Allah we shall meet again,' said Ahmed, as he helped him onto the carriage.

'Of course we will, Ahmed.'

The carriage trundled down the grieving streets. They were now in Lucknow, passing through Chowk. Rachael remembered how she had been jostled by the crowd three years back as she made her way to Bade Miyan's shop. The street was bare now, the silence unnatural. The shops were either shuttered or broken and bare. A pariah dog, the sole inhabitant of the bazaar, looked up at the sound of the carriage, then went back to drinking the muddy water in the drain.

Rachael touched Salim's hand as she remembered the first time his had touched hers, in this same bazaar. Salim pressed her hand reassuringly. She wondered what was going through his head.

He started singing softly:

'Babul mora naihar chuto hi jaye,
Chaar kahar mil mori doliya sajave,
Mora apna begana chuto jaye.'

'It sounds beautiful. Pray tell me what it means.'

Salim's lips moved as he began to recite: '"O father, I'm leaving my home behind, four men have gathered to lift my palanquin. My near and dear ones will soon become strangers, my home unreachable . . ." Abba Huzoor wrote these lines when he was leaving Lucknow.'

Rachael looked at him. His face was blank as he stared straight ahead. She brushed aside her tears with the back of her hand. She looked around at the city she was leaving behind. A city that had resounded with the sound of dance and music, poetry and revelry, a city she had grown to love with its numerous palaces and gardens. In their stead stood ruins and innumerable slums and a silence so loud as to tear one's heart apart.

And for once she was glad Salim could not see.

Chapter Thirty-Four

SALIM

Salim plucked the strings of the sitar one by one. No, the last one didn't sound right. He tightened it and listened to it again. Yes, brilliant. He played the tune he had composed the night before. Then put down the sitar with a satisfied smile. Yes, it would be the perfect piece to play at the finale of the concert. He leant back against the window sill and listened. He loved this time of the day, when his little cottage slowly woke up and started getting ready, while he sat in front of the huge window, practising his music.

He could hear little Haydn. He was banging the door. 'Melody, hurry up, I need to go badly.'

'Come along all of you, breakfast is getting cold,' Rachael called.

'Stand still, Sargam,' Daima grumbled. 'How many times have I told you to stand still when I plait your hair?'

Yes, he had settled down in his new life in Nainital. Sooner than Rachael had expected. Perhaps it was his stoicism that had helped. Or perhaps it was the strength he drew from Rachael's presence . . .

He was content, surrounded by RayChal and his four children. Even the children in the neighbourhood loved him. They called him 'pirate uncle' because of the black patches he wore over his eyes. But once in a while, when it rained heavily and memories invaded his brain like the children invaded the kitchen cupboards as soon as they got back home from school, he thought of his life in Lucknow, of Abba Huzoor, Ahmed . . .

He had gone to Lucknow a year back with the children and had enquired about Ahmed. No one had seen him for a week. Together with some of the neighbours, Salim had broken into his house. He had found Ahmed's dead body on the floor. Apart from the velvet curtain that hung over the doorway, the house had been bare. Everything had been sold. Ahmed had been too proud to admit that he did not have enough money to buy food and had died of starvation.

Salim swallowed. He heard a patter of feet and the scraping of chairs as his family gathered around the dining table for breakfast. Soon all of them would be off to school, giving him a couple of hours to practise for the concert before his students arrived.

Sometimes he wished he could see again – watch Rahim play cricket, watch Melody's golden pigtails bob up and down whenever she ran, or see how little Haydn's face reddened whenever he spoke.

He wondered what RayChal looked like. Had her

hair begun to turn grey? Did she have lines around her mouth and eyes? She would look beautiful even when she was ninety, he was sure of that. She still smelt of lavender and fresh starch. And kept her hair long. Did she still fiddle with her ring?

Salim sighed, covered his eyes with his palms and groaned loudly, 'Ya Ali.' Rachael was at his side within seconds. 'Salim, what happened?' She tugged at his hands. 'Oh pray tell me you're all right.'

Salim gave a sudden roguish grin and pulled her onto his lap. 'You haven't given me a kiss all morning!'

'Oh, you wicked . . .' She boxed his chest playfully as she scrambled to free herself from his grip. 'Pray let me go. I haven't finished preparing for my lecture today.'

'What are you teaching?'

'We are doing Shakespeare's *Romeo and Juliet*.'

'Ah, I could help you with that. I could even act it out for you.'

Rachael pulled his nose. 'That's kind of you, Mr Romeo, but no thanks.'

He smiled. He knew she was smiling and crinkling up her nose as she ran to collect her notes.

'Rahim, Haydn, hurry up and get your bags, otherwise we'll be late today,' she called over her shoulder. Soon the sound of feet running down the steps died down and Salim went back to his music. His forehead creased in concentration as the strains of *Raaga Bhairavi* wafted across the room.

Author's Note

All the main characters in *The World Beyond* are fictitious, other than Nawab Wajid Ali Shah, the last ruler of Avadh, and his wife Begum Hazrat Mahal, who played a prominent role during the uprising of 1857.

Nawab Wajid Ali Shah did not come back to Lucknow after he left the city in March 1856. He built a mini-city called Metia Burj on the outskirts of Calcutta, where he lived until his death in 1887.

Begum Hazrat Mahal carried on her struggle against the British from various parts of the country for almost a year, even after the uprising had been crushed. Finally she took refuge in Nepal with her son, Birjis Qadir. There she lies in an unknown grave, quite forgotten. She was the only Indian leader who did not surrender and lived in exile for the rest of her life.

Most of the palaces and gardens in the book are real,

as also are most of the historical events that take place. I have fiddled with the geography of Lucknow a bit, in that I have shown Marion Cantonment and Kaiserbagh to be much closer to each other than they actually are, for the sake of the story.

GLOSSARY

Abba/Abba Huzoor/Abbu	father
abkhora	an earthen vessel used for drinking water
angarkha	a tunic worn by men
angrez	the English
ayah	maidservant
baba	baby; also used for addressing a father, grandfather or an elderly man
balai	clotted cream
barre	big
basti	a place inhabited by poor people
begum	a Muslim woman of rank
beta	son
Bhagwan	God
bhang	cannabis
bhai dooj	a Hindu festival for brothers and sisters
bhai jaan	brother
chachi	aunt
chador	cloak
chand	moon
Chand Raat	last day of Ramzan
charpoy	bed made of wood and rush grass
chatai	woven mat
chatri	umbrella
chaupad (chaupar)	board game
chillum	hookah
daima	wet nurse
darbar	court
dastarkhwan	food set out
dhobi	washerman/woman
dhoti	loin cloth

dhol	drum
diwan	seat
doli	palanquin
domnis	storytellers
dupatta	long scarf
Eid Mubarak	greeting
eidi	loose change given by elders to the younger ones on Eid
firangi	foreigner
gharara	woman's skirt-like garment
ghunghroos	anklets with bells, worn by dancing girls
gujia	an Indian sweet
gulab	rose
hakim	doctor
hammam	bath
Holi	the Hindu festival of colours
howdah	a seat on the back of an elephant
huzoor	majesty
Inshah Allah	God willing
ittar	perfume
jaagte raho	stay awake
jalebi	an Indian sweet
janaza	dead body wrapped in white cloth
jannat ki hoor	an angel from Heaven
jelo-khana	the courtyard of a palace
jogi	a holy man
kafir	infidel
kaka	uncle
Kanhaiya	Lord Krishna
karela	a bitter vegetable
kathak	a classical Indian dance
kavi samelan	gathering of poets
keema	minced meat

kesar	saffron (a spice)
kheer	rice pudding
khurd nau	shoes
khus	an Asian grass
khwabgah	bedroom
kotha/kothi	house
kotwal	police officer
kurta	collarless shirt
lehenga	long Indian skirt
lakh	a hundred thousand
lathi	stick
lota	water jug
lungi	loin cloth
machan	a hunters' shooting platform built on trees
mahout	the keeper of an elephant
matka	earthenware pot
mem	madam
missy baba	little miss
mogra	a flower
mohur	gold coin
moulvi	a Muslim religious teacher
Muharram	first month of the Islamic calendar; also the month of mourning
namaz	a Muslim prayer
Navroz	celebrated by Muslims in Lucknow as the festival of colours
nautch girl	courtesan
nikaah	marriage contract
nikaahnama	a document of the marriage contract
nukkedar	pointed
paan	betel leaf
paratha	Indian bread
phupha	uncle

phuphi	aunt
pitara	tin box
punkah	fan
purdah	veil
qaba	cape
qatat	four-lined verses hung on walls
raat	night
rajnigandha	tuberose
rakhi	thread tied on the arm of a brother by his sister
rakshas	giants
Raksha Bandhan	a Hindu festival that celebrates the love between a brother and a sister
Ramzan	Muslim month of fasting
risaldar	Indian officer
ruh gulab ittar	rose-scented perfume
sarod	a musical instrument
sepoy	soldier
sharara	an Indian dress for women
shehnai	a musical instrument
surahi	earthenware pot
takhat	a low wooden platform for sitting
talukdar	landholder
tantric	a person who practices black magic
taslim	offering respect by bowing low and raising one's right hand to one's forehead
tatties	mats
tawaif	prostitute
tesu	rhododendron
zarda	rice dish
zenana	woman, often refers to women's apartments

Acknowledgements

My heartfelt thanks to:

Nawab Jafar Mir Abdullah for giving me an insight into the lives and times of the nawabs as well as for the handwritten notes.

Shri Ram Advani, Mrs Asma Hussain and Prof. Salim Kidwai for giving me their precious time as well as some invaluable information.

Susie Dunlop and the rest of the team at Allison & Busby, especially Chiara, Lara, Lesley, Georgina and the copy editors for doing such a thorough job and for providing me with this wonderful opportunity.

Christina Griffiths for the exotic cover design.

Jane Conway-Gordon for believing in my book even more than I did. Thank you for your support and for being such a positive influence on my life.

Siobhan Curham, not just for the guidance and for

plodding through the first draft, but also for pushing me – 'Stop revising and send the damn thing off,' she said.

My teachers, especially Miss Flynn, Ma'am Chakravarty and Ma'am David for instilling in me a love for literature and writing.

Simon, who is sadly no more, but whose words and encouraging smile will always be with me.

My fellow writers – Anna, Barbara, David, Gabriela, Indra, Jan, John, Kay, Maneesha, Mike, Oscar, Phil, Richard, Robin and Salil for their useful feedback and support, which has made all the difference.

Gaurav, for encouraging me to blog and for not letting me give up on my dream.

My extended family, my punching bags, my moral support – AnjaliB, AnjaliR, Anju, Bindi, Gouri, Madhu, Meena, Neelam, Neha, Nupur, Pooja, Prachi, Prerna, Pratichi, Rupali and Vimla – for always being there for me.

My family, my pillars – my parents, my in-laws, Tauji, Sameer, Monica, Nikeeta, Shilpi and Promit.

Karn and Diya, for not fighting and keeping the volume down when Mamma was working on a difficult scene.

My husband Bhaskar, my strength – for taking care of the kids as well as the cooking whenever I had a deadline, for making me what I am today and for showing me the way to a world beyond.

An Interview with the Author

Q. Rachael and Salim come together through their love of music. How important is music to you?
G.S., London

A. I was born and brought up in India where music is an integral part of life. Much of Indian classical music, as has been referred to in the novel, has now given way to the more popular Bollywood music. But even so, music – whether classical or otherwise, is the voice of the soul. It is something that cuts across all barriers for it is a language that needs no words to be understood. So my answer would be – extremely important.

Q. How did you carry out your research? Did you spend much time in Lucknow whilst researching the novel?
Rachael Conway, Blackpool

A. I did spend a considerable amount of time visiting all the ancient monuments like the Residency, Kaiserbagh,

Bara Imambara etc. in Lucknow, where the novel has been set. I also met and spoke to the descendants of the last king of Avadh, historians, history professors and also had a lengthy talk with Asma Husain who designs period costumes for movies and theatre and had an in-depth knowledge about the clothes, shoes and jewellery worn in those days. Then I trolled through some of the old bookshops in the city, which proved to be a treasure trove of books on Lucknow and its historical past. I had them shipped to my home in London where I spent the next three months rummaging through them.

Q. What came first – the idea to write a novel set in Lucknow during the Mutiny, or the desire to write a love story?
Yara Hortzig, London

A. The desire to write a love story. I have always been a sucker for romance.

Q. What other novels set in India would you recommend?
R. Bell, Berkshire

A. Novels set in India – the first ones that come to mind are *God of Small Things* and *A Suitable Boy*.

Q. Will your next novel be set in India too? Would you even consider setting your books somewhere else?
M Hale, Leatherhead

A. My next book has already been written so I can tell

you that it *is* set in India. But for the rest – who knows? If a place outside India inspires me sufficiently to set an entire novel there, then why not?

Q. I understand you previously wrote a book about pregnancy and babycare – how difficult and different was the experience of writing a novel?
Mary Gordon, France

A. Although I found writing the novel much more enjoyable than writing the book on pregnancy and babycare – for the simple reason that every single character, every single scene, every single detail was completely my creation – it was for this very reason that I found it more daunting as well. For the book on pregnancy, I had all the facts, all the notes, all the journal entries; I just had to put them nicely together. But when writing a novel – one has to build the entire book word by word.